DATE DUE   3/02

4-24-02			
10-30			
8/17/13			

GAYLORD   PRINTED IN U.S.A.

THE LOST COAST

BOOKS BY ROGER L. SIMON

Heir

The Mama Tass Manifesto

THE MOSES WINE DETECTIVE NOVELS

The Big Fix

Wild Turkey

Peking Duck

California Roll

The Straight Man

Raising the Dead

The Lost Coast

THE LOST COAST

A Moses Wine Mystery

ROGER L. SIMON

HarperCollins*Publishers*

HarperCollins books may be purchased for educational, business, or sales promotional use. For information please write: Special Markets Department, HarperCollins Publishers, Inc., 10 East 53rd Street, New York, NY 10022.

FIRST EDITION

Designed by Ruth Lee

Library of Congress Cataloging-in-Publication Data

Simon, Roger Lichtenberg.
  The lost coast : a Moses Wine mystery / Roger L. Simon.
    p. cm.
  ISBN 0-06-017707-1
  1. Private investigators—California, Southern—Fiction.
I. Title.
PS3569.I485L67   1997
813'.54—dc20   96-18374

97 98 99 00 01 ❖/RRD 10 9 8 7 6 5 4 3 2 1

For Sheryl

THE NIGHT I LEARNED MY SON was wanted for murder was like a wake-up call from hell. Actually, the charge could have been manslaughter or murder two, but what did it matter? They were just escalating degrees of horrendous.

Ironically, up until that evening, I had been feeling pretty good. Great, in fact. I was busy packing for a two-week vacation in Vietnam—a place I had done everything in my power to avoid twenty-five years ago. But now I was ponying up about eight grand to an outfit called Wilderness Travel to go there. Wilderness Travel would escort me and my girlfriend, Nancy, on a cushy "overland cultural adventure," through its dense jungles and bright green rice paddies from the Mekong Delta to the far north hill-tribe country, including a stop for snorkeling at Nha Trang Bay and a tour of the bountiful vegetable gardens at Son My—site of the infamous My Lai massacre.

The occasion of our trip was Nancy's thirty-second birthday, but I had something of my own to celebrate. After a period of incredible frustration I had finally had a breakthrough on the Dexter Reynolds case. Dexter, a twenty-three-year-old nurse and father of two, had been falsely accused of rape (oral, genital *and* anal, no less) by Olga Nazimova, an eighty-seven-year-old Russian émigré he was tending in the intensive care unit of Midway Memorial Hospital in Santa Monica. Despite Olga's advanced years, eczema, shingles-scarred face and shriveled physique, the DA persisted in believing her tales of sexual assault by Dexter (a handsome former power forward for UC Santa Barbara) for seven months until just yesterday. Pretending we were scouts for a talk show, my associate, Jane Ellenbogen, and I got Olga's cousin Maxim to brag into a tape recorder that his family, including Olga, came from a long line of Odessa confidence artists who had entered this country by tap dancing through a phony political asylum plea. Twenty minutes later we played our tape for the DA, saving Dexter from doing a four-year minimum for sexual assault and Midway Memorial from the sixteen-million-dollar lawsuit Olga had filed.

So I suppose, when the bell rang as I was packing for my Southeast Asian adventure, I could be excused for going to the door and blurting "Ho . . . Ho . . . Ho Chi Minh . . . Vietcong is gonna win!" into the intercom. It was eight o'clock, after all—past usual working hours, even in a business like mine. Besides, I had been expecting Nancy.

"Is this the home of Moses Wine?" said the voice on the other end, male and distinctly unamused.

"Yes," I said, frowning. "Who is it?"

"Detectives Jackson and Ramirez of the Los Angeles Police Department."

I opened the door to reveal two men—one blond and too big for his suit, the other Latino, wearing a sweater. He was holding up a badge.

"*I'm* Moses Wine," I said, as the pair stepped into my foyer. "What's this about?"

"You're the father of Simon Wine?" asked Ramirez.

"Yes, I am." I felt myself tighten like a wary parent. Simon was twenty years old, but it was still the same.

"Do you know where he is?"

"He's away at school. . . . Is there something wrong?" I had visions of my son splayed out on some Northern California freeway or floating under the waves beneath the Golden Gate Bridge, where he often surfed.

The cops ignored my question. "Would you come with us, please?" said Jackson. He started back out the door, giving me no real choice but to grab my jacket and join them. Ramirez indicated I should follow them down to Parker Center in my car, assuming correctly that I knew where it was. "I hear you're a private eye," he added in a bemused voice, glancing around my house before he left. "You sure don't seem like one."

"What're they like?" I asked, but he was already out the door with his buddy, heading for their squad car. In any case, I knew damn well what most PIs were like and so did he—retired cops in hairpieces and polyester warm-ups, padding their pensions working for personal injury attorneys or insurance companies. Sometimes, if they got lucky, they did a little marital surveillance or electronic debugging for a company rich enough to go the extra mile to fend off their foreign competitors. It was about as glamorous as phone sales.

But Ramirez was right. I was different. At least I started that way back in 1971, when I saved Marty Ross from being busted for throwing a brick through the front window of the Berkeley Bank of America. It was the height of the Vietnam War, the October Days of Rage, and I saved him by locating some tourist photos that showed the guy standing behind Marty, handing him the missile in question, was actually a plainclothes sergeant in the Berkeley police. In truth, my motivation for this deed wasn't so much Movement solidarity as getting into the tight-fitting bell-bottoms of Marty's younger sister, Emily (unsuccessful, unfortunately). Still, I soon got a reputation as the Sam Spade of the student left. A year or so later in Los Angeles, I unmasked a plot in which some gamblers were trying to sabotage an antiwar senator's campaign by pretending the candidate was being supported by a violent leader of the Weather Underground. The senator got reelected and my reputation soared. I wound up in *Rolling Stone* for my fifteen minutes of fame: THE PEOPLE'S DETECTIVE—ON THE CASE WITH MOSES WINE.

By then I was a (small) legend in the making and what began almost as an accident, a mix of youthful political idealism with unrequited lust, became my life. And I enjoyed it, playing Robin Hood through the American seventies. Unfortunately, I discovered that most of a detective's cases weren't rescuing the downtrodden underclass from a vicious system, and those that were barely paid bus fare in Los Angeles—a city where no one ever wanted to take the bus anyway. I had kids and a wife and I had to grow up and take things more seriously. Slowly, almost without noticing, I turned into something painfully close to a normal private investigator, even if I didn't want to admit it, working for lawyers and mixing in the occasional pro bono case when time would allow. But I was good at it, good enough at least to fend off the competition (which, in L.A., where the subject heading "Investigators" fills almost as many columns in the Yellow Pages as auto detailers and pool cleaners, was considerable). By the time

I was halfway through the eighties I was living the kind of bourgeois life I once reviled. And then, in the early nineties, I found myself almost inevitably across the table from a loan officer at Glendale Federal. I was going to expand, run my own detective agency—MW Investigative Services—with a half dozen employees including associates and clerical assistants, computers, modems, Infotek databases, photocopiers, fax machines, postage meters and a refrigerator stocked with Calistoga water and designer beer, all ensconced in an industrial space near Little Tokyo, between the Museum of Neon and a trendy sushi bar with minimalist paintings and cardboard furniture. The small company thrived and I became something of a manager as the source of our business ranged with the times, from industrial espionage (decreasing) to sexual harassment (increasing) to that recent favorite—juror misconduct. Sometimes I thought all that was left of the old Moses Wine were the fading portraits of Marx (Groucho) and Lennon (John) under the collection of original Big Brother and the Holding Company LPs I kept in my desk for sentimental reasons. I had long since given up a turntable.

But Janis Joplin and Papa John Creach were the furthest things from my mind that night as, thirty minutes later, I followed Officers Jackson and Ramirez into the cavernous lobby of Parker Center, a bland, sixties structure that looks like an oversized motel but is actually LAPD headquarters. I was thinking, of course, of my son Simon.

The last time I had seen him was about a month before, when I was up in San Francisco for a day on business. We had met for dinner at the Hunan, a somewhat grimy, diner-like place in Chinatown that had been popular for a while but now had been passed over for the Szechwan restaurant up the street. Simon and I still liked it, however, and we sat there drinking Tsingtao beer and eating spicy pork but not having that much to say to each other. Silences between us were commonplace and they often made me feel uncomfortable. They also made me think he was angry at me about something and I usually was the one to break them.

"How's school?" I said finally in this case, a pathetic gambit.

Simon shrugged and made a face. "Fuckin' art history," he said. He was studying to be a painter at an art school and was loaded down this semester with academic requirements he had been postponing. "Got two papers in Baroque," he added, as if he were being sent to a penal colony.

"Well, there're always the studio classes. . . . What're you painting?"

"Self-portrait. It's called *Double Man*."

"*Double Man?* Interesting title. What does it mean?"

But Simon didn't care to elaborate and we fell silent again.

"What's the girl situation?" I asked, half a beer and a plate of lo mein later. "Any cute models in studio?"

He shrugged again. Simon was exceptionally handsome, dark with a moody furrowed forehead that bore an uncanny resemblance to the young Brando's, and you would think he would be swatting the women away, but he was shy and seemed to spend most of the time by himself. It had been a couple of years since he had a girlfriend. "There's someone around," he said a minute or so later, almost as if it were an afterthought. He usually didn't like to go into details on these matters, at least with me, but I sensed this time he wanted to talk.

"Great," I said, trying to be encouraging. "What's her name?"

"Karin."

"Karin? . . . Where'd you meet her? Surfing?"

He shook his head. "She's a student at Cal. Philosophy."

"A high-brow . . . "

"Kind of. Yeah." He cracked a smile. "She's helping me with my papers."

"Lucky you. . . . Not bad looking either too, I imagine. . . . Does she ski?" Simon and I went skiing together every winter.

"I think so," he replied. "But I haven't gone with her yet."

"Maybe we could all go. The two of you and me and Nancy."

Simon grinned. "You two still on, Pop?"

"Ye of little faith," I said, and he laughed. Simon found my erratic social life amusing. I thought one of the ways he would eventually rebel against me would be to find one woman and stay with her for life. Who knew? Maybe he had already found her.

We agreed to go skiing as soon as the snow was good enough at Tahoe. Then we had another round of beers with the rest of our food and talked of the coming basketball season. We had barely finished when he checked his watch and said he had to leave. He had to be someplace unspecified in half an hour. I hugged him good-bye ten minutes later at an airport limousine stop.

A week after that I spoke with him briefly on the phone. He needed some extra money because he had overspent his monthly allowance. The acrylics for his painting class had cost more than expected and he had to repair the clutch on his pickup.

"Sure you haven't been spending it on Karin?" I said, meaning to tease him, but he didn't take it that way.

"We have better things to do," he said. And left it at that.

Now he was missing.

And I was being led by the cops into a fourth-floor conference room in Parker Center, where a tallish man in his early thirties sat with a woman stenographer. The man's name was Nicholas Bart and he introduced himself as a special agent of the FBI. He wore a modish black-and-white knitted jacket and a tie with French wine labels on it that I recognized from a mail-order catalog. He sounded educated for a cop, even an FBI cop, and had an easy manner about him, treating me like an anxious parent, even while saying with a smile that, as a private investigator, I was scarcely the average parent.

He asked me some questions about my son, and I replied quickly. Simon was twenty. He was a full-time student at the California Arts Institute at Walnut Creek. He lived by himself in an apartment a few blocks from the school.

"Do you know where he might be at this moment?" Bart asked.

"I haven't talked to him in a few weeks. I don't keep day-to-day tabs on his activities, Mr. Bart. He's not a kid anymore."

"I understand," he said. "So that means you don't have any idea at all where we could locate him?"

"No, I don't." I felt a sudden tightening about my chest, a shortness of breath. I glanced over at Jackson and Ramirez, then turned back to Bart. "What's this about? If you want me to talk to you, you're going to have to tell me."

He frowned for a moment, choosing his words carefully.

"Your son is wanted in connection with the death of Leon Erlanger."

"What?!"

"I'm sorry." He tilted his head sympathetically.

"I don't understand. This is crazy! Who's Leon Erlanger?"

"A logger with the Allied Lumber Company."

"How'd he die?" My heart pounded.

"Someone spiked a redwood tree he was sawing."

"Spiked a what? . . . You mean like those eco-terrorists who hammer steel rods in tree trunks . . . ?"

Bart nodded. ". . . to stop them from being cut."

"I didn't think anyone actually did that."

"Someone did," said Bart, reaching into a folder. "And Mr. Erlanger paid the price. Chain saw flew back at him like a boomerang. Practically cut the poor man in half." He slid a couple of photographs across the table to me. One showed a man lying in a pool of blood. His head was tilted oddly forward just above a huge gash that exposed the inside of his chest from the top of his lungs to his gall-bladder, almost as if his entire upper body had been split in two like a log. The second photo showed a mangled chain saw and the twisted remains of a giant steel nail perhaps a foot in length, the two items lined up together as evidence. The nail's head appeared to have been clipped off with cutters.

I looked up at Bart, who was staring at me with a pair of deep-set blue eyes. "Horrible," I said. "But I don't know what you think my son has to do with this. Simon's the most pacifistic person I know. He doesn't step on insects."

"He's a member of the Guardians of the Planet."

"Who are they?" I was starting to feel angry, but I tried to control it.

"The group that claimed responsibility."

"How'd they do that?"

"E-mail. Direct to the Bureau on the Internet. . . . Do they mean anything to you?"

"The Guardians of the Planet?" I remembered Simon had joined some environmental group—a couple of other surfers were part of it—but I shook my head.

"There are perhaps a dozen members. Your son is one of the leaders."

"I never heard of them."

Bart looked at me curiously. "Well, I can see why you don't know where he is then." There was the slightest hint of accusation in his voice. "That's what we needed to find out." He stood and extended his hand. "Please let us know if—"

"Wait a minute. Even if my son is a member of these, uh . . . Guardians, why is he the one responsible for spiking the tree? Did they announce that on the Internet too?"

"Unfortunately, he was the only one sighted in the vicinity of the Jack London Redwood Grove—where the spiking occurred—in the last week. In fact, he was sighted there twice."

"That's it? That's all you have?"

He shrugged and started for the door, as if to escort me out.

"Who saw him?"

"That's privileged information, Mr. Wine. I couldn't tell you, even if I wanted to."

"Was he under surveillance?"

"We're in an ongoing investigation here." Jackson was about to open the door. Bart nodded for the policeman to wait before he continued, resting his fingertips gently on my arm. "I can guess how you feel. I imagine you're very proud of your son . . . considering your past and everything."

"You're damn right I am," I said, staring Bart straight in the eye.

"He's kind of a chip off the old idealistic block, you might say."

"I couldn't be prouder."

"Then don't worry." He smiled with a forced pleasantness. "I'm sure this will sort itself out. If, as you indicate, he's such a pacifist . . . there must be some mistake."

"You can depend on it!" I said.

"Of course. Good-bye, Mr. Wine. We'll be in touch. . . ." This time he opened the door himself. "And by the way, congratulations on solving the Dexter Reynolds case." Always good to know your work was appreciated, I thought. Bart guided me out with another smile and the warning not to take the matter in my own hands. "I know you'll be tempted," he said.

Before I knew it I was back in my car, feeling disembodied from shock and heading home on automatic pilot. Almost immediately, I grabbed the cell phone and dialed Simon's number. I was pulling onto the Hollywood Freeway when his answering machine picked up. I left a message, although I knew I shouldn't. His line was almost certainly being tapped. Then I felt a paranoia I hadn't experienced in years. I checked my rearview mirror to see if I was being followed. A green Chevy was visible directly behind me and I slowed to let it pass, replaying my conversation with Bart as if it were a haiku I had to explicate. It was certainly short enough. And subliminally coercive. *"Considering your past and everything . . ."* Under other circumstances I might have been flattered or amused that the federal government continued to take so much interest in my political background after all these years. But at the moment I found it chilling.

I took a deep breath and called Nancy at her house in Nichols Canyon. She hadn't left yet and I told her what had happened. When I arrived home, she was waiting in front in her Saab convertible. She jumped out and gave me a reassuring hug. I hugged her back hard. Nancy and I were at that precarious point in our relationship where we were "trying" to make it work, but I needed her that night and she knew it.

"It must be awful," she said, as we headed through the patio toward the front door.

"Sorry you'll have to take a rain check on Ho Chi Minh City."

"Don't worry about it. I'll see if I can get the deposit back. . . . Is there anything I can do?"

She kept her arm around my back, consolingly, as I reached for my keys. "I wish there were," I said. "I think I'm going to have to go find him before the police do."

"Do you want me to come with you?"

"That'll make three of us then," said a voice from across the patio. It was a woman's voice, much huskier than Nancy's and considerably more caustic. I turned slowly, staring into the darkness to where a yellow bulb illuminated the bougainvillea. I could see a woman's form dimly silhouetted against the terra-cotta wall. "Don't you recognize me?" she asked, and laughed, holding some strands of long black hair up toward the light. "See. They're not all gray." She walked toward us, the features of her face, more lined than when I had last seen it, becoming more visible with each step.

"Suzanne?" I said.

"Who else?"

It was my ex-wife.

"Suzanne Wine . . . Nancy Wing. Nancy Wing . . . Suzanne Wine."

Nancy and Suzanne looked at each other, a Chinese-American woman in her early thirties who still had a career as a fashion model and a Jewish-American woman approaching fifty. I could see the slightest curl of an ironic smile around Suzanne's lips. "It's not Wine anymore—it's Greenhut," she said, extending a hand to Nancy. I had forgotten she changed back to her maiden name a couple of years ago.

Everyone went silent.

"I guess you won't be needing me," said Nancy after what felt like an hour but was probably closer to thirty seconds. She smiled politely at Suzanne. "I hope we meet again under easier circumstances."

"So do I," said Suzanne. They both seemed as sincere as a couple at the end of a bad blind date.

Nancy faced me with a smile. "Good luck," she said. "Call me when you can." She kissed me softly on the lips. Then she turned and left without looking back.

"She's pretty," said Suzanne, a few minutes later. We were in my living room and I was pouring us both some Stoli over ice.

"She's also intelligent. She's studying for her master's in psychology."

"I'm sure. . . . When do we leave?"

"As soon as possible. When'd the FBI notify you?"

"An agent visited my office this afternoon. They wanted me to come up here. So I took the next flight out and talked with that Bart character. I must have seen him a half hour before you."

I nodded. It made sense—as if the government planned to track us both so we could lead them to Simon together. So far it was working, assuming we could find him.

"How're we going to get up there?"

"I guess we can't take that," I said, glancing outside

toward my Beemer. "They probably already have a bug under the hood. We'll have to figure something different."

Suzanne smiled. "Like the old days, huh?"

"Sort of," I said. "I think I already have an idea. . . . Have you spoken to Jacob?" He was our other son, a fledgling writer in New York.

She nodded. Then suddenly her face broke. "Is this our fault, Moses?"

"What? We don't even know what happened."

"Did we do something wrong? It's almost as if he's imitating us." She started to cry.

"Simon's a great kid. You know he is. He couldn't do anything that crazy." Suzanne looked at me, wanting to believe what I said as much as I did. Neither of us dared to say the unspeakable—that somewhere, in the most remote reaches of our imaginations, there was always the possibility he was guilty. I wrapped my arms around her. I was starting to cry too.

Suzanne and I hadn't seen each other in three years, ever since she moved her law practice to New Mexico. We were divorced seventeen years ago, when Simon was three years old. By that time, we had left our first home in Berkeley, less than a quarter of a mile from the original People's Park on Telegraph, for L.A.'s Echo Park district. That was the ethnic neighborhood of choice for Cal exiles forced to move to L.A. for economic reasons but eager to continue their idealistic lifestyles in the less hospitable South. We lived next door to a Peruvian couple. The families across the street were first-generation Mexican and second-generation Japanese. Everybody loved our boys— Jacob because he was witty and verbal in an adult way from an early age, Simon because he was remarkably handsome and athletic even then as he ran naked through the field by the Griffith Park merry-go-round, carrying a placard protesting the cause of the moment in his little toddler fist. He was photographed that way for the back page of the alternative *L.A. Free Press,* with his proud mother and father chasing right behind him, making sure he wouldn't trip. He always had a reckless streak. We caught him just in time then. But this time, obviously, we hadn't caught him. And I didn't know if we could have, if we had tried.

"Are you sure you want to do this?" I asked Suzanne. I was continuing to hold her as much for my own reassurance as for hers. "Are you sure you really want to come?"

"I'm his mother," she said, and then she broke away. Her tears were gone.

2

"I HAVE JUST THE CAR FOR YOU, Señor Moses. A brand-new Mercedes SI Class convertible, never driven, pearl white with six tweeters, four woofers and—"

"No, no, Jorge. I want something obscure, get it? *Obscuro*."

"*Obscuro?* How about a Lexus? Dark brown. Not so old . . . "

"Not *obscuro* dark! *Obscuro*–obscure!" I was screwing up my Spanish again. "You know what I mean—inconspicuous. . . . Turn down the Home Shopping Network, you capitalist dupe, and listen for a second." I heard him grunt and press his remote, to the dismay of some kids who were probably sitting close to the TV screen. I was talking with Jorge Alvarez, a second cousin of my housekeeper, Gioconda, and former mechanic for the Sandinistas, who now ran an auto rental business in the Pico Union district. Though it was nearly eleven o'clock at night, I knew I could call him at home, and his prices were extraordinarily low, especially if you didn't ask him where the cars came from. "Oh, I get it," he said, without my having to repeat myself. "You want something no one will notice. Like that other time."

"Exactly."

"Trust me—I got just the car for you."

"Does this one work? I'm in a hurry."

"Does it drive?" He hesitated. "I think so. . . . . Yeah, it drives. I give you *my* car," he added hopefully.

"Great," I said. I told him I'd be over in a few minutes and hung up.

I dropped another quarter in the pay phone and dialed Jane Ellenbogen before nodding to Suzanne—so far so good. We were standing at the back of the bar of the Hollywood Roosevelt, using their phone, which I assumed was safer than mine at the moment, although there wasn't a line in Hollywood someone didn't want to listen in on for some reason. We had left my house twenty minutes earlier, slipped out the back door anonymously and come down the hill on foot. Before leaving I had packed an overnight bag with my cellular phone and laptop, clipped on my beeper, drawn the shades, switched on some extra lights and placed a Dizzy Gillespie big-band CD in rotation with Haydn's Surprise Symphony and Buckwheat Zydeco's *Live in Creole Country* on automatic replay on the stereo. I don't know why I selected those particular albums, except they all seemed jaunty and upbeat. And I thought it was considerate of me to give the cops some variety.

Jane's girlfriend, Harriet, picked up the phone in about six rings and passed it over to Jane. It was obvious they had gone to sleep early but Jane laughed and said, "Still up celebrating Dexter? I've already moved on to the Freeman jury. That number nine's got 'reasonable doubt' written all over him. I bet he lied in the voir dire."

"It'll have to wait," I said, and filled her in on what
had happened. For a moment she was so astonished she
couldn't speak, but when she could she was extremely
sympathetic—she liked Simon and had one of his draw-
ings hanging over her bureau—and promised to look
after everything at the office. "Don't worry," she said.
"Take as long as you need. I'm sure there's been some
mistake."

"I'm sure," I said. After hanging up, I hopped a cab
with Suzanne over to Jorge's.

A half an hour later we were speeding up the 405 to the
5 freeway in Jorge's personal vehicle, a Trans Am with
black scalloping, shiny vinyl top, chain-link steering
wheel, leopard-skin upholstery and an L.A. Raiders skull
in the rearview window between decals of Los Lobos and
the Virgin Mary. It was five years old and already had
172,000 miles on it. The windows rattled and the driver's
side-view mirror was missing, but one thing was certain—
it worked. In fact it moved like a son of a bitch.

"Keep it down," said Suzanne, indicating the speedometer needle, which was bouncing erratically between seventy
and ninety. "After the effort we've gone to."

I nodded, taking my foot off the accelerator and checking for cops in the rearview mirror. We were alone on the
405 except for a middle-aged Asian couple in a Maxima
and a black guy in a pizza delivery van. None of them
looked like cops, but you never knew. In my present mood
I suspected everybody. But I couldn't let any of them stop
me from finding Simon. "When was the last time you
talked to him?" I asked Suzanne.

"A week ago. He said you visited him." She flicked on
the radio, searching for a country station. Suzanne liked
country music, although she grew up in the center of Los

Angeles with parents who listened to opera and socially
conscious folk singers like Paul Robeson and Pete Seeger.

"Did he tell you about his new girlfriend?" I asked.

"Karin. . . . Did you meet her?"

"No. We talked about going skiing but . . . "

"Think she's involved in this?"

"He wouldn't be the first guy who joined a political
organization to meet the opposite sex."

Suzanne looked at me pointedly.

"Hey, I wasn't the worst offender. Remember Mike
Rigrod? He went underground for six years just to get in
Linda Scheckman's pants."

"I thought *he* was a police agent," said Suzanne.

"Another one? God, I hated those people."

"We all did," she said. The news had come on the radio
and the announcer, after some tedious bullshit about wel-
fare reform, was updating the story of the death of the
thirty-eight-year-old Humboldt County logger and father
of three named Leon Erlanger. The state police in conjunc-
tion with the FBI's International–Domestic Terrorism
Squad had put out an all-points bulletin on the group
known as the Guardians of the Planet, who were said to be
armed and dangerous. Roadblocks had been erected
throughout Humboldt and Mendocino Counties and an
800 hot line had been set up. The FBI offered a $500,000
reward for information leading to the whereabouts of this
group. Until their apprehension, the FBI warned citizens
of Northern California to be on special alert for further
potentially violent acts of so-called ecotage.

I looked at Suzanne, who glanced over at me with a
wan smile. I smiled back at her as she adjusted her shoulder strap. Her clothes were considerably more elegant
than the hippie batiks and gauze skirts she preferred when

we were married. Now she wore nicely tailored slacks and a stylish, loose-fitting burgundy sweater that looked as if it came from an expensive designer. Her law practice must have been treating her well.

"How're things with Monroe?" I said. Monroe was a carpenter about fifteen years her junior she had met while remodeling her house in Laurel Canyon. She kept him with her when she moved to Santa Fe.

"The same," she said. "He never ages."

"Lucky you," I said, suddenly noticing something in the rearview mirror. It was a black-and-white CHP car bearing down on us. By now we were climbing the Grapevine, the steep freeway switchbacks that led over the coastal mountains into the San Joaquin Valley. I couldn't have been going much over sixty, but the highway patrol car was moving with the kind of intensity they get when you know they mean business. So I slowed down to below fifty-five, trying to be as innocent as possible, but the CHP car kept coming. Soon it was right behind us, its brights blaring in my mirror like the evil spaceship in some sci-fi movie. Then it pulled alongside, driving parallel to us for what felt like minutes but probably was more like seconds while the officer stared in at us—two obviously bourgeois people in the leopard seats of a distinctly unbourgeois Trans Am. I turned to the officer and smiled, nodding to him ever so slightly. My heart was in my mouth as I noticed the monitor of his onboard computer blinking away in the night. Suddenly he floored his engine and the black-and-white disappeared over the top ridge of the Grapevine faster than even a Trans Am, in its liveliest hot-rod imagination, could dream of going.

Suzanne and I looked at each other and shivered. We remained mostly silent for a long time after that, wondering,

when someone would come for us, while crossing the San
Joaquin Valley and then heading west on interstate 580 into
the Bay Area. Nothing happened. It was nearly 5 A.M. when
we pulled off the freeway into Oakland.

Simon's apartment building was straight ahead of us in
the predawn light, a standard four-story stucco affair more
typical of Southern California than of the more folksy
North. I pulled up across the street and stared at the
façade. A lot of the stucco work had been patched, either
because of age or the latest earthquake, and a number of
windows retrofitted with cheap aluminum molding. The
front entrance had an iron mesh gate guarding an open
stairway that ran up the side to exterior walkways on the
upper floors. Simon's apartment was on the third.

Suzanne and I got out of the car, crossing to the iron
gate. I tried the handle. It was locked.

"I guess we're going to have to break in on our own
son."

"Police?" said Suzanne, still convinced we were being
followed.

"Not unless it's them." I nodded up the street toward a
couple of homeless people sleeping by a cappuccino
stand. Then I let a delivery truck pass and reached over
the top, flicking the button below the latch bolt. The gate
opened easily. Suzanne smiled and followed me up the
stairs to Simon's apartment.

"You know for once I'm glad you're a detective," she
said.

"Actually, I haven't been doing much breaking and
entering lately." We arrived at Simon's door, which was
also locked, but with a deadbolt and a steel escutcheon
blocking the latch assembly. I chose one of his windows
instead and tried to jimmy the sash frame with a credit

card. "Shit!" I said as the credit card snapped. "See what I mean." But the sash broke anyway and the window slid open.

I pushed aside the miniblinds and we climbed in. I shut the window behind me. We were in Simon's bedroom. It was like a beach cottage after a hurricane—clothes and dirty laundry in every corner, books and papers sticking out of rumpled sheets, magazines littering the floor with old junk-food packages. Nearer the bed itself were a half dozen empty beer bottles and some ripped condom wrappers with cutesy logos advocating safe sex.

"Didn't we used to call this the 'disaster area'?" said Suzanne, picking up a half-eaten can of moldy chili with a broken-off plastic spoon sticking out of it. "You can't tell if he's been gone for a year or left a minute ago."

"You should have seen my room," I replied.

"I did," she said. "It was worse than this."

We walked into his living room expecting to find the same thing, but oddly this room was neat, almost anal. It was his work space apparently, his atelier, with an easel in a corner by the front window and his paintings, in various states of completion, stacked in an orderly row against the opposite wall. I stepped closer and examined them. They were carefully painted realistic scenes in that brightly colored Chicano style derived from the Mexican muralists. But the surface of each one had been defaced with graffiti, as if the work had been violated by some tagger after the artist was gone. Only this time the tagger was the artist himself.

"Have you seen these?" I asked Suzanne, gesturing to the first canvas, which showed a man not dissimilar to myself smoking a cigar and wearing a Che Guevara beret while riding in a Mercedes convertible next to a topless blonde with a coke spoon around her neck. There was a peace symbol on the door of the Mercedes that had been painted in camouflage colors with the word "Hipochrissie" sprayed in orange across the door.

"Did you have a girlfriend named Chrissie?" asked Suzanne.

"I do now," I said, staring at the next canvas, which showed a group of nude long-haired men and women enjoying mud baths and sunning themselves at a woodland spa. One of the women, a young Suzanne with daisies ringing her hair like Botticelli's Venus, was pregnant, an arrow with the word "Simon" pointing at her distended stomach. She was holding his three-year-old brother Jacob in one hand while clutching what appeared to be a peyote button in the other. A lascivious expression on her face, she was playing footsie with a nude man whose face was obscured by an X. To their left, a younger version of me was cavorting in the baths with a buxom black woman in an Afro who was sprinkling holy water on my Prince Valiant while reaching down with abnormally long fingers toward my crotch. Other couples flirted and frolicked in the background. Floating above all of us, and flanked by a pair of angels brandishing matching shimmering gold wedding rings, was a mock biblical scroll. "Ha'open Marritch—1974," it said, carefully inscribed in imitation Hebrew letters.

"Well, that's, uh . . . something," I said, turning to Suzanne who was staring at the painting with a look of repressed anguish.

"It's not fair," she said. "We didn't really have an open marriage and I never took peyote while I was pregnant."

"Don't worry about it. It's artistic license," I replied, not sounding entirely convincing, and headed immediately to the next painting.

I started to look at it when I heard footsteps on the walkway. I froze for a second, then picked up the canvas and, nodding to Suzanne, walked with her quickly out of view into the kitchen, shutting the door behind us just as there was a knock on the front door. Then silence. Then the doorknob started to rattle.

"Harry, open this sucker up," someone said. "I thought you had a pick. The fucker's probably off giving head to a tree."

"Better get that warrant," said another voice. Suzanne and I looked at each other. The cops were up early, eager to nail Simon. The one called Harry gave a number and the other one punched what must have been a cell phone, calling the duty judge for a warrant.

Standing stock-still, I glanced down at the painting in my hand. It contained two apparently unfinished self-portraits of Simon, one ochre and one black, both created with bold strokes and truncated in the manner of Francis Bacon. But the black one was going up in flames, its mouth open in a scream of agony. *Double Man*, I thought.

I turned to Suzanne, who was standing three feet away, staring in the direction of the refrigerator. Outside, the cop had already made contact with the judge's office. I followed Suzanne's gaze to the refrigerator door. A calendar for the month of November was taped to it. It only had two entries: For November 1—"Karin/meeting." For November 6 a yellow Post-it had been stuck on with a phone number—"(415) 555 0173."—printed in Simon's distinctive graffiti-style calligraphy.

Suzanne frowned and pointed to the last entry. "Today," she whispered.

I nodded. Through the door the cop was audible, taking down the details of the warrant. His buddy was already fiddling at the doorknob with his picks. I could hear the lock slip. I put down the painting and removed the Post-it from the calendar, folding it and stashing it in my jacket pocket. I slid a couple of feet to my right and carefully pulled back the bolt on the kitchen door. It gave onto a dank rear stairway. I nodded to Suzanne and, stepping softly, we headed quickly down and out through the garage area behind the building and turned the corner toward where our car was parked—when I stopped dead in my tracks again. Two more cops had stationed themselves ten yards away from the Trans Am while yet another wrote down the plate number. We were goners.

I screwed an apologetic smile on my face and waltzed straight over to him. "Officer, I'm sorry. Is this a no-parking zone? Me and the missus were just waiting for that cappuccino joint to open." He stopped writing and looked at me. I leaned over and whispered, gesturing to Suzanne. "She's got PMS worse than a menopausal mare. If I don't get some caffeine in her, I'll never make lunch."

The cop nodded sympathetically and put away his pad. "Try the Denny's. It's open."

"Thanks. You're my hero." I opened the door for Suzanne and got in, waving to all three cops as I drove off around the corner out of sight.

"You liked saying that, didn't you, 'PMS'?" said Suzanne.

"Not at all. It was the first thing that came into my head."

"That's what I mean."

"Sorry if it bothered you, but I was probably just pissed off." I turned down Ashby toward the bay. "That was Gabriel, wasn't it?"

"What?"

"The guy with the X on his face. In Simon's painting."

"Oh, come on, it was symbolic."

"He had Gabriel's hair—wavy, black."

"Moses, that was twenty years ago. Do we have to rehash that now?"

"What's he doing these days?"

"You know—he writes those television mysteries. The kind you hate."

"You see him?"

"No." She sounded irritated. "Where're we going? I'm tired. I need some sleep."

"We have to go down to the Golden Gate Bridge first. Otherwise they'll be gone."

"The surfers," she exhaled.

"Yes, the surfers. They're all gone by eight o'clock." I checked my watch. "That gives us an hour. Before that I'm going to try this number." I tapped the Post-it in my pocket.

"Look, Moses." Suzanne turned around in the passenger seat, facing me full on. "If this whole trip is going to be about your idea of retribution or expiation or something for events that went on thousands of years ago, you can stop right here. I'll hire my own investigator to find Simon myself. We can go our separate ways."

"That won't be necessary," I said.

3

SURFING THE WAVES UNDER the Golden Gate Bridge is definitely for the hard core. The water temperature averages in the forties and the swells, which range from twenty to thirty feet, crash with a brutal force on some forbidding jagged granite outcroppings best left to the seals. The first time I saw Simon surfing there I thought I would have a coronary. He was riding a particularly long pipeline straight under the bridge between two concrete pylons as if they were the flags in some ocean-going slalom course. I averted my eyes, holding my breath until he emerged on the other side and climbed back on the beach, laughing and clutching his foot, which had suffered minor abrasions from the concrete.

"You should try it, Pop," he said, grabbing me playfully around the shoulder.

"After I've climbed Everest," I replied. Actually, I had tried surfing with him once, in Malibu a few years earlier. The ocean was warmer and more civilized, but even there I had fallen from the board before I could get to my feet. I barely could ride on my knees. Simon just said I needed

more practice, but I was skeptical. I was already forty, not
the time to begin surfing, even though, through him, I had
begun downhill skiing at thirty-five.

In truth, I related to Simon mostly through sports—tennis, bicycling, basketball. Every year I'd take him to a couple of Laker games and we'd stop for dinner at this old-
fashioned Italian place on La Brea that served the kind of
food they did before anybody heard of sun-dried tomatoes
or risotto con funghi porcini, chicken cacciatore or veal
parmigiana. One dish was enough to feed the entire Laker
team, the guards anyway. Good thing too, because I rarely
had that much to say to Simon, other than the usual
hosannas to Magic and Worthy. Unlike his brother, he was
never a verbal kid and never much of a student either. I
don't think I ever saw him read a book for pleasure, at
least not a book that wasn't 90 percent pictures. He was
diagnosed as dyslexic when he was in the third grade. But
like many dyslexics, he could draw superbly and draw he
did. From age three on, he was always sketching something: trees, birds, rockets, little cartoon characters with
sad faces, as if he were trying to tell us something incom-
municable through speech.

It was the same face that appeared in *Double Man* and
the same one that would often appear in the "bombs," the
clandestine graffiti murals he and his friends threw up on
the walls of inner-city Los Angeles. The investigation of
Leon Erlanger's death was not Simon's first brush with
the law. From junior high on he was a member of the KGB,
the "Kings of Graffiti Bombing," sometimes known as the
"Kidz Gone Bad," a pure L.A. multicultural group of Jews,
Chinese, Chicanos and some black kids, who roamed the
streets of the city looking for an empty wall on which to
register their protest. Sometimes it was an elaborate mural

of surprising beauty and political sophistication, but too often it was the simple ugly tag "KGB" scrawled indiscriminately on telephone poles, billboards, delivery trucks, shopping malls or school buses or anyplace else they could find a few inches of unused space. One even ended up on my garage door.

Simon was first arrested when he was fourteen. It was illegal for under-sixteens to buy spray paint in L.A., so he and a friend shoplifted a couple of cans from a hardware store on Santa Monica Boulevard. I got a call from the West Hollywood sheriff's department and had to bail him out at ten o'clock at night with the promise that he would see a counselor and that nothing like this would ever happen again. Fat chance. I knew, and he knew I knew, he would be at it again within a month—not the stealing but the devotion to his nocturnal art. (He also must have known I secretly admired him for living out my fantasies of being a renegade for social justice.) A few years later I got the call at 4 A.M. He and his buddies had been caught flagrante delicto essaying a thirty-foot-high portrait of Rodney King being beaten by the police on a bank building in the Wilshire district. It was great work, but the DA was no art buff. I had to use all my pull with a couple of friends in his office to get them out of it with no more punishment than two weeks whitewashing graffiti along the Miracle Mile.

All that seemed pretty paltry by comparison to a possible manslaughter charge or worse as I stood next to Suzanne that morning at the water's edge watching the surfers do their oceanic dance. The fog was thick and it was hard to see them as they materialized out of the waves like holographic images before receding again. Hard to see any police agents too, who, I knew, were probably perched on rocks or up on the palisade above us, scanning the area with binoculars for any sign of Simon or his fellow Guardians. Were they watching us?

I was all the more suspicious because only ten minutes before I had stopped at a pay phone, taken out Simon's Post-it and dialed the anonymous number. It turned out to be the San Francisco switchboard of the FBI. It was closed until 9 A.M., but the recording left an alternative number in case of emergency. I chose not to call. But I couldn't figure out what the number was doing there. What was Simon planning to do? Take credit for the spiking? Turn himself in? Turn someone else in? What?

"Recognize any of them?" I asked Suzanne, gesturing to the surfers. She shook her head as a couple of them came out of the water, walking toward us with their boards over their heads. One was tall, with long, stringy black hair like Howard Stern, and wore a full wet suit. His partner was shorter and stockier and looked Hawaiian. All he had on was a pair of Speedo briefs. I could've gotten pneumonia just looking at him, but he wasn't even shivering.

"Morning," I said.

"Cops," said Howard Stern to his buddy, continuing right past us and leaning his board against a rock. "All we get here these days is cops. It's worse than a fuckin' Winchell's."

"We're not cops," I said, walking toward them.

"Promise," said Suzanne.

"Oh, great, tourists. We haven't seen one of those in about ten minutes," he said to the Hawaiian, who grunted and reached behind the rock for a paper bag, taking out a jelly doughnut.

"We're somebody's parents," I said. "Simon Wine. You know him?"

Howard stopped and looked straight at us, his expression suddenly wary. "You Mr. and Mrs. Wine?" he said.

"This is Mr. Wine. I'm Ms. Greenhut," said Suzanne.

"Uh-huh," said Howard.

The Hawaiian was staring at us silently.

"Can we buy you guys some breakfast?" I said.

"We didn't really know your son," said Howard quickly.

"I thought he hung out here a lot."

"He was quiet, kept to himself."

"He's in deep shit," said the Hawaiian.

"We know," said Suzanne.

I looked up the barren beach to some figures way off in the distance, then back at the Hawaiian, who had a pensive expression. "I think I'll take you up on that breakfast," he said.

Ten minutes later he was sitting in a coffee shop by Seal Rock in front of a large orange juice, three eggs over easy, four sausage links, hash browns, sourdough toast and butter, a side of blueberry pancakes and an oat bran muffin. His buddy was having the same cardiologist's nightmare with Belgian waffles in place of the pancakes and two apple-cinnamon muffins instead of the oat bran. Such was the cost of information along the San Francisco Bay.

"The problem with Simon is. . . is . . ." said the Hawaiian—whose name, I found, was Donald—as he added another round of syrup to his pancakes in little concentric circles, "he takes things too personally. Isn't that right, Lewis?" Lewis—that was Howard's real name—nodded, his mouth too stuffed to speak. I glanced around the coffee shop, which was empty except for a bald man sitting at a corner table with his back toward us. He didn't seem to be eating anything but held a newspaper folded in the center as if he were riding the subway. "Like for instance," Donald continued, "a coupla years ago a lot of us surfers started noticing how polluted the bay was. Every time you got a little nick from your board or something—it wouldn't even have to be a deep cut or nothing—it would infect like a son of a bitch. . . . Remember that, Lewis? How you was walkin' around like you had a clubfoot for three months after that PG & E spill-off?" Lewis remembered. "Now Simon was pissed as hell about that. He didn't say much at first. He's the silent type, as I don't have to tell you, but you could see he was fuming."

I looked over at the bald man whose order still hadn't come.

"Personally, I don't get that way," said Donald. "Probably 'cause I'm used to it. When I was a kid on Maui, the place was a stone paradise. All the birds and whales and shit. Surfin' Honolua Bay in the morning—smokin' weed in the afternoon." He smiled, shaking his head and smearing some marmalade between the pancakes. The bald man turned the page of his newspaper. "Then more *haoles* come along, build the place into fuckin' Miami Beach except Miami is art deco and looks cool and Maui is a sewer with bullshit condos with weird Hawaiian names even us Hawaiians don't know. They might as well bring on the casinos—but you know what? I don't give a shit. This is only *one* planet. We could lose it. There's a zillion of 'em out there." He pointed skyward with his fork. "And who's to say pollution *itself* isn't part of nature's grand plan? It's just human shit. Like guano is bat shit. . . . Of course, Simon didn't take it that way. Eventually he went ballistic from all the garbage and—"

"Just a second," I said before he could go any further and turned to the waitress, who was standing by the cash register. "Could you tell that gentleman I'd like to buy him breakfast?" I gestured toward the bald guy, who glanced in my direction and pretended to smile. "Try the blueberry pancakes," I said, staring straight at him. "They're great with the guava jelly."

"Are they?" he said coolly, eyeing me for a second before checking his watch. "I'll have to try them next time." He stood and deposited a couple of dollars next to his coffee. "I have a breakfast across town. Good-bye." He walked out the door without looking back.

"Who was that?" asked Lewis.

"Fuckin' FBI," said Donald. "I recognize 'em ever since they arrested my cousin in Lahaina."

"Good eye," I said, watching through the window as the bald man drove off in a Pontiac. "Now tell me about Simon."

"You probably already heard what happened," Donald replied. "Everybody on the beach did."

"I'd like to hear your version," I said.

"Well, you know, about a month after the bay spill, he stole a huge barrel of raw sewage from a processing plant—shit, bloody syringes, old condoms, the works— broke into the PG & E high-rise on Market Street in the middle of the night and dumped it all over the floor of the CEO's office!"

"He did?" I said.

"You didn't know?" Donald looked surprised. "Man, did it make a stink!"

I shook my head and glanced over at Suzanne. She didn't know either.

"They knocked out a couple of security guards in the process," he continued.

"I heard they just tied 'em up," said Lewis. "And wrecked their elevator system for a month."

"Right, right," said Donald.

"Then what happened?" said Suzanne. She seemed stunned. I put my hand on her shoulder.

"Nothing," said Lewis. "They got away with it, as far as I know. . . . Your son's a lucky guy." He laughed. "Or he knows someone important."

I exhaled slowly, stood and walked over to the bald man's table, picking up the newspaper he'd been reading and walking back with it. It was that morning's *Chronicle*. The headline in the lower left corner read, GARBERVILLE FUNERAL PLANNED IN DEATH OF LOGGER. Lewis and Donald glanced down at it and frowned, then sat there silently for a while.

"Wish we could help Simon," said Donald finally, his voice suddenly quiet and sympathetic.

"Yeah," said Lewis. "He was a righteous dude. You shoulda seen him surf. Awesome. He coulda gone professional."

"We've seen him," said Suzanne.

"But those Guardians," said Lewis. "They were a piece of work. Like an eco-Gestapo."

"You met them?" I said.

"A couple."

"When was that?"

He looked over at Donald. "Are we supposed to talk about this?"

"Cops didn't say nothing." He shrugged.

"It was a long time ago anyway. Last year. In September sometime. Maybe November. They came down to visit Simon. Didn't surf though. I don't think they could've even if they wanted to."

"Who were they?"

"Woman and a girl. I never got their names."

"Well, what'd they look like?" asked Suzanne.

"Girl was kinda cool. Grunge type. Woman wasn't much though. Old, you know. Over thirty."

"Sure," I said.

"But the girl was real cute. Great figure, you could tell, even under all them clothes. She wore two rings in her nose on the left. I like it when they're like that, on the left."

"Was her name Karin?" I asked.

"I told you. They didn't give their names. . . . The older one was kind of a leader. Probably a chief tree-hugger or something. She walked with a limp."

"It's a secret group," said the Hawaiian. "That's what the police said. Underground-terrorist style."

"I hated to see it," Lewis added. "My man Simon messin' around with illegal shit like that. Waste of a good surfer." He shook his head and took a final stab at his pancake. "I saw that Gingrich dude on television the other night. It's a new era. Lots of opportunity. No more government interference and that crap. If you wanted to save the redwoods, you could buy your own."

4

"WASN'T THE TREE-SPIKING ENOUGH?" asked Suzanne.

"No one got hurt at the CEO's office. You heard what he said. They just tied the guards up."

"And if everybody knows about it, how'd they get away with it?"

"Who knows if they did?" I said. "Anyway, let's sleep."

I had been trying for a while, lying in a single bed facing Suzanne, who was in a bed of her own only a few inches away. Despite the now obvious fact we were being tailed—at least from the surfing beach, maybe all the way from L.A.—we were too exhausted to do anything about it. After some coded discussion about whether we should take one room or two, we rented a double at the old Seal Rock Inn to get an hour or two of shut-eye. But I couldn't get my eyes to close for more than a minute. I just lay there, staring at the seals on the famous rock. There must have been a hundred of them, barking away. I sighed deeply.

"Can't do it, huh?" she said.

"It's those FBI bastards. They always keep me awake with their loud music—looking for dirty words in rap lyrics."

Suzanne laughed softly and turned around in the bed, facing me. Rings had formed around her dark brown eyes and there was the tiniest smudge on the top of her cheekbone where her mascara had run—the same spot, I recalled, where it always did when she was too tired to take off her makeup. I could smell her musky odor, reminiscent of the patchouli scent most of the women I knew wore when we were young, but this was distinctly Suzanne's own smell and not perfume. It was an oddly familiar sensation, being there opposite her with nothing but a few sheets and blankets between us, something out of the distant past that seemed never to have gone away, even though I often had forgotten about it completely— something I tried to repress even on those increasingly rare occasions when it would come back to me. I wondered what it would have been like spending the last seventeen years with her, whether we could have stood each other, whether it would have gotten better, whether I could have ever overcome the feeling of betrayal. I didn't know. All I knew was this was not the moment to find out.

"We better get up," I said, sliding my feet off the bed. "We don't want to be late for the funeral." I gestured to the copy of the *Chronicle* I had brought from the coffee shop.

"The funeral?" said Suzanne, sitting up suddenly. "What're you? Crazy?"

"The good citizens of Garberville won't know who we are."

"Yes, but our minders will." She pointed out the window to our orange Trans Am, parked by itself in the hotel lot and about as subtle as a stripper in a convent.

"You know," I said. "That car could sure use a wash. We oughta do it."

"Now?"

A half hour later we were watching the Trans Am being doused with its first blast of recyclable suds at the Bay Vista Car Wash on Van Ness. "Blue Coral polish wax, Armor-All, full engine steam cleaning and pine forest aromatic upholstery shampoo," Suzanne told the attendant.

"The longer the better," I added, taking her by the arm and escorting her quickly down the glass corridor. "Besides, Jorge'll appreciate a cherry vehicle when he comes up here and picks it up." We continued through the auto accessories aisles without looking back, then out the side door behind a parked semi and around the corner to a MUNI station. I wasn't sure which of the four or five cars that had followed us up Geary to Van Ness was our tail, but it really didn't matter as long as they were waiting for the Trans Am to finish its elaborate beauty treatment. All we were doing was buying time, maybe even enough to get up to Garberville before they picked up our trail again.

But first I wanted to see what I could find out about the mysterious Karin. So as we stood in a Budget place near the Presidio, waiting for them to bring around our newly rented maroon Buick with velour interior, I borrowed the phone and called the philosophy department of the University of California at Berkeley.

"Karin Maxwell," I told the secretary. "She's a student there."

"We don't have a Maxwell," she said.

"Well, I thought it was Maxwell. . . . I'm sure it's Karin—with an *i*."

I heard the secretary sigh on the other end, but it was the kind of sigh you give when you're actually doing someone a favor, like scrolling through a computer. "We don't have a first name Karin," she said at length "Not with an *e* or an *i*."

I thanked her and hung up. Our car was pulling up. I didn't tell Suzanne the results of the conversation until we were heading out over the Golden Gate Bridge on 101 North. The weather was crisp with good visibility. I couldn't see anyone behind us, but I still couldn't relax.

"Maybe I should have tried another philosophy department . . . UC Davis or Santa Cruz."

"Maybe Karin's not her real name," said Suzanne.

"A *nom de guerre*? Like Carlos or Abu Nidal? I don't think it's likely."

But what did I know? The possibility my own son was a lot more than I thought he was had thrown all my assumptions into question. Clever pranks like dumping sewage in a CEO's office were one thing, but the specter of violence had been raised once again, not as severely as with the death of a logger, but it was there nevertheless. Had Karin drawn him into this, or was he at least partly responsible himself? Or worse yet, could he have been the instigator? But why? In the radical groups I had known, the most extreme elements were usually the police agents.

"I'm sure he was framed," said Suzanne, as we passed the Sausalito exit, continuing into the Mill Valley. "And the Internet's the place to do it. My partner André's on-line all the time. He says it's a den of liars—men posing as women, women posing as men, ten-year-old boys pretending they're dominatrixes. . . ."

"No kidding," I said, deciding to omit my adventures using a phony password to log on to a lesbian bulletin board in Santa Monica. It wasn't my most politically correct moment, although it may have been my finest hour as

a novice hacker. When we first arrived at the motel, I had
been less successful. I had made a frustrating attempt with
my laptop to log on to the FBI server to see if I could
download any files concerning the Guardians. It took me
about six tries before I got past the HOST DOES NOT RESPOND
message, only to find there was no listing for GUARDIANS of
any sort in their data base. Then I typed the name
NICHOLAS BART, made another five passes only to get the
message CANNOT RETRIEVE FILE—INSUFFICIENT LEVEL.

"If your partner's such a dedicated nerd, maybe he
could break into the FBI server for us."

"I don't know if he's *that* good," said Suzanne. "And
his wife's getting fed up."

"A 'Net widow, huh?"

"She claims she hasn't talked to him in months. She's
threatening to burn his modem."

"Tell him we'll buy him a new one. Also see what he
can find out about the Guardians in general. Maybe some
show-off on one of the news groups will tell him something interesting."

"It's worth a try," said Suzanne. We both had cellulars
but that would have been like broadcasting our private
business on *Larry King Live*, so I drove off the freeway into
a service station for her to use a pay phone. The tires of
the Buick felt low and I took the opportunity to check
them before we continued north. It was then I began to
suspect that for all our efforts we were still being followed. A dark blue Mercury Sable pulled to a halt in the
parking lot of the Jack in the Box across the street. The
same vehicle had been two cars behind us as we came
through the toll on the Golden Gate Bridge and I thought
I'd seen it during a gas stop we'd made along the I-5
around three that morning, when we were in the Trans

Am. Only this time I noticed a small remote aerial on the roof, the kind that look like little wire baseballs. The driver, a beefy blond in a gray warm-up, didn't look especially eager to get out to cop some fast food or even to roll down his window to tell the inanimate Jack what he wanted. He just took out a copy of *People* and began to read, turning the pages in a haphazard fashion that led me to believe he wasn't paying excessive attention to the text.

I got back in the car, trying to figure out where he had picked us up again. The car rental place? I had used their line to call Jorge and tell him where to recover his Trans Am. Were they tapping *his* phone too? Or had they put a bug on me right at the start, some new high-tech tracking device I couldn't see or recognize? I started to pat myself down, but stopped, feeling ridiculous, just as Suzanne got back in the car.

"I got a hold of André," she said, staring at me strangely. "His wife just moved out. She's filing for divorce."

"What timing . . . I guess we'll have to get somebody else."

"No, no. He says he has plenty of time to be on-line now."

"Great," I said, as I pulled out of the station. "All the better for us if not for him." Glancing in the rearview mirror, I had another reason to be pleased. The Sable was paying no attention to our departure. Not only that, the driver was leaning out his window, placing an order through the intercom. Maybe I had been mistaken. Maybe we weren't being followed and I wasn't some hot-wired homing pigeon leading the radar wizards to my son.

But the moment I got out onto the freeway, my mood

darkened again. "I hope they make it," I said. "André and his wife."

"That's nice," said Suzanne. "But you don't even know them."

"Sure but . . . I can sympathize. I know what happens to marriages in our generation."

"I imagine."

"Sure. And so do you. Look at what happened to us. What it did to Simon."

"I thought you said we weren't responsible."

"Who else could be? We're his mother and father. Look at the way we lived."

"How *did* we live?"

"Come on, Suzanne. Free drugs, free love . . . 'Two, four, six, eight. Fight the System. Smash the State.'"

"We talked about that stuff. Just like everybody else. We didn't really do it."

"That's the point. We talked about it all the time. It's all Simon heard."

"Kids hear all kinds of things."

"And we did do it some of the time too."

"Did what?"

"Fucked around. Under the cover of some social philosophy by Bertrand Russell." I looked over at Suzanne, who was staring at me coldly.

"Will you keep your eye on the road?" she said.

"I am keeping my eye on the road."

"No, you're not. . . . And I didn't fuck around, as you say."

"Right, right. . . . You were in love. I'm the one who had a one-night stand. I didn't give a shit about Faye Ebersol. . . . But you had a *soul* connection with Gabriel Levine."

"If that's what you think."

"Of course it's what I think. You told me so yourself. It lasted for years."

"And you believe that?"

"Why wouldn't I believe it? It broke us up!"

"How do you know?"

"Oh, I know, all right! I sure as hell know!" I was almost shouting.

"No, you don't. You don't at all!" she shouted back.

"Yes, I do! And I thought you didn't want this trip to turn into a rehash of our relationship!"

"I don't."

"So don't turn it into one."

"I won't." She stopped for a moment, then started to smile. "Peace," she said, acting more maturely than I was. But after another moment, I cooled down too and started to smile back. "Okay," I said. We were in the wine country by now, up toward Healdsburg, miles of vineyards stretching out toward rolling hills of oak and sycamore. "Sorry I got carried away like that. It was just displaced anxiety—about Simon."

"I know," she said. "I feel the same way, obviously." And then she added, "But I do have some other ideas . . . if you're interested . . . about why we really broke up."

"I hope you'll share them with me."

"I will. . . . But right now we have to find Simon."

"Okay. . . . But we better do it carefully."

"Why?" said Suzanne, eyeing me curiously.

"Because we're still being followed."

"Shit," she said, turning around in her seat and looking through the back window. A Mercedes convertible had just cut in front of us, revealing the Mercury Sable cruising discreetly along about six car lengths behind, the affectless blue eyes of the blond man staring straight at our rearview mirror.

"Don't worry," I said, flooring the accelerator. "It's only the federal government." I smiled and waved at the blond man as the Buick kicked into overdrive, shooting out in front of the cars beside it and weaving through the pack ahead. For a moment the Mercury kept pace, but I maintained my pressure on the gas, picking up speed from seventy-five to eighty-five. Soon I was going ninety and gaining, passing another cluster of cars and flying flat out on the open highway, heading for the redwood country. It was almost fun, but after another minute or two, the Mercury slowed and ducked into the crowd again.

"He'll be back," said Suzanne.

"Depend on it," I replied.

5

WE REACHED THE FIRST POLICE CHECKPOINT five miles south of Willits, where the 101 passes through the first of the major redwood groves and temporarily comes together in a two-lane country road. We barely had a moment to admire the magnificent trees when we were waved over by a state trooper who stopped us in front of a barrier and signaled for my I.D. I handed him my license and he looked at it, betraying no particular reaction to my family name. Then he scrutinized Suzanne and me for a moment.

"Passing through?" he said.

"Tourists."

"Be cautious and stay on the main roads. There have been problems in this area you may have heard about."

"No kidding," I said. "I understand there's a reward."

"Good luck," he said with a laugh as he returned my license. "Maybe you'll get it."

I gave him the high sign and drove past the barrier, searching in my mirror for the reappearance of the Mercury in the long line of cars at the checkpoint. Although we were in full daylight, most of them had their headlights on as a precaution against the thick fogs that could instantly enshroud the area like flash floods. These were the *coastal* redwoods, after all.

Willits itself, tucked into a narrow valley, was cloaked in one of those fogs and I could only make out some of its storefronts as we drove through—a health food store, a tiny import shop with Moroccan jewelry, a café named Tsunami offering Zen and North Indian cuisine, an ecology information center. We were in the land where the sixties never ended, where aging hippies and their followers battled loggers and their families over moral truth and economic survival.

And the center of that battle was Garberville, the next decent-sized town up the line from Willits, where the various conflicting forces in the North Coast wars—pot farmers, loggers, fishermen, small businessmen, real estate brokers, ecologists, lumber barons, DEA agents—collided like alien ingredients in some giant stew that would never coalesce, no matter how long you cooked it. And this was the town where the death of Leon Erlanger—supposedly at the instigation of my son—was being marked by a solemn ritual.

But Garberville didn't seem much like Sarajevo as Suzanne and I drove slowly down its main street, Redwood Drive, at ten minutes to noon that day. On the surface it seemed little more than your usual California one-horse rural town—three blocks long with gas stations at each end, a convenience store, some fast-food chains and a couple of motels with cutesy names in the middle to ensnare tourists. It did seem to have two real restaurants though. One, called the Café Garberville, advertised pork chops, ribs and "killer slaw" and had a sign on the front door saying "No Backpacks!" above a bumper sticker reading "Are You an Environmentalist or Do You Work for a Living?" There was no question which crowd they were appealing to. Ditto its competitor across the street, the Woodrose Café, which featured organic linguini for lunch and had a chalkboard in the window recording the latest figures on the numbers of spotted owls extant on the planet.

The only similarity between the two joints was that at that moment they were both completely empty. Not a soul was around, as if there had been an air raid alert or a flood warning. Indeed, there seemed to be only one or two cars around in the whole town.

"What happened to the Mercury?" said Suzanne.

"I don't know. I haven't seen it since before the check-point. Maybe they realized we spotted them and they're tag-teaming us in some way. Now it's another car."

I glanced at a Jetta parked on the corner ahead with its back sticking out of a side street. But as we reached the street, I saw it was only the first in what looked like a long line of several hundred cars all parked and double-parked on a road leading up to a church at the top. So that was where everybody was—the funeral. I glanced at Suzanne and parked the Buick. Then I took out an old floppy felt hat and pulled it down far over my head with some horn-rimmed dark glasses, for a perfunctory disguise that made me look like Woody Allen gone fishing. Suzanne wrapped her head in a black scarf and put on some sunglasses of her own. We got out and walked up the hill.

In a couple of minutes we arrived at the white-clap-board church. It seemed as if the service had been going on for some time and it was so crowded we had to push our way into the back through a side door. "Where do

they all come from?" Suzanne whispered to me. "It's hard
to believe there are so many people around here." The
church was indeed overflowing, with people of all
descriptions packed together on benches or standing in
back, stepping on the bottoms of pillars or standing on tip-
toe as we were to get a better view. A couple of dudes who
had the look of rich growers in ZZ Top beards and expensive Tony Lama cowboy boots stood near us, close to some
younger guys still wearing their uniforms from the local
Chevron station. Several of them stared at us, wondering
who we were, and I nodded and smiled politely, trying
not to arouse suspicion. Up front a minister was finishing
a blessing before a closed coffin near where a slightly
plump, dark-haired woman in her thirties, veiled and
dressed in black, stood with her children, a girl about fourteen and two boys under ten. They all looked as if they
had been crying. The younger boy was hiding his face.

"The family," said Suzanne. Her voice sounded
strained and hoarse. I could imagine how she was feeling.
My heart was pounding. It wasn't easy attending the
funeral of a man allegedly killed by your son's misguided
zeal.

I felt nauseated. I swallowed and turned away for some
air when I noticed a tall, birdlike man in his late twenties
with a heavy green sweater hanging loosely on his thin
frame, standing by the wall. He was studying me with a
startled expression, as if he were about to accuse me of
something, and I turned back to face the front quickly.

"For our final speaker," said the minister, a prematurely bald man in his early thirties with hazel eyes and a
slight stammer, "I would like to introduce to you someone
who—as the cliché goes—needs no introduction for any of
us, indeed whose family has needed no introduction in

this community for the better part of this century—Mr. Lawton Stanley."

A man in his fifties stepped slowly forward. He was tall and patrician with dashes of silver at his temples and wore a traditional black pinstripe suit with a black and orange regimental tie that made him look like one of the trustees of Princeton, an odd sight in such a rough-and-ready context.

"Vice-president of Allied Lumber," another man leaned over and whispered to me, noticing my puzzled expression. He was about my age and wore a brown bomber jacket not unlike mine and had his gray-streaked hair in a ponytail. In his left hand he carried a new canvas attaché case from Land's End.

"This is a tragedy," Stanley said. "And since I am not a poet, there is no way I can find to express the depths of anguish we all feel for the death of Leon Erlanger. Although we are not members of the immediate family"— he nodded toward the women and children—"we are all family here in Humboldt County, all recipients of God's bounty in this incredible and magnificent region which is the envy of the entire world. So the question is, Why has it come to this? Why do we fight with each other? Why is it that some believe those of us who were born in this place, who grew up here, whose families grew up here, whose parents and grandparents grew up here, are so callous we would destroy the extraordinary gifts of nature that provide our livelihood? Some of the people who believe that—not all of them but some; it would not be fair to say all—have shown themselves to be the true destroyers, the truly callous about human life. They have shown they care more for clear-water-jumping fish, spotted owls and brush rabbits than they do for Ethel Erlanger and her beautiful

children Lorraine, Edward and Raymond. God save their
souls and ours. And God rest the soul of Leon Erlanger."
The wife began to cry again.

Five minutes later it was over. "It's a tragedy all right . . .
for the environmental movement," said the man in the
ponytail as we filed out. Suzanne and I looked at each other.
Groups of loggers were all around us, consoling the
bereaved family.

"You're Moses Wine, aren't you?" continued the man in
the ponytail. I stopped and looked at him, warily. So much
for my Woody Allen disguise. He put out his hand.
"Daniel Springer, I'm the editor of the *Humboldt Herald*.
We met once before. I interviewed you when you were
security director for Tulip Computers in the Silicon Valley.
I was with the *San Jose Mercury News* then."

"Sorry," I said. I didn't have the slightest recollection,
but that didn't mean much. It had been ten years since my
brief stay at Tulip and all I remembered about it was how I
blew what amounted to three million dollars' worth of
stock options by quitting early.

"I heard about your involvement in this," said
Springer, nodding his head sympathetically. "It must be
awful. Can I buy you lunch? There isn't much except for
the Woodrose. I can recommend their linguini though."

I glanced at Suzanne, who shrugged. I doubted she was
any more hungry than I was.

"You're together, I take it," said Springer.

"This is Suzanne Greenhut," I said, when my beeper
went off. The sound was jolting. I looked at the number
quickly and clicked it off.

"That's some beeper you've got," he said. "You're a
long way from your office."

"Satellite. They can get me in Vermont, heaven help me. . . . Is there a pay phone in here?"

"In the back." He pointed to a door near the altar.

"I'll meet you both at the Woodrose?" I waited for Suzanne to nod her agreement before I walked quickly through the door. I may have had a sky beeper capable of delivering messages from anywhere in the world, but this one didn't come from far off. It had a 707 area code, from that very area of Northern California. Who knew I was there—unless it was the FBI?

There was a line to use the phone in the corridor, and I had to wait a few minutes before I could drop a quarter in and dial the number. After a couple of rings, I heard the other end pick up, but nobody answered.

"I believe I've been paged," I said finally, keeping it anonymous.

"Go away, Pop," said the voice on the other end.

"Simon!" I looked both ways to make sure no one was coming. Suddenly, my hand was trembling.

"Go away," he repeated. "You don't have any business here."

"What're you talking about? You're my son. You're in trouble." I tried to keep my voice down but I wanted to scream.

"I can handle it."

"How'd you know I was even here?"

"I have my ways."

"Your mother and I—"

"She's here too, isn't she?"

"We came up together."

"That's a first."

"Look, whatever's going on, whatever happened, you

have to know first and foremost I'm on your side. We're on your side. What do you want me to do?"

"Nothing. Go home."

"I can't go home. They'll arrest you and. . . . Are you on a secure phone?"

He laughed. "I'm on a pay phone out in the middle of nowhere. No one can see me except for a couple of cows."

"Good, good."

"So leave, Pop, okay? You guys had your chance. Now it's our turn. Go home to your Beemer and your girl-friends."

That one stung. "Maybe I can help you," I said. "I'm still on the side of the angels in my own way."

"It's over your head. There're heavy actions going down."

"Is that what you told the FBI?"

"What?"

"Their phone number was on your calendar."

"You were in my apartment?!" He sounded outraged.

"What was I supposed to do? Let you—"

"I can't believe you did that!"

"I'm sorry, I . . . "

"I gotta go."

"No, wait. Where are you?"

"I can't say."

"Well, call me or something."

He didn't respond.

"I love you," I said. But he had already clicked off.

6

"BAD NEWS?" said Springer as I slid in next to Suzanne at a booth in the Woodrose Café. He must have read it on my face. The place was already filled up with people from the funeral, obviously of the tree-hugger sort. The food was seventies vegetarian, a cuisine I always found particularly unappealing, with an emphasis on seven-grain sandwiches and guacamole. A note on the recycled menu reminded us, "Every year the average Californian consumes the equivalent of one 100-foot tree in forest products."

"One of my employees got caught photographing the wrong husband," I said, wondering if I sounded as transparent as I felt. "I think I'm losing a client."

"Tough luck," said Springer. "But when the cat's away, as they say."

"Try some linguini," said Suzanne, gesturing to her plate. "It's not entirely inedible."

"No alfalfa sprouts?" I said.

"No. Cilantro and I don't know what."

"Hemp pesto," said Springer, trying to make a joke. I signaled to the waitress to bring me a plate.

"Well, I gather you two are exes. I'm impressed." He exhaled and shook his head. "'Course, in our generation there's no reason we should hold on to some old-fashioned feud out of *I Love Lucy*. We've all had too much group for that. Besides, you never can tell what will happen. Friend of mine married and divorced the same woman three times before he gave it a rest. How's that for optimism?" He turned to me for a reaction, but I wasn't giving any. My mind was on the phone call from Simon. "So, look, as I told Suzanne here. . . . You don't mind if I don't call you Ms. Greenhut, do you? My first old lady always wanted everybody to call her Ms. and it's got bad associations for me."

"Whatever you want," said Suzanne.

"Anyway, I didn't invite you here for an official interview or anything. It's easy to imagine the stress you're under. I just thought maybe we could both profit from an exchange of views. Completely off the record, of course. You might want to know what's going down here and if I want to put anything in the *Herald*, I'll ask you in advance, in writing if you want."

"I don't think we have much time," I said. "Unless you can tell us how to find the Guardians of the Planet."

"If I could do that, I wouldn't be the editor of *this* rag," he said, pointing to a copy of his small-town journal, which was on the table in front of us. It was a mixture of local gossip and alternative press reprints with what looked to be a dash of hard reporting, all with an overly inky layout that smudged the type from one article to another. "I'd be back at the *Mercury News* with a shot at the city desk. The Guardians are big news hereabouts, I'm sorry to say."

"Who are they?"

"Nobody knows—that's the thing." He lowered his voice. "Except for your son, of course. And Claire Hannin, if she's still a member. There have to be others, maybe a half dozen more."

"What about a girl called Karin . . . a philosophy student?"

He shook his head.

"Who's Claire Hannin?" asked Suzanne.

"You don't know?" Springer gave her a surprised look. In an almost reverential tone he continued, "She was a leader of Earth People—one of the original eco groups, very peaceful."

"I thought that was Amos Manling," said Suzanne.

"Manling was the founder, one of the pioneer environmentalists. But that's one thing I'm sure you do know. He and Claire were a couple for a while, until they had an ideological disagreement—the kind of thing that happens in political movements, as I'm also sure you know—and split up. Claire took over the group from him."

"What does she have to do with the Guardians?" I asked.

"Everything, you could say. Or nothing. Depends on who you're talking to." He paused while a girl with rings in her nose walked toward our table. For a moment I wondered if it could have been Karin, but the rings were on the wrong side. "Remember back in 1990," Springer continued after she was past, "there was something called Redwood Summer? . . . Anyway, it was supposed to be the crowning glory of the Earth People, a return to community action. Well, that was all Claire's idea. . . . But just before it, a bomb went off in her car on the way to a meeting in Mendocino. The police and the FBI said it was her own bomb, that the

Earth People were going militant and accidentally blew themselves up. Hannin denied that, of course, but she vanished into the underground almost immediately. And then the Guardians made their appearance."

The woman with the limp, I thought. The story was coming back to me now, something I skipped over in the center pages of the *L.A. Times*. It wasn't the kind of thing I was paying much attention to in those days. "Wasn't there somebody else in that car explosion?" I asked.

"Yeah, fella named Ned Sayles. He didn't fare so well. Some shrapnel took his head off. . . . So I've been blabbing away here. What've you got to tell me?" He leaned in closer and smiled. "Do you know where your son is?"

"If we did, we wouldn't be sitting here," said Suzanne.

"Touché," said Springer. "Well, look, would you mind if I tagged along with you? You could use someone sympathetic showing you around up here and—"

"No dice, Springer," I said. "This is family business. I'm sure you understand."

"Sure."

My linguini finally arrived and I stared down at it. Someone had sprinkled sesame seeds and mung beans on the top along with some red stringy stuff that looked like ginger or, worse, shredded beets. "I don't think I can handle this," I said.

"It's probably someone else's order," said Springer.

"They have my condolences. . . . Anyway, I'm not hungry for once." I glanced over at Suzanne, who hadn't touched much of hers either despite having recommended it. "Ready?" I said. We stood and I deposited a ten-dollar bill. "Thanks for the offer of lunch, Springer, but I can't accept what I didn't eat."

"Another time," he said. "There's actually a good

Chinese place down in Ukiah. . . . Take the paper." He handed me the *Herald*, pointing at the masthead. "You'll know where to find me. . . . And careful of the back roads. The pot farmers don't ask for a background check before they shoot."

"He sure wanted to talk," said Suzanne, after we had left the restaurant and walked most of the way to the Buick. I had parked it at the corner opposite a fishing tackle shop.

"No kidding."

"I wonder why."

"My guess is we'll find out." I opened the car doors and we got in. "There's something I have to tell you."

"It was him, wasn't it?" she said immediately. "Simon. . . . I knew the minute you walked into the restaurant." She sounded angry. "Why didn't you tell me?"

"In front of that guy?"

"You could have excused yourself."

"It didn't seem like a smart thing to do."

"You could've thought of something."

"I assumed it could wait."

"Wait? Why didn't you come get me when you were talking to him in the first place? He's my son."

"You were gone already, Suzanne!" I was raising my voice. "What was I supposed to do? Leave the phone dangling there in the church?"

"How'd he sound?"

"I don't know," I said. "It was weird."

"Where was he?"

At that moment, Springer walked by, picking his teeth with a toothpick. He looked in the car and waved, waiting for a response. I turned on the motor and pulled out as if I hadn't seen him.

"I don't know . . . out with the cows somewhere. . . . He said we should go home, that we didn't have any place here. They were into something heavy."

"What was that?" She sounded alarmed.

"I don't know. I offered to help."

"Help?"

"You know . . ."

"No, I don't know. Jesus . . . what is this? Some sentimental bullshit about the—"

"Don't worry. He was having none of it. He said it was over my head. . . . I asked if he'd called the FBI."

"The San Francisco number?"

I nodded.

"What'd he say about *that*?"

"He hung up."

"God! What's going on? I don't know who he is. . . . Maybe we should call that guy Bart."

"We can't do that now. . . . Look, calm down, Suzanne, okay? All I was trying to do was make contact. Keep him on the phone."

"I wish I'd talked to him." She was starting to cry.

"Next time. I promise."

"What next time?"

I didn't know what to say. I reached out and touched her arm.

"I'll be okay," she said, biting her lower lip to stop crying and staring straight ahead. We were coming to the end of Garberville. I paused for a moment, checking for the presence of the Mercury before continuing. I hadn't seen it anywhere but I didn't find that any more reassuring than if I had.

"Do you have the map?" I asked Suzanne. "See if you can find the Jack London Grove. Before it gets dark, we ought to visit the scene of the crime, if that's what it was."

She found the grove on what looked like a dirt road headed east from the Avenue of the Giants, the famous reserve of old-growth trees contained within the borders of Humboldt Redwoods State Park. It wasn't that far from Garberville and when we turned off 101 on Mattole Road we were soon among the big trees, hundreds of them. We had passed what I thought were remarkable examples on our way up, but these were different, far more majestic, as if we had visited a few country churches and suddenly stumbled into Notre-Dame or Chartres. Even in my anxiety, there was a pathos to them, a natural poignancy, that calmed me. And they were so exquisite you felt that to harm them in any way would have been a desecration.

We drove past the visitors' center, and slightly over a mile later I almost missed a tiny sign. It read, "Jack London Grove—4.2 mi," pointing off to the right. It was already getting dark in the middle of the afternoon, and I wondered if we had made a mistake going too late. But I turned down the narrow road anyway, which was half dirt and half paved, with numerous large potholes marring the paved part. I held the speedometer well under twenty, sometimes nearer ten, and we crept along for about an hour, the tall trees looming over us, obscuring the already diminished sunlight.

"It's hard to believe it's real," said Suzanne, staring at our surroundings. Wisps of fog hung motionless in the air. A fallen tree in front of us was overwhelmed by moss and ferns.

"It's hard to believe any of this is real," I said when the left front tire bounced into a pothole and started to lose traction. I stopped, slipped the transmission into reverse and gently rocked back and forth, trying to get us out.

"Maybe we should come back in the morning," said Suzanne. "It's almost dark." She was right. Night had begun to fall, suffusing the forest with an eerie blue-gray light.

"I don't know," I said, finally rocking us out. "Maybe." But I continued up the road anyway to where a sign reading "You Are Now Leaving Humboldt Redwoods State Park" was hammered onto a tree. At that point, the road made an immediate sharp turn to the left and became pure dirt, and only the width of a bridle path. Just beyond, a pair of similar paths, which looked as if they had been recently cut by Caterpillar trucks, led off in opposite directions into the woods. I slowed to a near halt, feeling distinctly urban and out of my depth. I knew it was crazy to be out there without a four-wheel drive or at least a topo map, but even if I had one, I doubted I'd still remember how to read it. I was just about to give up and turn around when I saw a band of yellow police tape tied to a temporary metal pole, a weirdly reassuring outpost of big-city life suddenly materializing in the wilderness. It led off between some trees, disappearing down the side of a hill. "I guess this is it," I said, pulling over on a mound between two trees.

Suzanne and I got out. We walked around the front of the car and ducked under the police tape, following it into the forest. The tape ran along the side of an old stone fence, parts of which had fallen down or crumbled; other sections were painted with what looked like surveyor's marks, some fresher than others. We continued along the fence as it circled down into a gully and in a minute we were in an area where about a dozen huge old-growth trees had been cut and removed along the Caterpillar paths. All that remained were stumps, which were themselves ten to twenty feet high, and the thick beds of brush and pine needles that had been put there by the loggers to cushion the redwoods' fall and avoid breakage to the precious trunks. It looked as if there had been a scalping in the forest.

Just beyond was another mammoth tree still lying on its side. At its base, near its stump, were four other metal poles where more police tape had been tied off in a larger square, delineating what must have been the formal crime scene. Suzanne and I walked up to it. A small shrine had been created where the tree split; a bouquet of flowers, daffodils and irises, leaned against a cross fashioned of branches with the words "Leon, forever in our hearts . . ." carved into the bark.

I turned away and stared into the nearby trees. Had they been spiked as well? It was impossible to tell. And what about the one they chose? Why that one? Had they put up a warning? A flag? A mark? Some indication that mortal danger awaited the unsuspecting logger? I looked along the trunk but saw nothing. And how would someone die this way anyway? It was easy to understand a serious blade cut, perhaps, or a maiming from an errant chain, broken bones or even blindness. But death? It seemed unlikely, but then maybe I was looking for a simple way out.

"Where do you think they put the spike?" I said, quite confused now. Suzanne shook her head. "They'd have had to climb up fifteen feet or so in the first place," I continued. "And then how do they know where the loggers are going to cut?"

I reached for the police tape, starting to lift it to go through for a closer look when I heard a voice from behind.

"Excuse me, please."

I looked to my right. Three people were walking deliberately toward us. They stopped in a couple of steps and planted themselves about ten feet away. One of them was a tall, ruggedly handsome man in his early forties. He wore a gold pin with the initials CFP on the lapel of a green felt shirt and a holster on his belt containing what I guessed was a .38. A shorter man next to him wore a baseball cap and a down vest over a palm tree T-shirt that said, "Souvenir of Kuwait City." He had a thin mustache and carried a shotgun. The third person, a woman with close-cropped dirty-blond hair, kept her hands in a lumber jacket. She was doing the talking. "Excuse me," she repeated. "Do you have permission to be here?"

"I didn't know we needed it," I said.

"This is private property."

"I thought it was Humboldt State Park. I'm sorry." I looked at the three people, who were staring at us expressionlessly.

"We got lost," said Suzanne. "We're tourists."

"Can I see some I.D?" asked the woman.

I glanced at the guy with the .38; his hand was positioned on his belt an inch or two from his holster. "Sure," I said, reaching slowly into my jacket pocket and taking out a special business card I kept for emergencies. "Whose land is it, if I might ask?" I passed the card over to her.

"Allied Lumber Company."

"And you work for them?"

"We're a private security company . . . California Forest Protection." She gestured to the initial pin on the tall man's shirt. "What do you do, Mr. . . ." —she looked from the card to me— ". . . Lucas?"

"Advertising."

"I see you're from Los Angeles."

"Yes, I am."

She passed the card over to the tall man who also looked it over. "Well, since you're from L.A.," she continued. "I'm sure you know what a crime scene is. Can you tell us what you're doing here?"

"Like she said. We got lost."

"The address on the card's a post box," said the tall man. "You have some formal I.D., Mr. Lucas? Driver's license or California identification card?"

"Back in the car," I said.

"How about you, ma'am?"

"Same."

"Is that what you always do, Mr. Lucas?" the tall man asked. "Keep your I.D. in the car?" He looked over at his partners. They didn't seem impressed. The man with the mustache glanced down at his shotgun. I couldn't tell if it was loaded.

"I'll get it for you," I said, taking Suzanne by the arm. "Be right back."

We turned around and started walking up the hill, slowly at first, then faster and faster, hoping they wouldn't come after us, but not looking back for fear of appearing suspicious. There were some voices behind us, then some laughter, then nothing. Everything seemed all right when, just as we had rounded the bend out of sight, a shot rang out, shattering some branches. Suzanne gasped. I grabbed her hand and ducked, breaking into a run and pulling her with me all the way up the hill to the car. I didn't stop until we reached the door of the Buick. As I fumbled with the keys, I glanced back down the trail, but I couldn't see anyone.

"Jesus," said Suzanne, when I finally managed to get

the car open and we jumped in. "Was that meant for us?"

"I don't want to wait to find out," I said, spinning the car around with a loud screech and heading for the main road. In a few seconds, we were well inside the park again.

I looked over at Suzanne. There were big rings around her eyes and the bottom part of her face had nearly gone concave from fatigue. I must've looked the same way. We had barely slept in almost thirty-five hours.

Without saying anything, once I had turned onto 101, I started looking for a motel at the north end of the Avenue of the Giants. But as I did so, a blue Dodge van suddenly appeared in the rearview mirror. Were these CFP characters already following us too? I raced ahead and pulled into a gas station beyond the forest gate, waiting for the Dodge among the tourist vehicles. It slowed down as it approached, then sped up and disappeared over the ridge. After a few minutes, I made a 180 and headed back to a motel I had spotted along the way—the Eel River Lodge. This time Suzanne and I took separate rooms. Then we went out and finally had something to eat before we retired early.

But tired as I was, I couldn't fall asleep. I sat there staring at a broken-down portable TV—first an old movie and then the local news. I was finally about to drift off when I was startled awake by the announcement of a homemade videotape just arrived from the Guardians of the Planet. A spokesperson, his face completely covered with a terrorist kerchief which was dark green instead of the traditional black, read into the camera from a prepared statement in a voice that was unmistakably my son's:

"The Guardians of the Planet regret any loss of life or personal injury in the ongoing struggle for the preservation of the world. However, the self-righteous hegemony of the human species over all other animal and plant forms has caused and continues to cause more destruction on this globe than all other factors combined. The Guardians of the Planet hereby vow to continue their all-out war on polluters and despoilers in all their manifestations. In the battle to save the Earth, there can be no compromise!"

I stared at him, wondering who had written those words (Karin? the FBI? Simon himself?), when the video faded to the encouraging countenance of the local newsman. He reassured his listeners that, according to the sheriff's office, it was only a matter of hours before these heinous criminals would be apprehended. By way of illustration he showed some clips of police dogs sniffing around an abandoned shack in the mountains while helicopters roared overhead.

I turned the TV off and tried to sleep, but my mind was racing now from this latest report and my eyes wouldn't stay shut for more than a couple of seconds. I tossed and turned in the bed for a few minutes, when I started to have the yet more unsettling feeling that I was being watched. I stopped moving and looked in the direction of the picture window, which gave onto the second-story walkway outside my room. A pair of eyes was peering through a crack at the edge of the miniblinds.

I lay there for another minute, holding my breath and rehashing my resolution never to carry a handgun because I might, once again, have to pay the moral and emotional price of using it. Then quietly, with painful slowness, I rolled over to the opposite side of the bed and, careful not to disturb the pillows, lifted the blankets an inch or so and slid off onto the floor. I lowered my head and was crawl-

ing across the carpet toward the bathroom, when I heard
steps racing across the walkway.

I jumped up and ran to the front door, fumbling with
the lock and finally sticking my head outside. I didn't see
anyone and I ran out farther onto the steps, recklessly continuing halfway down the stairs, when I saw two shadowy
figures streaking through the trees fifty yards up from the
motel. I couldn't see their faces or anything about them,
but they got into what seemed—in the headlights of an
oncoming car—to be the same Dodge van I had seen earlier. They drove off up a dirt road that disappeared into
the woods.

I stood there for a moment, shivering in my T-shirt and
pajama bottoms, then turned to head up the stairs again.
Suzanne was standing in front of my room in her night-
gown.

"What was that?" she said, her hands clutching the rail-
ing.

"We're being watched again."

"By whom?"

"The feds, those forest protection characters we ran
into . . . Who knows?" I opened my door, waiting for her
to go in. Then I bolted it behind us and slid the chain in as
well before turning on the light. Suzanne leaned against
the bureau.

"Did you see Simon?" I said, indicating the TV.

"Who's writing his dialogue? I never heard him use the
word 'hegemony' before." She sounded even more
exhausted than she had in the car.

"Have you been able to sleep?" I asked.

She shook her head.

"Me neither. . . . Do you want to stay here?" I gestured
to the bed. She hesitated, then nodded, walked over and

lay down. I turned out the light again and slid down beside her.

"I can't stand it, Moses," she said.

"I know," I said. I took her in my arms and held her. We remained motionless and silent for a while. I felt her body against mine. It was warm and consoling and I exhaled slowly, letting myself go, my overloaded mind drifting off, unable to focus. But, then, as we lay quietly for ten or fifteen minutes, the inevitable first dim stirrings of arousal appeared. I didn't know how to deal with them, but I lowered my arm and wrapped it around her back. It felt good, but confusing, oddly incestuous after all this time.

"What did we do to deserve this?" Suzanne said finally, almost in a moan.

"I don't know," I said. "Remember how Simon used to run away all the time when he was little? But he would always come back. That time when we were at Exposition Park . . . he disappeared behind those rosebushes and we looked and looked until we were halfway out of our minds, but he was just sitting back at our picnic table, waiting for us, laughing. . . . Maybe it's the same thing now. . . . Of course, he's not four years old anymore, is he?"

Suzanne didn't answer. She was fast asleep.

7

"HAVE YOU HEARD FROM YOUR BROTHER?"

"No, not in weeks. Where are you?"

"In a motel in the redwood country."

"Together?" said Jacob, his voice registering both irony and shock.

"Yes, we're both here," said Suzanne. She was sitting on the edge of the bed. I was in the bathroom, using the extension. It was about seven-thirty in the morning, ten-thirty for Jacob in New York.

"Do you think he's all right?" he said.

"Yes, he sounds okay. I talked to him once."

"You know where he is?!"

"He beeped me."

"Oh. Of course."

"You sure he never said anything to you, Jacob?" asked Suzanne.

"About what?" he said. He sounded uncomfortable. "I haven't seen him since summer. When we went down to Tijuana together."

"I just thought there might be something," she said. "I

know you guys talk. He's got a new girlfriend called Karin? Did he tell you anything about her?"

"Oh, Mother, please. Am I getting the third degree here?"

"You tell each other things you'd never tell your parents," she said.

She was right.

The two boys were close, even though in many ways they shouldn't have been. Jacob was a witty intellectual who enjoyed gossiping until dawn with artsy types on the lower Manhattan scene. Simon was by instinct a loner. But despite their differences they had remained confidants since childhood. Only when Jacob came out as gay was there a rift between them, and that was short-lived.

"What about Karin?" I asked. "Or someone named Claire Hannin?"

"If I knew anything, I doubt it would be relevant," he said.

"Look, we're desperate here," I said. "Any scrap of information is a help."

"Not that desperate," said Jacob. His tone was exceptionally mordant.

"What's that supposed to mean?" said his mother. I could see her posture through the bathroom door. She was sitting up straight on the bed with her neck stiff and elongated.

"Well, some things create more problems than they solve."

"Can we be the judge of that?" I said.

"Especially with you guys doing this together." Jacob added, "He once told me something about Claire Hannin."

"Jacob, what is it?" said Suzanne sharply.

"Well, you asked," he said. "All I know is the way Simon got to know her is through Gabriel Levine."

"What?!" I said. The name gave me immediate stomach palpitations. Even during a crisis like this, the feeling of betrayal overwhelmed everything. "Did you know about this?" I said to Suzanne, cupping the phone and looking at her. She shook her head. "How'd that happen?" I asked Jacob. "I didn't even know they were in contact."

"Well, you know Gabriel moved up north to get away from L.A. . . . "

"Uh-uh. Sort of." Actually I knew damn well he had moved. I had kept closer tabs on Gabriel Levine than I cared to admit.

"Simon ran into him at an eco rally in Mendocino a couple of years ago. The Grateful Dead were playing with some grunge band and Claire Hannin was there, giving a speech."

"I thought she was in hiding," I said.

"Up to a point. I guess she surfaced to rally the troops or something."

"And Gabriel introduced them?" said Suzanne. I studied her expression for some sign of feeling, but I couldn't read any.

"I guess," said Jacob.

"How'd he know Claire?" I asked.

"Research on some movie he was writing, I think. I'm not sure."

"What movie was that?" I asked disingenuously, knowing full well that most of Gabriel's movies never reached the screen and unable to resist the bitchy snipe. In truth, the thought of my kids in contact with this man after all these years was a wound I had no idea how to heal.

"What else do you know?" asked Suzanne.

71

"Nothing. Simon never said any more about it and I never asked him. I didn't think it was important. . . . You guys going to check it out?"

"Yes," I said. "Right away." I could see Suzanne tense up. "We'll call you back as soon as we know anything."

"I'll be here."

We all said our good-byes and hung up.

I walked into the bedroom and asked Suzanne, "Where does he live? I'm sure you know."

"Willits."

"Willits? We drove right by him and you didn't say a word."

"What was there to say? I haven't talked to him in some time. . . . Shall we go?"

"In a minute . . . I need to speak to Nancy. I owe her a call." I smiled and nodded toward the door. "If you don't mind . . . "

Suzanne got up and left before I dialed. "Hello. It's me," I said when she picked up.

"Oh, God. I thought you'd call earlier. I've been so worried. How are you?"

"In hell."

"I should imagine. Have you found him yet?"

"No. But a lot of people seem to have found me."

"What does that mean?

"I'm not sure."

"Is there anything I can do?"

"I don't think so. . . . I wish there were but . . . "

"I guess you've got help." Nancy sounded disappointed. "She's not like I expected."

"Who?"

"Your ex."

"What'd you expect?"

"I don't know. Different."

"Everyone's different when you meet them. . . . Nancy, I've got to go."

"I understand. . . . Call me."

"Yes."

"Promise."

"Yes." I said good-bye and hung up. Then, before I went to fetch Suzanne, I decided to make another call, to the San Francisco branch of the FBI, dialing the number I had found on Simon's calendar.

This time there was no recorded message. But I got a surprise from the live voice on the other end: "Special Agent Bart's office," the woman said.

I hung up. After a moment, I went outside to join Suzanne. She was waiting on the walkway outside our rooms. She must have noticed the mildly stunned expression on my face.

"Everything okay?" she asked.

I told her what had happened, that Simon had had Bart's phone number.

"What do you make of that?"

"I wish I knew," I said, but I could see in her expression we both had the same awful suspicion. A feeling of dread came over me.

I shrugged it off and surveyed the area around the motel. I wanted to be sure we weren't being watched before we headed out in our car to visit Gabriel Levine.

When we arrived at his place about a half hour later, I was surprised and more than a little jealous at the way he was living. At the end of a steep private drive just east of Willits off 101, Gabriel's house was a splendid three-story redwood in the Craftsman style with intricately carved dormer windows and an entry walkway flanked by bronze lanterns with celadon leaded glass. A new Land Rover Discovery and a vintage Morgan stood in the garage next to a pair of Peugeot mountain bikes. Off to the right were a hot tub and a Japanese gazebo in their own individual redwood stand, fronting on what looked like a hundred acres of virgin land. The whole compound was a Northern California dream, the kind of place where'd you expect Ken Kesey or Jerry Garcia, had he survived, to be spending his dotage, swapping memories of the Merry Pranksters while jetting in macrobiotic rice bowls from Nepal.

Gabriel was waiting at the front door wearing a green and black Pendleton shirt and holding a thick, restaurant-supply coffee mug when we walked up. I assumed he had heard us pulling up the long gravel driveway. He looked good for a man I knew would be fifty in February. He had a bit more salt in his pepper-and-salt hair. Other than that, he hadn't changed since I had last seen him, a few years ago at a Franco-Japanese restaurant in Santa Monica. There didn't seem to be a pound more on him and I had to stop myself from patting my stomach self-consciously as we shook hands.

"Hello, Gabriel," I said.

"Hello, Moses . . . Suzanne . . ." He was smiling broadly, although I couldn't imagine he was glad to see us, or at least me. *That* had changed drastically in the nearly thirty years since we had been inseparable college room-mates. "What a surprise," he continued. "Come on in and have a cup of joe." He held the door open for us, and we entered the foyer. "It's Sumatran, my specialty. Amy does the scones." He nodded through the dining room into the kitchen, where a very attractive Asian woman of about thirty was extracting a muffin tin from the oven. "Amy,"

Gabriel called out. "Can you believe it? It's Moses and Suzanne. I told you all about them."

"Hello, there," she said. "With you in a minute."

I glanced at Suzanne, whose expression made clear she had picked up on the irony that both Gabriel and I were spending our midlife-crisis years with younger Asian women. She probably thought it was in reaction to a life-time of being guilt-tripped by liberated Western women, but I could tell her she had the stereotype all wrong.

Gabriel poured us some coffee and led us into the liv-ing room. "Why don't we sit here?" he said, nodding toward a Stickley-type sofa arrangement that faced French doors with a view of the snow-capped peaks of the north-ern Sierra.

"Nice place," I said. "The script business must be look-ing up."

"So-so," said Gabriel. "Cash just goes a lot further around here. I put in a large down from *Satan in Mendocino* and now I do my best to make the payments off what comes up." He was referring to the one script of his that had actually been made in recent years, a hocus-pocusy business about devil worshipers along the California coast. It was shown a few times on cable. "And Amy helps out, of course. She's teaching tai chi up in Garberville." That sounded like a real money maker.

Just then Amy arrived with the scones. "We've been wondering if you'd show up," she said. "We've been watching what happened to your son on television."

"They've used Simon's name?" said Suzanne, startled.

"Didn't you know?" said Amy. "You must be in a terri-ble state. I'm so sorry." She offered us some butter for the scones. I wondered how much Gabriel had told her about our mutual past.

"I guess you have some involvement in this too," I said to Gabriel. "I'm told you introduced Simon to Claire Hannin."

"That's true," he said. "I'm to blame, as usual." He forced a curious little smile. I had a quick flash of him and Suzanne in bed together, all those times she said she was going to her gym class and headed over to his apartment for her real exercise. "Actually, I feel quite guilty about it," he continued. "If I'd known it would have gone this far, I never would have done it. I had no idea Simon was so impressionable. He always seemed so levelheaded in a quiet way."

"Where do you think he is?" I said.

"Oh, I have no idea. I don't follow the Guardians of the Planet. It's not my kind of thing. You know I was never militant like you and Suzanne were. Even when it was fashionable."

"But you knew Claire Hannin."

"Some producer wanted to do a script on eco-terrorism. I didn't think it was commercial. Too sixties. But he had some money for a treatment so I met her. It wasn't hard to find her then."

"Do you know where she is now?"

"Well, you hear rumors but . . ." He shrugged evasively and looked over at Suzanne with a smile. "More coffee?" he said to her. "There's Key lime marmalade for the scones. I know you like that."

Fuck you, I thought.

"Something wrong?" he asked, turning toward me.

"What rumors?" I said, ignoring him.

"Nothing substantial. It's surprising, actually. When I was doing my research, I found the ecologists to be not as lily-white as they're supposed to be. And the big lumber-mill owners ... well, Lawton Stanley turned out to be quite a decent guy. In fact, the Allied Lumber Company and the Stanley family in general have a history of treating their employees extremely well, putting their kids through college, giving them better health benefits than the union and so forth."

"That's because they don't *have* a union," I said.

"I figured you'd say that. . . . Anyway, they made an effort. They even made the first deal for forest conservation back in the twenties, with the Save-the-Redwood League, I think they called it. . . . Of course that all changed when FOXAM came in."

"FOXAM?" I asked.

"The conglomerate that bought Allied Lumber. A real eighties deal with junk bonds and everything. The forests are owned by foreigners these days, gray men in high-rises."

"What does this have to do with Claire Hannin?"

"Nothing, as far as I know. I just thought you might be interested in the history. I find it a lot more intriguing than the likes of Claire. To my mind she was just another of those professional paranoids out to blame the system for her own—"

"What?!" I said. I found myself on my feet, staring down at Gabriel, who looked up at me with an expression of disdain tempered by a hint of anxiety.

"What's your problem, Moses? I can't help you. I don't know where your son is. Or Claire Hannin."

"I don't believe you."

"Why not?"

"Because you lied to me when I was your best friend. Why should I believe you now?"

Everyone went silent. Outside a crow swept by one of

the windows and disappeared into the trees, flashing me
back for an instant to the first time Gabriel and I took
mushrooms together, thirty years ago. It had been a great
experience until I had visions of myself tied to a post,
being attacked in the face by wild birds.

"Look, Moses," he said, standing and walking toward
me. "All this anger about something that went on between
Suzanne and me years ago—it's pointless. Why don't you
just let it go? I can assure you it's over. Amy can vouch for
that. . . . And so can Suzanne. Can't you?"

"Yes," said Suzanne, a dull emptiness in her voice.

"So there you have it," said Gabriel, putting his hand
on my shoulder and squeezing.

"Take your hands off me," I said.

Gabriel withdrew and looked at me with an amused
smile. "What do you want to know, the rumors about
Claire Hannin?" he said. "They're useless anyway. . . . Once
I heard she was hiding at her daughter's nursery school.
Now I hear she's on a pot farm somewhere in the hills. "

"Where?"

"Oh, please . . . I wouldn't know."

"Would you tell me if you did?"

He stared at me a moment. "Great to see you again,
Moses. As always. But now you'll have to excuse me. I
have a deadline. You won't mind if I don't see you out."
He walked over to Suzanne and smiled. "Bye, love. Cheer
up. I'm sure everything will be all right." Then he kissed
her on the cheek and exited through the patio door to
what looked like a studio out back.

"Where're we going to find a pot farm?" said Suzanne five
minutes later. We were driving down from Gabriel's
through a forest of Douglas fir. "Much less *the* pot farm."

"Assuming he's not lying about that too."

"Come on, Moses."

"Sorry. I'm still jealous, okay? . . . He just pushes every button. And I don't like the idea of him living in a place like that . . . Jacuzzis . . . gazebos . . . a Morgan."

"It is pretty well equipped, isn't it? Did you get a whiff of that candy smell coming from downstairs?"

"Candy smell?"

"Like bubblegum . . . coming from the basement."

"What's he got? A movie theater down there too? . . . You really do still have a crush on the son of a bitch, don't you?"

I slapped on the brakes before she could reply. The blue Dodge van from the previous night was parked across the road, blocking our path. I started to back up, looking in the rearview mirror. An old dump truck was emerging from a dirt fire road. It too stopped in the middle of the road. I hit the brakes again and looked at Suzanne. "Shit!" I said.

"Who is it?" she said.

"Those bastards from yesterday, I think."

"California Forest Protection?"

I nodded, looking at the two trucks. Although the windows of the van were tinted, I could see the shadow of what appeared to be a shotgun barrel through the glass of the side panel. "What do we do?" asked Suzanne.

Before I could think of anything, the side door of the van slid open and four people poured out and ran toward our car. They wore leather gloves and dark green kerchiefs over their faces. I spun around to see three others coming from the direction of the dump truck. In seconds, they were swarming us.

"Get out! Get out!" one of them yelled—he was a

man—as another pulled open the door on the passenger's side, removing Suzanne. I reached out for her but a third person was already leaning in on my side, taking me by the arm while a partner twisted my head backward and tied a green bandanna around my eyes. We weren't under attack by California Forest Protection—or any other security group, for that matter. These were the Guardians of the Planet. We were being kidnapped by our own son.

A minute later we were in what felt like the van, bouncing along a dirt road I assumed was the one the dump truck had come from. I was flanked on both sides by Guardians, Suzanne in the seat behind me. "Simon, you here?" I called out.

"No." It was a woman's voice. Who was this? Claire Hannin? Karin? I started to reach for my blindfold. "Don't!" she said. I felt cold steel push hard into my side just below the rib cage.

"What's this?" I said. "The ecology movement packs a rod?"

"By any means necessary," she said.

8

"I TOLD YOU TO GO HOME, POP."

I was sitting, still with my blindfold on, tied to a shaky stool in what I took to be a room in a cabin somewhere deep in the backcountry. We had been deposited there after a forty-five minute or so drive over some of the roughest, most winding mountain roads I had ever experienced. Twice the vehicle stopped and gates were opened and shut again; once it pulled over briefly while a helicopter buzzed overhead and disappeared. It parked, finally, tilted forward in what seemed like a ditch, and we dismounted to be led for another twenty some minutes on foot, sightless, through thick woods, slipping and sliding on rocks, banging into trees, fording a couple of streams and crossing a fragile rope bridge until we reached a flatter, gentler area. I smelled manure and thought I heard sheep. Then Suzanne and I were ushered up a couple of steps into the cabin and tied onto the stools. All this with barely a word spoken. Simon finally broke the silence. He must've been standing there, waiting.

"This isn't your business," he continued. "It never has been and it never will be."

"Simon, I know this sounds corny, but there is such a thing as parental responsibility."

"Stop being pompous, Pop. That's not your style. You're afraid of what I'm doing. Both of you."

"Simon . . ." interjected Suzanne. She sounded exhausted.

"I'm not afraid of it," I said. "It's . . ."

"It's what?"

"It's . . . I just want to make sure it's thought out."

"Who are you? The ideology police?"

"I'm your father."

"And . . . ?"

"Maybe we can help you out."

"You think so, do you? . . . You know that's just the way it was, growing up with your generation. You did every-thing first—sex, drugs, rock and roll, politics. You think you know it all. Well, you don't always."

"I never said we did."

"I know you didn't. You never do. That's what I mean, Pop. Everything's supposed to be okay, but nothing really is that isn't your viewpoint." I heard him start to pace. "Follow your star. Everything's cool. Do your own thing. Well, look where it got you . . . got us. Homeless on the streets and Gingrich in the Congress. You failed, Pop. And, Mom, you're worse . . . almost . . . wasting half your life in New Age fads, gurus and psychics, and then when you finally get your shit together and go to law school to help immigrants, you end up doing bankruptcy cases for branch banks and loan companies because you say it's hard times and you gotta make a living. Well, you know, some people really have hard times."

"Is this over?" said Suzanne. "Can we take off our masks now?"

"I don't know," said Simon. "I don't know if it will ever be over." I had never heard him so articulate. It almost sounded as if he had been taking lessons from his brother.

"Are you in charge here?" I said, not knowing if there was anybody else in the room. "Subcomandante Marcos or something?"

"We have no leaders."

"Ah, yes, the old rhetoric."

"There you go!" said Simon bitterly. "Co-opting. Knowing. Been there . . . done that. The king of all experience." He sighed with disgust. "You know it's attitudes like yours that are the most reactionary of all. Petty. Self-protective. At least with the fucks who own the mills and the FBI you know who you're dealing with."

"I'm sure you do," I said flatly.

He stopped still.

I waited a moment before I said, "Special Agent Nicholas Bart among them."

Silence. Somewhere in the distance I could hear a horse whinny.

"Why didn't you tell me about the break-in at PG & E?"

Still no response.

"Was that your idea or Karin's?"

"I don't have time for this," said Simon finally. "We're in the middle of a war here."

"So what're you going to do with us? Keep us here until it's over?"

"If we have to."

"We love you, no matter what," said Suzanne.

"I know," he said. And he walked out of the room, shutting the door behind him.

Five minutes later, someone came in and removed our blindfolds. It was the birdlike man from Erlanger's funeral. We were in a bigger room than I had thought, with a dining table and a cookstove. "Follow me," he said, quickly untying our hands and feet. He led us out the door into a small clearing in the woods, where four cabins had been erected. We had been in the largest one, which had two floors. The others were one-room affairs with a single door and a couple of windows. No one seemed to be around, although where they had gone I had no guess. "This way." The birdlike guy led us toward the cabin near a fence where some sheep were grazing. Suzanne and I followed and entered behind him without comment.

Inside were a couple of cots and a camp table with a chair. Our overnight bags, obviously taken from the rental car, were stacked in the corner. "Simon said you two might want to sleep separately, but we don't have enough room," he said. "Shower's behind the main house. Latrine's over there." He pointed between the opposite cabins. "We'll bring your meals to your cabin. Keep as far from the windows as possible, stay inside unless it's absolutely necessary and no night candles. We don't want to attract helicopters. Any questions?"

"What's your name?" I asked.

"Bill," he said, and exited.

Suzanne and I looked at each other. Out the window we were supposed to keep away from, Bill was visible, heading around the main house. I stood there watching until he disappeared. We were under some form of house arrest and I was already feeling stir-crazy.

I turned back to Suzanne. "What's wrong with Simon?" I said. "He wouldn't answer any questions."

"He doesn't trust us."

"Trust *us*? He never told us anything in the first place."

"Maybe he couldn't."

"Who's stopping him?"

"I don't know. I. . . ." She shook her head in frustration.

"If he's an FBI undercover, I'll fucking kill him. That's the most disgusting behavior I could—"

"We don't know that."

"But if he isn't, it's even worse. He's gone off the deep end!" I walked over to the window and looked out again. "Who do you think she was?"

"Who?"

"The one with the gun."

"I don't know. I don't even know if it was a gun. . . . Karin?"

"What about Claire Hannin?" I said.

"Not here, I guess."

"Right. She's the *non*violent one."

"You don't believe it?"

"I don't know what to believe. All I know is we're not learning anything waiting here." I turned back to Suzanne. "I'm going to have a look around."

"You heard what Bill said. You want to bring down the helicopters?"

"I won't bring down helicopters. I'll stay in the trees. You want to come?"

"It's not what Simon wants."

"Yes, but it's what he needs."

"That's what you think."

I stared at her, feeling that ugly competitiveness that often comes between parents where their children are concerned. Who will do the best for the child? Who does the child prefer? It was the original no-win situation. "Yes, it's what I think," I said finally. "I'm going out there. I don't feel like I have a choice."

"Suit yourself," she said.

"You *sure* you don't want to come?"

She shook her head. I hesitated a second, then smiled and touched her shoulder—did I want her to reassure me in some way, the way I did when we were twenty-five?—before I peered out the door and, looking both ways, slipped out.

I walked swiftly into the trees, hiding under the branches as I skirted the perimeter of the clearing. I stopped behind each cabin to peer in through the back window. They were almost identical to ours, except each had three cots jammed together instead of two. As a result, they had barely any open floor space, making them look like rooms in a woefully underendowed college. The only personal effects visible were a couple of sweaters, a hand mirror and a ski parka. The walls too were bare, as if the Guardians had agreed to eliminate any revealing evidence of their identity. The only exception, in the last cabin, was a teddy bear on one of the cots and a Polaroid of Kurt Cobain in concert taped to the ledge of the window.

I continued on to the back of the main cabin, standing there a moment to detect the presence of Bill or anyone else. I could see through the window past a hallway into the living-dining area, all the way to the front door. No one appeared to be around. Where had they all gone? I took a step backward and looked up at the second floor. A wood stairway ran up the side of the house to a door beside a window, where a Coleman lantern stood on a desk with a black ski mask draped over its lid. Was this where Simon lived, my son the subcomandante?

I was about to make a run for the stairs when I saw Bill walking from the direction of the latrine with a copy of *Wired* magazine. I waited until he crossed into another cabin before I crept forward, climbed the stairs on my toes

and tried the door. It was locked with a deadbolt. I
glanced through the window. Inside was a large room containing two cots and the desk I'd seen from below; there
was a closet off to the left side. The Power Book I had
bought Simon two Christmases ago was on top of the
desk, next to a neat pile of papers. A large U.S. Geological
Survey topo map of Humboldt County was attached to
the far wall with aluminum pushpins. Several distinct
areas—were they forests?—had been outlined with a yellow marker. They had black ink notations along the border, in Simon's distinctive graffiti-like style. I strained to
read what they said when I heard laughter and talking.
The Guardians were returning.

I backed up and sped carefully down the stairs from
my son's room with a dirty, cheating feeling I hadn't
had since I was a kid myself, stealing change from my
father's bureau drawer to pay poker debts to my high
school buddies. At the bottom, I looked both ways. For a
second, I looked home free, but when I turned the corner, I ran straight into one of the Guardians coming
toward me. She had a tool of some sort in her left hand
and was in the process of pulling off her ski mask with
her right. I stopped dead in front of her like a trapped
animal.

"Hello," she said.

"Hi . . . I was, uh . . . "

"Looking around?" she said, and finished removing
her mask. Beneath it was the face of a truly gorgeous nine-
teen- or twenty-year-old girl with a pale, almost translu-
cent complexion, short rust-colored hair and the most
extraordinary hazel eyes I had ever seen. Even the two
rings in her left nostril, which normally might have
seemed a cliché, heightened her attractiveness, giving her

a primitive sexuality that was almost tribal, despite the fact I knew she was a philosophy student.

"You must be Karin," I said. "I'm Simon's dad."

"I know . . . Moses. Do you mind if I call you that? I've heard so much about you I feel as if I know you." She took a step closer and flashed a smile. She was obviously one of those young women who sensed everything about men by the time they were six.

"No, not at all."

"Find anything interesting?" she said. She gestured casually about the compound. I glanced down at her body, which was nearly flawless.

"Not especially. Is there anything interesting to find? . . . What's that?" I nodded toward the tool in her hand.

"A thirty-two-inch bolt cutter, good for de-heading spikes of ten inches or larger—even spiral helix nails, which are normally quite difficult."

"I take it that's what you were doing, spiking trees."

"You could assume that."

"Was Simon with you?"

"Not in this case."

"Do you know where he is?"

"Not at the moment."

"I thought you and he were close."

"We are. Very. Your son's a special person, Moses. With global concerns. . . . You're to be commended for the way you raised him."

"Thank you. . . . He thinks very highly of you too. . . . Actually, I was trying to find out something about you yesterday. I checked the Berkeley philosophy department, but they didn't seem to have record of a Karin. I didn't know your full name."

"It wouldn't have mattered. I dropped out a while ago.
. . . Fascinating as they are, I don't think Kant and Hume
are particularly relevant when the ozone layer is being
destroyed, do you?"

"I see your point," I said. "So what *is* your name?"

"My real name or my political name?"

"How about both?"

"How about neither?" She flashed the smile again.
"Aren't you supposed to be in your cabin, Moses?" Before
I could answer, she walked off around the main house and
disappeared.

9

"A GRUNGE HELEN OF TROY," I said.

"That good?" said Suzanne.

I nodded. I was back in our cabin, pacing about and feeling caged already.

"But who is she? Is Karin even her real name?"

I shook my head. "She wouldn't tell me anything. Not even where Simon is. Only thing I know is it's true she once studied philosophy. And she knows a helluva lot about spiking trees."

There was a knock on the door. Before I could say "Come in," Bill entered, carrying a tray.

"Dinner," he said, depositing it on the small table between our beds. I checked my watch. It was only four thirty. "We eat early, while we can still see our food."

He exited, leaving Suzanne and me staring at our dinners—tinned fruit cocktails and a couple of reheated sausage pizzas that looked as if they had just come out of the bottom of the freezer. Not particularly healthy fare for a group of eco-freaks, but then this was a war zone and I was famished. I hadn't eaten since our unappetizing visit to Gabriel's.

Suzanne was hungry too and we sat and started cutting into our pizzas when we heard the dull whirring of
helicopters somewhere in the distance. After a few
moments the sound grew louder, the copters seeming to
come closer, drift away, then come back again, louder
still. They weren't directly overhead, but near enough.
Suzanne and I looked at each other without speaking. I
could see the tension in her face. It was that generational
reaction we all had, even those of us who never saw battle, to the whir of the helicopter—a nightmarish sound
calling forth maimed images on the six o'clock news,
body counts and violence in the streets and, for me, my
own head bashed and bloodied as I ran, not once but several times, from the police. So Suzanne and I waited there
frozen, not eating, not talking, until the sound seemed to
go away.

Suzanne smiled. "Probably a traffic reporter," she said,
and I laughed when Bill walked into the room again without knocking and wearing a ski mask.

"We have to leave," he said, grabbing our still
unopened bags. "Take your own bedrolls and come with
me, *now.*"

"What happened?" I blurted out as I jumped to my
feet, the helicopter sound suddenly roaring at us out of
nowhere as if the whirlybird were that minute about to
strafe our little cabin.

"They found our camp," said Bill. "Hector picked it off
the police band."

Who the fuck was Hector, I wondered, but I didn't
have time to ask because Bill was already gone, the door
slamming behind him. The helicopter zoomed off to the
right, as if it had taken pity on us at the last second and
granted a temporary reprieve. Suzanne and I shared a

look, then quickly rolled up our sleeping bags and followed Bill outside.

The group, those accounted for anyway, had gathered
at the edge of the trees behind the main house. Suzanne
and I walked rapidly around the perimeter toward them.
There were three men and two women, all wearing black
ski masks—the green bandannas had apparently been
replaced by something more anonymous—and carrying
backpacks with various tools hanging from lashes. I
walked up to the woman I suspected was Karin.

"Karin, I'd like you to meet Suzanne," I said.

I watched as they shook hands, Suzanne staring
directly at the younger woman as if she were trying to see
through her mask. Neither one said a word.

"Where's Simon?" I asked.

"Out there," said Bill, gesturing vaguely into the forest.

"He'll find us," said Karin.

"Put these on," said another man, handing Suzanne
and me ski masks of our own. "We can't take a chance
anyone will be recognized. Even parents." I pulled mine
over my head and adjusted it to fit my mouth and eyes,
tugging the bottom down all the way over my neck. The
wool was thicker than I expected, too hot and itchy
around the edges, but the mask itself was weirdly trans-
forming. It gave me an immediate sensation of power. If
there were any Latin American dictators in the vicinity, I
felt ready to take them on.

I stood there, peering through the narrow slits in the
wool and relishing my status as a newborn revolutionary
while Suzanne finished fitting her mask. We strapped our
sleeping bags to our backs and picked up our overnight
bags, which had been stacked by a tree. Then Karin nodded toward an almost indistinguishable trail that led off

along a gully behind the main house. She started for it and
the group headed off after her. I stumbled almost immediately, grabbing on to Bill to stay erect. The mask restricted
my peripheral vision and I had forgotten to look down.
"Che Guevara—not!" said Suzanne, mocking me. "Che
didn't wear contacts," I replied, but I was already beet red
beneath my mask.

An hour later I was walking through the forest like a sea-
soned *guerrillero*. We were coming to the top of a ridge of
redwood and Douglas fir interspersed with prickly horse-
tail brush. Up ahead, across what looked like several miles
of deep green rolling hills dotted with live oaks and occasional cattle, was the Pacific Ocean crashing in all its wild
splendor along the rock-studded shore of a seemingly
endless, empty beach. It was nearly a quarter to six and
the November sun was just starting to set, suffusing the
pristine landscape with a dazzling golden glow from the
mountains to the ocean.

"Where are we?" I asked Bill, who had stopped to
examine a topo map—the same one, I realized, that had
been taped to the wall in the upstairs room.

"The Lost Coast," he said.

"The Lost Coast?" I had never heard of it.

"It's larger than Big Sur and more spectacular," he said,
shielding his eyes against the sun as he tried to locate our
position on the map. "But they couldn't get Highway 1
through here so people don't know about it. The only
route in is a one-lane road out of Humboldt Park that
washes out half the time in the winter."

Karin came up alongside him and consulted the map.
"We're down there," she said, pointing to a valley with a
small river that disappeared in another grove of red-

woods. "Tired?" she added, her voice rising in a slight mocking tone.

"No, no, I'm fine." I wouldn't have admitted otherwise.

The group descended the far side of the ridge into the valley Karin had indicated. We were in a grove of mostly old-growth trees again, bisected by the rushing river, which made the only audible sound in the forest, drowning out all the others. The helicopters were long gone.

"Home sweet home," said Karin, as we arrived at a small clearing at the river's edge between two huge trees. Their trunks had been hollowed out by some pre-Columbian forest fire. Karin took off her mask and the rest of us followed suit. "I hope you don't mind, but there won't be any campfires tonight," she said to me. "It's too risky. You'll have to find some other way to keep warm."

"I'll manage. . . . Is this where Simon's going to meet us?"

"Of course. Why wouldn't he? He loves it here." She started to remove her backpack without taking her eyes off me. "The Lost Coast is a special place, Moses. People can still live here the way nature intended. . . . Relax and forget yourself."

She smiled at me another moment, then took her pack and stashed it inside the tree. The others did the same.

Twenty minutes later, after we had made camp, I walked with Suzanne along the river's edge. The light was diminishing fast. Among the tall trees, it was already almost pitch-dark.

"It must be flattering to still be attractive to twenty-year-old girls."

"What're you talking about?"

"Don't be coy, Moses. It's one of life's great unfairnesses."

"She was just having fun manipulating me."

"Maybe yes. Maybe no." She stopped in front of a fallen tree covered with germinating burls and faced me. In the half-light, she too seemed almost like a twenty-year-old girl, the one I had first seen being hoisted in a wicker basket by war protesters into the occupied Berkeley Administration Building while the crowd applauded both her guts and her beauty.

"I hate time," I said.

"Me too."

"Dinner," someone called out, and we walked back to the campsite. The group was sitting between the two burned trees. For the first time we were introduced to the three we hadn't met—Max, a man in his thirties who described himself as a failed yuppie; Sheila, a young Englishwoman who had a degree in biochemistry; and Hector, who turned out to be a fifteen-year-old whiz kid of mixed Chicano-Irish parentage from Van Nuys with two computers in tow, one his own IBM clone and one Simon's Power Book. I asked whether Claire Hannin was still a member of the group and got the kind of curt response that indicated it was pointless to pursue the question. So we sat around for a while, making small talk and sharing a makeshift supper of granola bars, jerky and hot powdered lemonade, until I said, casually as can be, gesturing to the several towering trees that surrounded us, "Are you guys planning on spiking here?"

That stopped the conversation. I waited a minute or two before continuing. "What I'm asking is . . . It's a big forest out here. How do you choose where you're going to do this? And do you leave a mark on the tree, some kind of warning that it's been spiked?"

"What makes you think we don't?" Karin asked. "Do you think we're killers?"

Suddenly the giant woods were as quiet as the Mojave at midnight. Even the rushing river seemed to stop momentarily in place as if we were all engaged in some cosmic game of freeze-tag. "Somebody died," I said.

"You, of all people, don't believe what you read in the newspapers, do you?" she said.

"What am I missing?"

"I don't know. We always tie red warning signs to the trees. Perhaps this person just didn't see it."

"That's possible," I said.

Karin eyed me skeptically. "Or perhaps you think there's another explanation for what happened."

"What's that?"

"A provocateur in our midst who has encouraged us to go so far as to endanger the lives of innocent people."

I glanced over at Suzanne, who was staring at her intently. "What for?" I said.

"To discredit us . . . naturally," said Karin.

"I wouldn't know," I said.

"Of course you wouldn't . . . although you might suspect." She looked around at the others—Sheila, Max, Hector, Bill. They were huddled together against the night chill, their faces dimly illuminated by a crescent moon just beginning to rise. "Which one would it be?"

"I don't make those kinds of accusations," I said.

"What about you?" said Karin, looking at Suzanne.

"I don't know what to think," she said.

"Well then . . . perhaps it's something entirely different," said Karin. "Perhaps someone else did it. Someone you don't even know about."

"Who would that be?" I asked.

"Someone strong. Someone beautiful," she said. Her voice was suddenly sad and preternaturally old. Then she

started to laugh. "Come on, Moses. Why are you so
solemn? In every revolution somebody must die. And saving the Earth is the biggest revolution of all, right?" She
looked at her comrades, who murmured their agreement.
"After all, we've all been living the other way since the
beginning of history, raping the Earth instead of loving
each other. Sometimes I think industrial pollution's just
another by-product of sexual repression. What do you
think?" She stared at me with a mocking smile.

"I think it's a load of bullshit," said Suzanne before I
could say anything.

Less than an hour later, we went to bed. It was cold and
there wasn't very much else to do. I walked around the
trunk of one of the largest trees and unrolled my sleeping
bag on a bed of pine needles. I slid into it and tried to close
my eyes but they wouldn't stay shut. I kept wondering
where Simon was and peering out into the night. Once I
thought I saw a deer lurking in the undergrowth, its
antlers outlined in the pale moonlight, but it was gone
before I could sit up.

After that, I laid back and stared up at the stars, noticing my old friend Arcturus, the red giant at the end of
Orion's sword, then drew a line in my mind's eye to Spica.
But the white dwarf was hidden by some bushes in the
foreground. As I strained to see, my attention was caught
by movement on the other side of the campsite. I sat up
suddenly and stared through the undergrowth. A figure
was crouched over a sleeping bag. It stayed there for a
moment or two, then stood, turned and disappeared into
the darkness. A few seconds later, someone else rose from
the sleeping bag and walked quietly into the middle of the
campground. It was Karin. She reached into her pocket

and took out a small flashlight, switching it on and shin-
ing it quickly over the other bags as if to make sure their
inhabitants were still asleep. I shut my eyes and lay back.
The light passed over me and went off. When I opened my
eyes again, Karin was heading off into the brush.

Curious, I carefully pulled apart the Velcro seal of my
bag and stood, following quietly after her along a narrow
trail. She had a lead of half a minute or so and I couldn't
see her at first, but I finally caught a glimpse of her silhouette moving rapidly upriver. Then I lost her again behind
the trunk of a massive redwood. I continued along the trail
anyway as it descended into a gully by a bend in the river.

I stopped at the bend. At the river's edge, Simon was
visible with his shirt off, his chest and shoulders glinting
white in the darkness. He was locked in a passionate
embrace with Karin who was herself topless, her breasts
tilted upward as they pushed against his skin. They fumbled with each other's jeans and sank to the ground
together, starting to make love. I was witnessing the pri-
mal scene in reverse. My heart beating in confusion, I
backed away. This was not for a father to see.

10

SIMON AND KARIN WERE HAVING coffee together when I woke up the next morning at dawn. They were sitting on a large boulder near the campsite, a coffeepot between them, talking intensely but inaudibly over the omnipresent river. They stopped the moment they saw me climbing out of my bag. I stumbled toward them, trying to shake off the sleep and still feeling guilty about having intruded on their personal lives and about whatever private attraction I had for Karin.

"Cup of joe?" she said, echoing Gabriel as she lifted the pot and poured me some coffee in a tin camp cup before I could formulate an answer. I accepted the coffee gratefully and she turned to Simon with a wry smile. "Your father doesn't approve of what we're doing," she said. I tensed immediately, then relaxed. She couldn't have any idea they had been observed. She was obviously referring to their political actions.

"Really?" I said. "I don't even *know* what you're doing. How could I disapprove?"

"Oh, so you don't think we were spiking trees?" said Karin.

"I don't know the specifics."

"Like what?" she said.

I glanced over at Simon, who was staring at me implacably. "Whether the land was public or private, to begin with," I said. "Whether you really have sufficient warning signs."

"Of course we do. Why would we want to endanger the lives of innocent people? It would be counter to everything we stood for." She got up and walked over to a backpack, taking out a cardboard tube and handing it to me. "This is your son's work," she said.

I looked over at Simon as I reached into the tube to pull its contents out. I unrolled a hexagonal red poster about the size of a stop sign. The words FORESTER . . . GRAVE DANGER! DO NOT SAW! THIS ANCIENT TREE PROTECTED BY THE GUARDIANS OF THE PLANET! were printed in bold type beneath a well-crafted drawing of a muscular young man with an owl's face spiking the tree with a giant nail. The style was clearly Simon's. It was a variation on the graffiti paintings he used to do.

"Nicely done," I said.

He didn't respond.

"We put them on every tree in three places *before* we spike," said Karin. "It's the rule. Someone double-checks each one."

Why was she telling me all this, I wondered. It was hard to decipher. "Could they have fallen off?" I asked.

"All of them? They're stapled to the trunk. Up and down each side." She took the poster back from me and rolled it up again, replacing it in the tube.

"So I guess that means . . ." I stared down at my cup. The coffee was almost gone and Karin poured me another cup. I smiled my thanks back at her. ". . . someone else pulled them down . . . ? What about a group called California Forest Protection? Do you know them?"

"This is bullshit!" said Simon suddenly. "Why are we even talking to him?"

"I want to help, Simon. I'm your father!"

"You don't want to help. You want to take over!"

"That's not true. I—"

"You don't have a clue what's going on here!"

"You're goddamn right about that," I said, my voice rising to a near shout. "And I'll tell you something else. I think tree-spiking is despicable. There's no tree in the world, no matter how old, worth one human life. I hope to God there's been a mistake here, because if there's not, we're all going to regret this as long as we live!"

"There's been no mistake. The only mistake is that *you* came! I don't want to talk to you anymore." And with that he walked away into the woods.

I stood there trembling when Suzanne walked up. "What happened?" she asked.

"Your son takes things more personally than he should," said Karin.

I stared off into the trees. Simon was barely visible, heading upriver. "I'll go talk to him," I said.

"No, no, no. Wait," said Karin. I turned to her. "Why don't you really help us?"

"What do you mean?" I glanced over at Suzanne. Then back at Karin.

"We thought that tree was on public land . . . inside Humboldt Park . . . and then it turned out to belong to Allied Lumber. . . . Maybe someone was setting us up."

"Who would do that?"

She shook her head. "Those California Protection people. Who knows? . . . Simon says you're this great private eye. Maybe you could find out."

"I don't think I could find out much here."

"Bill's going into town for supplies. He'll lead you out."

They were letting me go? I looked down in Simon's direction. He had disappeared.

"Don't worry," said Karin. "He'll be back. Just do what you have to."

I took Suzanne aside to talk to her privately. We walked down to the water's edge, where we couldn't be overheard. "What do you think?" I asked.

"What choice do we have?"

"Do you want to come?"

She bit her lip a moment. "I can't leave Simon now."

I nodded and wrote down my beeper number on the back of an old credit card receipt, handing it to her. "If there's any problem, try to get to a phone and notify me immediately."

We stood there looking at each other a moment. "Good luck," she said.

"Thanks," I replied, feeling overwhelmed by the situation. "You know, sometimes I think I just made up my whole life."

"Who doesn't?" she said.

I smiled and hugged her briefly, then walked off to join Bill, who was now standing a few feet away, waiting for me.

I followed him up a trail that snaked up the ridge in two quick curves. At the top, I turned to look back down at the camp. Simon had already returned to rejoin the others. It occurred to me then that I had never questioned him further about his telephone contact with Special Agent Bart. Had I stopped myself unconsciously? The thought that there was anything to this, that Simon could possibly be an FBI plant, was so abhorrent to me I didn't want to confront it even for a second. It would have been such a total rebellion against, such a thorough rejection of, everything I thought I ever stood for (however hypocritical those values or however naïve), that, were it true, I don't think I could ever have recovered. My heart would be forever broken.

So I dismissed even a micro-contemplation of this from my mind and continued on with Bill through a grove of newer redwoods thick with morning fog. Surprisingly, we were out at the main road in less than a half hour, emerging near a rinky-dink town called Honeydew that consisted of a handful of houses, a general store, a gas station and a fishing tackle supply place. It was one of the two towns on the entire Lost Coast, Petrolia being the other, large enough to make the map that was on the wall of the local general store.

"I have to talk to some people," said Bill cryptically, going to the pay phone in the back of the store. He waited for me to walk away before he dialed. I could hear him whispering unintelligibly into the mouthpiece as I wandered about, surveying the products for sale. It seemed as if the local customers were a mixture of Spam-eating rednecks and others with mysteriously richer tastes, running to porcini mushrooms in virgin olive oil and large slabs of fresh imported gravlax.

"Are we in the heart of the 'farm belt'?" I asked Bill when he got off the line and walked back to me.

"Not so much anymore," he replied, eyeing the gourmet items and catching my drift immediately. "Too many DEA helicopters. Only the hard core are left. . . . The rest of those greedy slime went into underground cellars, where they can make even more money," he added, apparently not overly sympathetic to his dope-growing brethren.

He told me he'd pick up his supplies on the way back and we continued two hundred yards down the road, to a dirt driveway next to a mailbox. Bill pointed to an old barn at the other side of a dandelion field. "See you," he said. I looked at him, puzzled. "Your car."

He reached into the mailbox, handed me the keys to my rented Buick and started off. I stopped him. "What do I do in case of emergency?"

"Send e-mail with no subject to N2690@earthlink.net. If you have time, do it anonymously through a remailer. We'll beep you."

He headed off, I assumed back to the store. I was watching, committing the computer address to memory, when he stopped and looked back at me. He clearly didn't like being observed. I walked over to the barn and pulled the door open. The car was sitting there. I got behind the wheel and turned the ignition. Those silly bells and chimes that sounded like the lingerie department at Bloomingdale's went off, but it fired right up.

I backed up and drove out the driveway onto the main road, heading for 101 and turning on the radio to an all-seventies oldies station. The dial was filled with them; it was Northern California after all. I felt relieved to be on the open highway again and on my own. But my rock-and-roll respite ended abruptly about an hour and a half later when I approached Garberville. The area seemed to be crawling with more police than South Central after the riot. I counted four sheriff's vehicles, including a van, three checkpoints and two CHP squad cars before I was even within five miles of the town and another half dozen along the main street when I arrived. I figured it wouldn't be long before one of them ran a make on my car, but I wasn't going to let it bother me now. I pulled into a parking lot behind a Laundromat across from the editorial offices of the *Humboldt Herald* just as a couple of DEA helicopters passed overhead. I got out and crossed the street, climbing the stairs to the second floor and entering the newspaper office without knocking. It was a tiny, two-room affair with a random, homespun decor, half hippie and half Chamber of Commerce, that mimicked the contents of the paper. I flashed a smile at the two reporters in the front room and walked straight past them without speaking into the editor's office in back.

Daniel Springer was standing behind his desk, staring into a window reflection and combing his gray ponytail. He put the comb away with a start when he saw me. "Moses, you've caught me in my vanity," he said. "But us midlife guys have to take any edge we can get, don't you think?" I nodded and shut the door to his office. "Getting confidential, are we?" He studied me and indicated that I should take a seat. "How're things going? Have you found your son? Popular boy, I see." He nodded toward one of the copters, which that second was visible, elevating to the firmament outside his office window.

"Not so far."

"God, it must be rough. If there's anything I can do at all . . . I'll put the vast resources of the *Humboldt Herald* at your disposal." He smiled and gestured toward a couple of battered filing cabinets in the corner. "I also have a friend at the *Bay Guardian* who knows some good private eyes, but"—he added with a chuckle—"I don't suppose you need that."

"Maybe I do," I replied mordantly. "Tell me about California Forest Protection."

"Where'd you meet *them*?"

"Out in the woods."

"Great name, huh? Sounds like a conservation society in the fifties."

"Smokey the Bear," I said.

"That's just what they want you to think." He took a seat opposite me behind his desk.

"Who are they?"

"'Wise use' freaks."

"'Wise use'?"

"Double-speaking assholes who turn ecology on its head by saying old-growth redwoods pollute the environment and don't allow healthy baby trees to grow. Or we shouldn't be saving spotted owls because they're destroying the native wild berry harvest. What they really want is a government payoff every time they're restricted from using a square centimeter of land they never had any intention of using in the first place. . . . What do they have to do with your son?"

"Who knows? Do you know where I can find them?"

"They're not exactly among the major subscribers to this paper. I wouldn't bother looking them up in the Yellow Pages either."

"I figured that. . . . Well, who are they then?"

He stared at me a moment. "Disaffected small businessmen, ranchers in Chapter 11, unemployed loggers with an ax to grind . . . no pun intended. A dangerous group. You wouldn't want to cross them."

"Paramilitary experience?"

"Possibly."

"Who are their leaders?"

"I didn't know they had any."

"Well, they work for somebody . . . Lawton Stanley? The heads of the other lumber companies?"

"Nobody employs anybody around here anymore, Moses." He leaned in as if he were telling me a meaningful confidence. "We're all working for the conglomerates, even Stanley. And they do their best to act like the CFP doesn't exist. I can promise you. Especially since 'ninety. . . . So, where have you tried to find your son? There's a coffeehouse in Ukiah called the Global Village. A lot of burnouts with backpacks. Some of them know something though. They might have connections to the Guardians."

"I'll look into it."

"There's a dude named Jasper who does the *latte*. You can tell him I sent you. The food's a lot better than the Woodrose too. How's your ex, by the way, the fabulous Ms. Greenhut? This must be hell for her."

"She's okay . . . What happened in 'ninety?"

"What do you mean?"

"You said they changed their minds in 'ninety."

"Did I?"

"That's the year of the Claire Hannin bombing, isn't it? Redwood Summer."

"Yes, that's right. You're sure up on your local politics."

"You're the one who told me."

"Oh, right."

Springer smiled blankly for a moment. One of his reporters, a young woman with short black hair wearing jeans and a man's shirt over a turtleneck, walked in and deposited an article in front of him.

"Hi. I'm Samantha," she said to me as Springer started to peruse her piece.

"You don't have to give your name," he said.

"That's okay. I'm Moses. I'm here looking into the CFP. Trying to get a hold of them."

"Phew, those guys." She made a face. "I wouldn't want to be in the same room with them. But, if you really care, first place I'd go is the Thurman fund-raiser."

"That's ridiculous," said Springer without even looking up. "They couldn't afford that."

"What do you mean? It's at the Old Cook House. They'll be lining up for him."

"If you say so," said Springer.

"Come on. He's the new king of the wise use movement." She turned to me. "It's in Samoa."

"I wasn't planning on going *that* far."

"Not that Samoa." She grinned. "This one's a tiny island a mile north of Eureka, across the bridge. They're having a dinner for Congressman Alan B. Thurman, one of the freshmen from the Gingrich Revolution. I hear the Newtman himself is going to be hooked up by satellite."

"I'll be sure to bring my checkbook," I said.

"I think I'll pass," said Springer, picking up a red pencil and making some marks in the article.

It turned out they were on a deadline, so I stayed only another couple of minutes, just enough to learn the subject of Samantha's article was "asset forfeiture" as a threat to the Constitution (whatever that meant) and to assure Springer that I would share my information with him if I learned anything.

"The *Herald* could use a scoop," he reminded me as he escorted me all the way down the stairs to the street despite his deadline, wanting to know my immediate plans. He also wanted a number for where I was staying.

"Well, let me know as soon as you have one, *compadre*,"

he said, putting his hand on my shoulder and smiling sympathetically. *"Hasta la victoria siempre."*

"Sure," I said. Once he walked back inside, I crossed the street again and, glancing around to make sure no one was watching, got into my car. I had time to kill before the fund-raiser and I wanted to have another look at the crime scene, this time in full daylight, and see that property line for myself. So I drove up through Garberville and along the Avenue of the Giants again, taking a circuitous route to the back side of Humboldt State Park to make sure I wasn't being followed.

It took an hour and ten minutes to get there, but nobody appeared to be around as I walked down the trail to the Jack London Grove once again. I came to the giant tree stump at the bottom and stopped. Everything was quiet. The crime scene tape had been removed but the little memorial flower arrangement to Leon Erlanger remained, just as it was two days before, although freshened, it seemed, by newly cut flowers. The loose stone wall over to my left, which I thought marked the border of the state park, had been covered in part with shiny, new concertina wire.

I started to go over and have a look at it when I heard a dull whirring sound. I stopped still and listened. A gull, having drifted in from the ocean, flapped its wings and flew off. Then nothing. What was going on? It was oddly quiet except for the whirring noise. There was something familiar about it. Why had Suzanne and I been discovered so quickly on our last visit? Without moving my feet, I turned slowly to my right, surveying the area behind the crime scene tape until I was facing the new flower arrangement. Then I froze, seeing the glow of a tiny red bulb reflected under an iris leaf. A lens stared straight at me from a miniature video camera hidden in the flowers. I was being taped.

I thought of the tall guy with the .38 and his buddy with the shotgun in the Kuwait City T-shirt. The woman with the dirty blond hair. Was this my first recording? Or had they already recognized "Harry Lucas"? I felt the dead weight of fear in the pit of my stomach. I looked into the trees but saw nothing. A squirrel jumped from its perch and scampered off into the bushes. Again without moving my feet, I rotated my trunk away from the camera and started to walk, step by step, back toward the trail.

But I hadn't gone ten feet when I heard footsteps behind me. "Trespassing again, Mr. . . . *Lucas*?" someone said. It sounded like the tall man. "This isn't a collective farm here. Or the Berkeley Co-op. Haven't you learned to respect people's property?"

Before I could say anything, I saw his partner with the shotgun coming down the trail straight at me. "Stop where you are, Mr. Wine," he said.

Mr. Wine?! I bolted to my right, diving over the stone wall, shredding my pants leg on the concertina wire and rolling onto the ground. I picked myself up immediately and ran into the woods. A shot went off, one that I knew wasn't a warning. The tall man shouted but I kept going, scraping my face on the branches of the young trees as I circled to my right and then left again to elude them, coming to a steep embankment. My heart pounding, I scrambled up as fast as I could. Up at the top I could see my car ahead of me. I ran straight for it, my head down, not looking back until I was in the front seat with my key in the ignition.

11

"HOW THE FUCK DID THEY know your name?"

"They knew enough about me to write my obituary. But I didn't think it was a great idea to hang around to find out how."

"Dad, aren't you getting a little old for this?"

"No shit." I was leaning against the wall by the rest rooms in the Woodrose Café, talking with Jacob on the pay phone. I couldn't stand up straight because my ribs hurt too much from the dive over the concertina wire. My chest and arms were scraped and my knee throbbed as if it were being repeatedly hit in the cap with a ballpeen hammer. In fact, my whole body was black and blue, as I had noticed when I changed my clothes back in the men's room of the ranger station. The old ones looked as if they had been mashed by a trash compactor.

"Did you find the property line?" Jacob asked.

"I think so. It's the same stone wall I saw the first time."

"Are you going to tell the police?"

"Not yet. They'll just try to get me to lead them to

Simon. I need some proof it's been moved first. Besides," I
said, keeping my voice low, "they still spiked a tree, even
if it was on government land and even it did have a warning sign."

"Fuck," Jacob said. He sounded as tense as I was.
"What're you going to do? What about this Claire Hannin
person? Maybe *she* knows something."

"I don't know where to find her. Gabriel says she's hiding out on a pot farm somewhere."

"You talked to him?" He sounded surprised.

"Son of a bitch is living the life of Riley up here in a
skillion-dollar dream house."

"How'd he do that?"

"Beats me." I glanced at the wall in front of me, which
was filled with ads for self-help and therapy groups. I
wondered if Amy's tai chi class was among them. "By the
way," I continued, "you don't know anything your brother
could have done that could . . . um . . . make him be working for the FBI?"

"What?!"

"Strike that. Forget it," I said. "You're a computer
junkie, aren't you? You know what a remailer is?"

"On the Internet? It's a way to send e-mail incognito.
You address your message to an anonymous computer and
they remail it to its destination without your name on it."

"That's what I thought. Stay close to the phone. Maybe
I'll need you to send one." It was a strange feeling bringing Jacob into a case for the first time, but this was a family matter. He was the only one I could trust.

"I'll be here. I have more time than usual these
days. . . . " His voice tightened. "Carlos and I broke up."

"Sorry to hear that," I said. It was his third relationship
in four years. "If there's anything I can do . . ."

"Don't sweat it. You've got your hands full with my brother these days. Besides, there's nothing you could do about *my* private life, even if you wanted to," he added with an ironic chuckle.

"I'm not going to argue about that. Me giving advice to the lovelorn is like Jackie Mason telling Gandhi how to meditate."

He laughed. Then he said "Be careful, Dad," his voice suddenly solemn and devoid of irony.

We said our good-byes and hung up.

For a moment I considered taking the opportunity to deal with my own love life and call Nancy, until I heard another squad car roar past and it seemed absurd. Obviously, this wasn't the time. I wanted to have more precise knowledge of the property lines near the crime scene. But I wanted to do it without going to the police.

Ten minutes later I was sitting in the offices of Redwood Empire Realty on Church Street just east of Redwood Drive talking to Carl Gribaldo, a member of the twenty-million-dollar club and a forty-year resident of the county, according to the framed proclamations above his desk. We were discussing building sites for my future vacation home.

"It needs to be right on the edge of a state park or government land," I told him. "It's my getaway in nature, you understand, so I don't want to find myself staring at a shopping mall in a couple of years. We have enough of those in L.A."

"I quite understand that, Mr. . . . ?"

I hesitated for a paranoid second, wondering if it wouldn't be safer to change aliases. Whoever told the CFP my identity, it probably hadn't been this guy. But you couldn't be too safe. "Watkins. Richard Watkins," I said.

"Did you . . . uh . . . have an accident, Mr. Watkins?" He gestured to my cheek, which was decorated with an unattractive purple shiner from my escape.

"Does it look ridiculous? I gotta tell you, Mr. Gribaldo, it's the way I feel. I'm driving along in the Beemer, looking for my dream property, when I think I've found something, gorgeous redwoods all around, old-growth trees, and I get out of my car to look at it and slide straight down the side of the hill. I guess I'm still a city boy at heart, huh?" Gribaldo chuckled with just the hint of condescension I was hoping for. "I can't believe anyone sells that kind of land," I continued. "Those trees are priceless."

"I wouldn't say priceless, but . . . pretty steep."

"How about property right on the edge of Humboldt State Park?" I leaned forward in my chair with an expression of poorly disguised expectancy. "I'm sure that's out of sight."

"You never know until you ask," said Gribaldo.

Soon enough, we were sitting together at his desk going over topo maps and a thick book of real estate listings. I traced with my finger down to Humboldt State Park, found the dirt road and then continued west until I came to the border. "Right about there," I said.

"That's the Jack London Grove," said Gribaldo.

"Amazing. My favorite writer when I was a kid. *Call of the Wild* . . . *White Fang* . . . I read it seven times. I'd kill to live in his grove!"

"I think it belongs to the Allied Lumber Company."

"They won't sell it?" I said eagerly.

"Not unless you're Bill Gates or someone like that." He looked at me guardedly. "You're not Gates, are you?"

"Me? No." I waved at the absurdity of the idea and Gribaldo chuckled again jovially, not anxious to lose a sale.

"And that's the location of that tree-spiking last week," he said, "if you heard about that."

"Really? . . . Maybe they'd want to get rid of it then."

"You've got a good point there, Mr. Watkins." Gribaldo smiled and picked up the phone. "Might cost you a lot though. . . . I'll call them directly in their Glasgow headquarters," he said. "They're just up the road. Frank Carpenter in their real estate department will know."

"Tell him I'm interested in any land in that London Grove. Maybe there's some that doesn't belong to Allied Lumber. . . . Jack London," I added, shaking my head in wonder. "Didn't he run for governor—or was that Upton Sinclair?"

"I'm sure it was London," said the realtor as he got on the line with Frank. I sat there a few minutes as Gribaldo asked him a series of questions. Finally Gribaldo broke into a broad grin and hung up.

"You're in luck, Mr. Watkins. Allied Lumber has an incredible piece of virgin land available on the banks of the Eel River itself they want to get rid of. No one could ever block your view."

"But what about the London Grove?"

"That's not for sale, I'm afraid. They're not selling a single tree."

I frowned, confused. "They own the whole thing?"

"According to Frank. Allied bought it all from the state a couple of years ago and they're foresting it. And he'd know. He's got all the latest maps on his computer. Straight from the County Hall of Records," he added with a wink. "So . . . can I show you the Eel River property?"

"Thanks, but I had my heart set on that other piece. Another time, Mr. Gribaldo." I stood and, shaking my head despondently, walked out of his office.

Actually, I was feeling worse than despondent. I was feeling dreadful. I didn't know what Simon and his friends had been thinking or where they had received their information. But it seemed as if, even if they themselves thought otherwise, they had spiked a tree on active lumber company land. There was no way out of it. At the very least, they were staring down the barrel at a manslaughter charge.

For the next twenty minutes or so I drove along 101 in a depressed stupor. I didn't think about anything. I didn't listen to music. I didn't even bother to look in my rearview mirror to see if I was being followed. I was in such a haze, in fact, I almost went plowing right past the massive billboard beckoning tourists to VISIT GLASGOW! in bright yellow and black Scottish-plaid type surrounded by bagpipes that played the explanation HOME OF THE ALLIED LUMBER COMPANY in a ribbon of musical notes. Even then I would have continued on had not the word "Glasgow" itself caught what was left of my reflexively ironic sensibility that, under other circumstances, had not always been my best friend. Glasgow, I thought—how bizarre this Northern California proclivity for naming towns for foreign locales that seemed to have no relevance whatsoever to their present location. First Samoa, that evening's destination, and now Glasgow.

At that point the massive structure of the lumber mill came into view, a looming presence out of an Edward Hopper painting seemingly plopped among pristine redwood hills by some renegade architect from the Industrial Revolution. It should have been a horrible scar on the landscape, but like a Hopper painting itself, there was a beauty in its bleakness. I stared at it, entranced by its weathered wood siding and rusted iron catwalks, as the off-ramp rushed at me.

On an impulse, I signaled right and drove off the highway and beneath the underpass, circling a rotary, which
took me out onto Glasgow's main street. Unlike the mill
itself, the rest of the town had a quaint, almost antisepti-
cally preserved feeling. It was the first company town I
had ever visited and I suppose I was expecting something
out of Dickens, but what I saw instead were meticulously
preserved streets with restored nineteenth-century row
houses, a tourist mall with cute souvenir shops, an old
vaudeville thee-ay-ter, a Museum of Lumber and a large
restored Victorian hotel called the Glasgow replete with
gaslit sidewalk lanterns and a carriage entrance. It
reminded me of Disneyland. The only thing lacking was
the monorail.

I pulled over and parked in front of the hotel. It was
only then I realized why I had come and felt that dread of
discovery I experienced when I investigated in places
where I suspected I wasn't welcome, like the Arab villages
of the West Bank or the crack houses of the South Bronx.
But this time the reason for my dread was more specific
than racial hatred or random violence. It was blood. I
checked my rearview mirror just to see how much I
looked like my son. People had told me there was a close
resemblance, but I never noticed it. Now it seemed as if we
were carbon copies, cloned off the same DNA without an
iota of alteration except age. Had that shown up in the
CFP's videotape—or had they made their identification in
another manner?

I combed my hair as differently as possible from
Simon's and put on a tie for respectability. Then I got out
of the car and walked over to the museum, which seemed
to be the center of activity at the moment, a handful of
tourists and locals walking in and out. It was in a well-

kept neoclassical building with Grecian columns that must
have once been the town bank. I was glancing at a sign on
the front door reading SORRY—NO MILL TOURS TODAY when a
CHP helicopter buzzed overhead. It seemed to hover for a
moment almost directly over my car, then zoomed off.

I watched it go, my heart in my mouth, then entered a
large room with marble floors and more decorative
columns. Objects and photographs from the history of
northwest lumbering were exhibited on the walls and in
glass cabinets, primitive saws and old silver prints of rag-
tag loggers looking like Lilliputians next to the felled
stumps of giant trees hitherto unseen by the white man.
Near the front was a rather prominent exhibit about the
area's ecology, showing the careful reforestation methods
now used by the company and the scientific programs
they had established to protect endangered species like the
coho salmon and the spotted owl. Above it all was a
poster asserting "The Allied Lumber Company Supports
the Environment." Just like California Forest Protection, I
thought.

"Would you mind signing our guest book?" said a tall,
good-looking man about thirty with rippling muscles
bulging from a polo shirt with the company crest embroi-
dered on the front. He seemed like a logger moonlighting
in public relations.

"Not at all," I said. I leaned over and started writing,
giving Richard Watkins an address in North Hollywood.

"I see you're from the L.A. area. How'd you do in the
quake? Come out pretty well?"

"Foundation didn't crack."

"Sounds good to me," said the man with a broad but
somewhat forced smile. "We get a lot of visitors from the

Southland. Man came in here from ... where was it? ...
Sherman Oaks. Half his garage fell in."

"It's tough," I said, forcing a smile of my own. Making
earthquake small talk was one of the more tedious
California pastimes.

"So, Mr. Watkins ... what brings you to Glasgow?"

I took a step closer and lowered my voice. I was a
reporter from the *L.A. Times*, I told him, on my way back
from covering a story on trade negotiations with the
Canadian government. The young man looked impressed.
I waited until a couple of tourists were out of earshot and
added that I would be remiss, considering my occupation,
if I didn't stop off here and look into last week's dreadful
tree-spiking, perhaps get some background on its victims
and its perpetrators. "There's a lot of anger down south," I
continued, lowering my voice still further, "about how far
these people have gone."

"The Guardians?"

I nodded.

"Have you talked to our public relations people, Mr.
Watkins? Their office is just across the street in the administration building."

"That'd be great but"—I looked down and made a face,
seemingly embarrassed, waiting while another tourist
came by and picked up a printed sheet of "Quick Facts on
American Forests"—"I'd have any story I did on this subject killed in a minute if I sent in something with the
slightest taint of company publicity. I need to talk directly
to the people involved . . . loggers . . . their families.
Someone who was there when Mr. Erlanger had this horrible accident. Otherwise there's no chance my editor would
run it." The man fidgeted, confused. Normally, deception
was the part of my work for which I had the least stom-

ach. But in this situation I had not a single qualm—neither
with Gribaldo nor with this guy. "I'm in an awful bind," I
continued, "I want to get the real story out but it's hard as
hell to get it by my editor. You know the media elite—they
pretend they're impartial, but they'd do anything to make
excuses for those terrorists or sweep it under the rug." I
glanced at him quickly, wondering if I'd gone over the top.
But I saw the hint of a smile and barreled on. "I know it's
not the normal channel, but if you know someone . . . anyone who was there, I'd be much obliged. You can tell them
they can tape me, do anything they want to make sure
they're not misquoted."

In a short while, I was at the front door of the
Ridgeway residence on Bristlecone Lane at the far end of
the small town. It was a newer stucco house within view
of a dock where huge redwoods were floated up the river
for milling. I hesitated a second before knocking, glancing
at the plastic jungle gym in the front yard and trying to
gather my emotions—or maybe push them away. The
dread still lingered from the image of the helicopter above
the Buick. But there was more. Dick Ridgeway—the owner
of the house—was Leon Erlanger's brother-in-law and had
been within thirty feet—I had been informed—of him
when Leon's chain saw flew backward and mistook his
torso for the trunk of a tree. So, standing at his brother-in-
law's door at five minutes past five that afternoon, I didn't
know if I was seeking information or absolution.

12

FOR SOMEONE WHO SPENT HIS LIFE defending the working class, I wasn't always comfortable among them, unless they were members of an oppressed minority who could slam-dunk backward or do endless variations of the merengue to a conga and timbale band. So, when I stood with Jo-Ellen Ridgeway in her kitchen that afternoon while she made coffee and her children played Sega games in front of the living room television, I wasn't quite sure what to say. Part of me wanted to wait for her husband to come home, but the smarter part of me knew that I would probably learn more directly from her.

"You must be feeling terrible," I said.

"No kidding. It's a mess. . . . Leon's daughter, Lorraine, cries all night and one of the boys won't get out of bed. . . . Black or milk?" she asked, pouring us each coffee.

"Black."

"Sugar or Sweet'n Low?" I shook my head. Jo-Ellen carried the cups over to a breakfast table and we sat down. She was a tall woman in a blue print blouse with a flag pattern. "This is a real human tragedy, Mr. Watkins. Even if it wasn't my brother."

"I know what you mean," I said, taking out a note pad and a pen. "I hope you don't mind my writing this down?"

"No. Sure."

"Now, Mrs. Ridgeway, Leon Erlanger and your husband were on the same logging team. . . ."

"That's correct. For three years. Dick operates the winches—you know, the puller—and Leon does the cutting."

"And how long had they been working at the Jack London Grove?"

"Let me think. . . . For the better part of a month."

"And what was their workday?"

"They're out there by eight. Done by four usually, while it's light."

"And what time did the accident occur?"

"I think it was like a little after three . . . but you should call the police about that. Jack Tidwell in the sheriff's office would have it. Do you want me to call him?" she added, reaching for the phone.

"No. That's okay," I said quickly. "I'm on a deadline. . . . So it was already getting dark when Leon cut that tree?"

"Well, not dark really but in the forest, the sun's hiding behind the trees by the middle of the afternoon. And the London Grove's in a gully."

"I know. Could you tell me what kind of saw he was using?"

"Shindaiwa."

"Japanese?"

"They're supposed to be good. My husband says they make great blades. Never break." Her little girl ran in and whispered something shyly in her ear. "Not now, Emily.

After Mr. Watkins leaves." The little girl stared at me briefly and exited. "She always wants more Oreos," Jo-Ellen explained, rolling her eyes. "I guess she's a sugar junkie like her mom."

"Who isn't? . . . So, Mrs. Ridgeway"—I put on my most innocent face—"there's something I don't understand here. . . . How could someone as experienced as your brother allow this to happen? I mean an injury, sure, maybe even a serious injury, but . . . I hope this doesn't offend you . . . that saw damn near cut him in half."

"I know. I've been wondering that too. There's always *some* kind of accident out there and Leon was in great shape. Ethel always complained she could never get him off the Nautilus on the weekends."

"Then what happened?"

"I don't know. Maybe those Guardians did something to the spike."

"What could they have done?"

"They're crazy people. I've heard all kinds of things. They put dynamite in there. They wired it. But who knows and who cares? Nothing's going to bring Leon back." She looked away and bit her lower lip.

"I know," I said. "But did anybody see it happen?"

"No. Of course not."

"What do you mean?" I sat up straight.

"Well, he was behind the tree and—" The phone rang. "Excuse me." She picked up. "Hello. . . . Oh, hi, hon. . . . Yes, he's here. He—" She stopped suddenly and looked at me, her lower lip dropping. Before I could say anything, she tried to mask her astonished expression with a half smile and stood, turning away and walking the phone back toward the bedrooms.

I sprang to my feet and ran past the kids out the door to

the street. I jumped into the car just as I heard the wail of a siren in the distance. I gunned the motor and headed off down the road in front of the mill, not having a clue where I was going and not pausing to wonder whether someone had called the *L.A. Times* for a Richard Watkins or if it was the copter or the CFP or how I had been discovered.

I made a sharp right behind a logging truck, cut left and sped through an alley that separated the mill from the shipping area. Just beyond, the road turned to dirt and I barreled on uphill into the redwoods, feeling the Buick bottoming out on its marshmallow suspension and trying unsuccessfully to catch a glimpse of my pursuers in its furiously jiggling rearview mirror. This car had the off-road capability of an antique unicycle, but I pushed the accelerator to the floor anyway and jackrabbited the car over the ruts. Immediately, I heard what sounded like a tie-rod break and the side panels started to shake like a washing machine on uppers. It seemed they were about to fly off and leave me stripped naked, driving through the trees like an older, frailer version of Mel Gibson in *The Road Warrior*. But I didn't let that stop me. I rattled on that way a mile or so into the woods, until I finally allowed myself to slow down and looked behind me. No one was there. I stopped the car for a moment and looked again. It was clear I wasn't being followed. A complete false alarm. I took a deep breath. Then I put my head on the steering wheel and thought of Simon somewhere farther off in the hills, an endless parade of helicopters and squad cars pursuing him until there were no more bushes and caves to hide in and he stood before the impartial wrath of the law, handcuffed for life. I pressed my forehead harder against the cold plastic wheel. I knew I had fucked up and I wanted to cry.

A few minutes later, I turned around and drove slowly

back toward Glasgow, skirting the town itself and returning to the freeway. No one appeared to be following me
there either, but if they were, I was almost beyond caring.
It was hard to dodge the forces of the state in a car that by
now would have had a hard time making it to the super-
market. In any case, it was growing dark, approaching the
hour of the Alan B. Thurman fund-raiser, so I headed up
101 for Samoa. Maybe I would be able to find out even 10
percent as much about California Forest Protection as they
evidently knew about me.

In a short while, I was in Eureka, seemingly the largest
outpost of civilization north of San Francisco, which meant
it had more than one shopping mall. The downtown was a
tarted-up old whaling village, bookstores, boutiques and
trendy micro-breweries replacing the rowdy fishermen's
saloons and brothels that used to occupy the nineteenth-
century brick buildings lining the streets of the dock area. I
drove past it and across the bridge to the California island
called Samoa, following the signs to the Old Cook House.
In a few minutes, I arrived at its sizable parking lot, which
was already nearly filled for this important event.

The restaurant itself was a large rectangular clapboard
edifice at the water's edge; with its own dock and exten-
sive loading equipment, even in the glow of the setting
sun, it looked more like a factory than an eating place. I
entered and found myself at the end of a cavernous room
supported by open joists filled with long tables surfaced
with white linoleum. Diners eating family style from plates
piled high with extraordinarily generous portions sat in
front of oversized ketchup bottles, massive loaves of white
bread, giant sticks of butter and huge pitchers of draft beer.
Behind them was an open industrial kitchen with the enor-
mous iron kettles and vats of the type one associates with

prisons or military academies. This was the last of the lumberjack cook houses, a haven of voracious communal eating where for decades loggers had mainlined cholesterol before going back to fell more giant trees.

But tonight the joists were laced with red, white and blue crepe paper and sitting at the tables with the loggers, and far outnumbering them, was a mixture of the small business people, aging yuppies, twenty-something media nerds and well-heeled retirees that could only be described as the shock troops—or more exactly, the "future shock" troops—of the new Republican majority. Over their heads, between two portraits of freshman Congressman Thurman, a tall man in his thirties with the practiced smile of an infomercial pitchman, was a video projection screen, where, at that very moment, Speaker Gingrich himself was reassuring the faithful of the coming millennium with the dreaded government no longer on their backs and the genius of modern technology turned loose like one massive virtual CD-ROM drive to erect individual toll stations for their personal economic enrichment along the information superhighway.

I took a few steps forward to survey the crowd for my friends in the CFP when I heard a woman's voice to my side saying, "I see you found your way."

I turned to find Samantha, the reporter from the *Humboldt Herald*, standing to my left with a drink in her hand. She had dressed for the occasion in a black cocktail dress that looked distinctly urban. "Where'd you get one of those?" I said, gesturing to her glass.

"There's a real bar in back." She nodded to a banquet room where a group of principally business types had gathered, watching yet another projection screen. "No host, of course," she added. Just then Newt mentioned something about a proposal he was supporting to increase compensation to property owners every time their rights were restricted by dubious federal regulations such as the Endangered Species Act. The room erupted in wild applause. We were definitely in the Kingdom of Wise Use.

"Good-bye, owl. Good-bye, salmon," said Samantha.

"I've put away a lot of salmon myself," I said. She looked down at my stomach and I sucked it in self-consciously.

"I've seen worse," she said, smiling. "Daniel says you're this terrific detective."

"Yeah, well, right now I'm feeling outclassed by some supposed country bumpkins with a video recorder."

"What do you mean?"

"California Forest Protection. They seem to be well connected. . . . Where *is* your boss, by the way?"

"Here someplace." She looked around, confused. "I saw him five minutes ago. He was talking with. . . . that guy." She pointed to a man in as superbly tailored a black pinstripe suit as I'd ever seen on a mannequin in Barney's in Beverly Hills. He was whispering to a woman with long curly hair wearing an Armani power suit. It took me a split second to realize the man was Nicholas Bart.

"I didn't know there was so much money in government work," I said.

"You know him?" said Samantha.

"What's more interesting is your boss does. . . . How about I buy you a refill?" I said, guiding her by the arm through the crowd out of Bart's view to the bar. "Stoli. Rocks. Olive," I told the bartender, and looked at Samantha. "Another gin and tonic," she said with a shrug, quickly downing what was left of hers. "Maybe this way I can bear the victory speeches." She nodded to yet another smaller monitor behind the bar, where the Newtman had now been replaced by a man in his late fifties, talking to us in his shirtsleeves from an office high up in downtown Los Angeles, looking out at the already aging glass cylinders of the Bonaventure Hotel.

"Who's he?" I asked, looking toward the man. His reddish brown hair was balding and his complexion pale, but his body seemed fit and wiry as a jogger's.

"Sean Handler, the president of FOXAM."

"Lawton Stanley's boss?" I tried to hear what he had to say, but he spoke in measured tones that were hard to distinguish over the increasingly boisterous crowd.

"Stanley hates him." She smiled mischievously. "I don't think they've talked more than twice in five years."

The crowd quieted for a second and I could hear Handler mention something about a return to the eighties and the creativity of venture capital. "Does he ever come around here?" I asked.

"Handler? Once. For a Fourth of July celebration in Glasgow. He wore brand-new Pendleton and Frye boots to the loggers' barbecue and fell backward into the Eel River."

I laughed and leaned closer to the monitor, trying to catch something more of his speech, when Bart walked up to me.

"Hello, Mr. Wine. I didn't know you were a supporter of Congressman Thurman."

"Go with the flow, Mr. Bart. How's your investigation coming?"

"I was just going to ask you the same thing."

"Couldn't be worse, to tell you the truth. Have you met Samantha . . . ?" I turned to her, waiting for her to fill in the rest.

"Backus."

"Ace reporter for the *Humboldt Herald*. I believe you

know her boss, Daniel Springer. Ms. Backus is doing a piece for him right now on 'asset forfeiture.' That should be right up your alley."

"Seizing a defendant's property before he has his day in court? Hardly Constitutional. It's the DEA that does that, Mr. Wine. Not the FBI. . . . Of course, it seems as if somebody's tried to seize *your* assets, if you don't mind my saying so." He nodded toward the shiner decorating my cheek.

"One of the congressman's opponents. Never turn your back on a sore loser."

"Why don't I believe that?" said Bart.

"Because you're paid to be suspicious."

"So are you." He took a step closer and studied me with an expression that was almost clinical. "I can understand a father's pain, Mr. Wine. And a son's. But it would be unfortunate if you were using it to justify actions you will later regret."

I was about to respond when I noticed the woman with the dirty-blond hair from the CFP joining the group to our right. Instead of her lumber jacket, she was wearing an attractive knit suit with a large Thurman button on the lapel, and she seemed to have paid a recent visit to the beauty parlor. I wanted to turn away, but she appeared already to have seen me. I smiled at her innocently, but it didn't work. With barely a moment's hesitation, she started to back up into the other room.

"I take your point," I told Bart. "I think I'm going to have a look for Springer. Do you know where he is?"

"Why would I?" He frowned.

"No special reason. See you all in a while." I nodded to Samantha and headed off into the main room after the woman. Even more people had arrived and I couldn't find her right away, but I made my way through the tables and finally spied her near the front just as everyone sprang up, blocking my view and shouting "Thur-man! Thur-man! Thur-man!" The real live self of the new congressman, a tall, bland man who looked eerily like a younger Michael Huffington, stepped out of a doorway and walked toward a dais, pumping the hands of his supporters as a Dixieland band blasted the traditional "Happy Days Are Here Again."

Where had they ever gone, I wondered, as I continued moving rapidly through the tables after the disappearing woman, nearly bumping into Thurman himself. As I was edged aside by a security guard, I caught a glimpse of her on the opposite side of the room, heading out a side door of the restaurant. The crowd was thick and I backed up, walking as swiftly as I could to the main entrance. I pushed through and emerged in the parking lot. The woman was already on the far end, getting into a Toyota. I ran down the steps after her. She started to pull out and I raced on, trying to get the number from her plate. She burned rubber and sped off. Even then I would have continued had my attention not been distracted by the yellow tape of yet another crime scene, this one much fresher and more grizzly than the first.

A young cop was gagging in horror just off to my left, where three squad cars had their headlights trained on a small fishing boat bobbing by the restaurant pier. I held my breath in dread as I followed their beams. Illuminated at the bow was the body of Daniel Springer splayed out on the deck with blood oozing from his mouth and a fisherman's hook through his now lifeless chest. It wasn't until some minutes later I found out there was a hand-printed note attached to it that read: "Lying Double-Agent Stoolie for the FBI! [Signed] The Guardians of the Planet."

13

I REMEMBER DISTINCTLY the first time I suspected Suzanne was having an affair with Gabriel. We had been living in Los Angeles for a few years, Simon was three years old at that time and Jacob about seven, and Gabriel had come out to visit from New York and see if he could make a dent in his ambition to be a screenwriter. He had been staying with us for about a month, taking every meal with us, picking up the boys from school when Suzanne and I were busy, going for family hikes every weekend along the bridle paths of Griffith Park. One night, when Suzanne and I were in our room about to go to sleep, quarreling about something superficial (which more than likely meant she didn't want to have sex), Suzanne got out of bed and said she was going downstairs. A few minutes later I could hear her in the living room, laughing and talking with Gabriel. Then there was a girlish shriek. A couple of minutes later I heard the door shut. They had gone outside. At that precise second I knew there was something wrong, but it took over a year and a half for me to do something about it. And by then it was too late. The family was on the way to disintegration.

"Why do you always blame yourself?" asked Samantha.

"Do I?"

"It seems like it," she said. It was after one in the morning and I had been sitting in her kitchen for the last hour
or so, drinking vodka from an anisette glass and compul-
sively telling her my life story, such was my anxiety.
"You're not responsible for everything in your life. The
divorce wasn't *all* your doing. That's a selfish way to look
at it really."

"Maybe you're right."

"And your children are grown up. They're responsible
for themselves a little bit. Your son could have decided to
become an eco-terrorist because he thinks it's the right
thing to do."

"I hope to God he's not really a terrorist."

"I hope he's not too. Especially now. But even if he is,
ultimately he's going to have to make his own choices
whatever they are."

"I guess you're right about that," I said, finishing my
vodka.

She picked up the bottle to pour me another. I was
about to wave her off when she smiled at me and said,
"It's okay. We both deserve it. Besides, there's nothing you
can do now."

We had been talking nonstop since about 11 P.M. when I
volunteered to drive her home from the Old Cook House
after it was clear that her original ride was forever dys-
functional and that his car and all his personal effects had
been impounded by the police. I had intended just to drop
her off at her cabin, which was on the banks of the Eel
River about halfway between Glasgow and Garberville,
and go on to a motel, but by the time I got there it had

been silently agreed that I would come in and, over the iced bottle of Absolut from her freezer, we would continue our conversation, which had started about her boss and veered off into other things as the alcohol worked its magical way through our nervous systems.

"How long have you known him?" I had begun by asking her when we were barely out of the parking lot, trailing Springer's ambulance over the bridge back to Eureka.

"Daniel? He's the reason I'm here."

I looked over at her. Her expression was almost as ashen as mine. "Professional or . . .?"

"Both at first. Then . . ." She made a gesture. "He was my boss at the *Mercury* . . . I was twenty-five. I thought he was this . . . cool older guy. All those sixties experiences. You all make it sound so romantic."

"It's just a memory."

"So I came over here with him and . . . I don't know." She took a deep breath.

"You don't have to talk about it."

"No, no . . . I have to. Or I'll just strangle. . . . He was kind of a disappointment, I guess you'd say. Or maybe I grew up."

"That happens. . . . Was he a double agent?"

"Who knows? Yes . . . no . . . maybe."

I laughed. "Make up your mind."

She didn't respond to that directly but pointed out a shortcut to the 101 and we continued up a road leading away from the city lights. It was a dark, humid night with the moon mostly obscured by low-hanging clouds. I couldn't see Samantha that well next to me, but I knew she was more attractive than I had first realized and it added to my tension, almost as if she were another vector pointing away from my mission to save Simon, a mission that, in the last hour or so, had become simultaneously more pressing and more impossible.

"Mostly Daniel was scared," she said as I negotiated a complicated turn onto the freeway, following a detour around an off-ramp that had been twisted out of commission during the latest quake. "He was always a scared person, even when I first knew him in San Jose, scared for his job, scared about his health, scared someone would carjack his Alfa when he used the ATM machine."

"He had a point there."

"He said a man had to make certain compromises to work within the system."

"So you think he *was* an agent?"

"I don't think anything. There are a lot of them around here. And if he was, I know he would have been ashamed to tell me. . . . But he also did everything he could to make the *Herald* a better paper. Taking on the most controversial subjects."

"Like what?"

"The Claire Hannin case."

"What was he doing with that?"

"Trying to discover what everybody wants to know, I guess . . . what happened to her and why."

"Did he find out?"

"If he did, he didn't tell me."

Later, as we approached her house, I asked her if she knew any of the members of California Forest Protection.

"No, I've only heard about them."

"What've you heard?"

"That they were a big deal a few years ago, but then sort of disappeared."

"Why was that?"

"I'm not sure. I think they were under some kind of investigation."

"By whom?"

Samantha hesitated. "I don't really remember. Maybe the state."

"What happened?"

She shook her head. I looked at her, trying to decide if she knew more than she was letting on. She was hard to read but whatever the truth was I had this weird sensation what and exactly how much she chose to say was for my own good. "Was that what they were always called?" I asked. "California Forest Protection?"

"As far as I know," she said. "You can park right here."

I stopped at the end of the driveway and we got out. Her house was a cute little redwood affair, the kind of place gangsters were always escaping to in old Ida Lupino movies. It had a screened porch with a rocker and a milk box by the front door.

"Half this place was underwater the year before I moved in, if you can believe that," said Samantha, nodding back toward the Eel River as she unlocked the door. "There was mud up to the top of the porch." I glanced back at the calm water fifty feet away before following her into the wood-paneled living room, walking up to the TV and switching it on. I wanted to see what was being reported about the murder of Daniel Springer, but we were too late for the local news and CNN hadn't picked it up yet. I sank down on her couch in exhaustion.

"You look almost as bad as Daniel," she told me.

"It's been a long day."

"What're you going to do?"

I shook my head, too far gone to have any plan at all. It was then she beckoned me into the kitchen and took out the vodka. "It's too late for anything but this," she said, sounding motherly despite the fact I was close to twenty years older than she was. I dropped into a chair and made the pretense of asking her a couple of more serious questions, whether she knew where Springer kept his notes (on his computer, but it had a password) and whether she knew the password (she didn't). But soon our conversation dissolved into personal matters and we talked with the openness of strangers on an airplane—only this airplane was flying precariously over jagged mountain peaks. I told her about my work, how I came to be a detective, and about my fractured family and the pain I felt. And she made fun of my guilt, in a gentle sort of way, and told me something about herself. She always wanted to be a reporter and, after attending Brown, roamed around Paris for a while trying to get a job with the *International Herald Tribune*. But it never happened and she came back and had to work for her father, a dentist in Van Nuys, for three years before landing the position with the *Mercury News*. "You're from the Valley?" I said, unable to suppress a grin. "Fer shure," she said, doing a fine imitation of the nasal whine that had once made Moon Unit Zappa famous.

Samantha went to bed and I fell into a fitful sleep on her sofa, having casebook reveries out of Freud's *Interpretation of Dreams*. "Father, I'm burning!" Simon called out to me in the night from a bed like a funeral bier engulfed in flames. I saw myself running toward him, arms outstretched but getting nowhere, my heart pounding as if I were being thumped in the chest by a sledgehammer. I awoke in a sweat, my body having made soggy damp indentations in the cushions of Samantha's couch. I turned one of them over and fell asleep again, this time almost as dead as Daniel Springer.

14

"TRY 'SUMMIT,'" said Samantha.

"What's that?"

"The name of his street." It was four minutes after seven and I was hunched over Springer's computer in the offices of the *Humboldt Herald*, staring at a password prompt. On less than four hours' sleep and half an Absolut bottle's worth of throbbing headache, it was a little hard to focus. But I managed to type in the letters and hit return. Nothing happened.

"Any other ideas? What's his mother's maiden name?" Samantha remembered it was Marino. I knew I was really reaching on that one, but I figured we might not even have an hour before the police arrived and confiscated the computer, so anything was worth a shot. I tried it and it wasn't. I also tried his social security number, which I picked up from a half-completed health insurance form on his desk. And his telephone number. And his fax number. And his birth date. And Berkeley, the name of his college. And Mercury, the name of his old paper. And Herald, for his present one. And Humboldt, for the record. And

Linguini, because he liked it so much. And Pesto, for the hell of it. And Grateful Dead, for nostalgia—it was too long. And Simon, out of hope. And Woodrose, out of desperation. And even Fidel, because the last words he had ever said to me were *"Hasta la victoria siempre."* Comandante didn't work either. I tried Claire and Hannin and California and Forest and Protection and about a dozen others I can't remember or justify, before I leaned back in his chair and looked at Samantha. She had a wan smile on her face as if to say, What could we do? It's out of our hands now. I sat there staring at her a moment, feeling the vodka still burning in the pit of my stomach like an ulcer struggling to be born, my eyes beginning to shut, when I said, "What about you? He liked *you* a lot." She waved her hand in embarrassment, but I typed her name in anyway. Instantly the hard disk rumbled and the "c" prompt came up.

"I guess I was right," I said. Samantha exhaled and looked away. But seconds later she was standing over me as I made a global search on the name Claire Hannin. A file came up filled with random notes about sixteen pages long.

I was still printing it out when I heard a car pull up on the street below us. I looked through the window. It was the police. I switched off the computer, took the pages that were finished and walked with Samantha out the side door. Down the street at the Woodrose, we took a seat at one of the booths—I ordered a double espresso, she ordered a *latte*—and we split up the pages of the printout. My part consisted of a history of the Earth People, Claire's now defunct ecology group, which mostly seemed obtained from a five-year-old issue of the *Bay Guardian*, followed by some notes taken from a pamphlet called

Middle Eastern Terrorist Bomb Designs published by the Paladin Press in Boulder, Colorado. It contained descriptions of such handy items as a "cassette box bomb" and a "fragmentation canister."

I had no clear idea what this all meant and looked up at Samantha, who was scrutinizing her pages with the intensity of a medieval monk.

"What're yours about?" I asked her, and she looked up almost startled.

"It's very rough. Something about Claire Hannin and a school."

"Bomb school?"

"Sounds like it. It's not really clear," she said, glancing down again when she started to smile, as if she had just discovered the answer to something. She pointed to a line at the bottom of the page. "'Only the bubblegum man knows,' it says."

"Bubblegum man?" I frowned, suddenly remembering the sweet smell coming from the basement of a certain California dream house.

"You know him?"

"I . . . maybe."

"Is he a grower?"

"A grower?"

"Yeah. Bubblegum's the hottest new cannabis seed hereabouts, imported from Amsterdam. Bred for its sweet odor to escape detection. Sells for a fortune."

"Son of a fucking bitch," I said. "That's where he got the Morgan."

"You *do* know him," said Samantha.

I was about to call for the check when the door opened and Nicholas Bart entered. He looked distinctly unsurprised to find us there as he walked directly over to the table. "Good morning, Mr. Wine . . . Ms. Backus. . . . Mind if I join you for a cup of coffee?" He sat down next to Samantha without waiting for an answer. "Difficult night, wasn't it?" he said to me. "How're you bearing up?"

"I've been better."

"Any word from your son?"

"Not personally." He was staring at the printout in my hand, so I continued. "But I do have some word from the Guardians. . . . This is their most recent communiqué."

"May I have a look at it?"

"With a search warrant." I folded the papers ostentatiously in half and slid them into my jacket pocket. Samantha stashed hers in her shoulder bag.

"Am I allowed to ask what it says?"

"They deny responsibility for the death of the FBI informant Daniel Springer."

"They've had a change of heart, have they?"

"Come on, Bart, you don't believe they do assassinations of that sort. They also deny culpability in the death of Leon Erlanger."

"How interesting. You seem to be up-to-date on their positions."

"They're in the communiqué."

"Of course." He smiled wryly and signaled to a waitress, who came over to the table. "Cappuccino," he said, waiting for us to order refills before continuing. We shook our heads and the waitress went off. "I understand you came up here with your ex-spouse, Suzanne Greenhut. Where is *she* at the moment?"

"Beats me."

"Three nights ago you stayed with her forty miles north of here at the Eel River Lodge on 101."

"Correct. But the next morning we had a battle royal

over breakfast. Woke up half the motel. We're not ex-spouses for nothing. She got into a cab and I haven't seen her since. Why don't you call her office?"

"I already have."

"She has a pager, doesn't she?"

"It's switched off."

"That *is* a problem, Mr. Bart. But I don't think I can help you." I deposited some cash on the table and turned to Samantha. "Shall we?" She nodded and we got up and started for the door.

"Mr. Wine," said Bart, his voice suddenly sharp, almost taunting. "There's something you might want to know."

I stopped and turned back. "What's that?"

"Someone who refuses to disclose knowledge of crimes such as these can be prosecuted for conspiracy under the RICO Act. . . . But I'm sure you're aware of that," he added with a smile.

"Are you arresting me, Mr. Bart?"

"I'm thinking about it."

"Let me know when you come to a decision," I replied, and exited with Samantha.

"Why don't we go find the bubblegum man?" she said when we were ten feet away from the restaurant.

"I don't want to drag you into this."

"Don't be silly. I'm already in it. Besides, I'm a journalist. This is a story. . . . And you need help. You can't go anywhere in that." She gestured ahead, where the Buick was parked just across from the very same Mercury Sable that had been following me way back in Marin County. The driver was sitting at the wheel reading the morning paper. "You might as well attach an ambulance siren to your roof. . . . It's a useless vehicle around here anyway," she added, tugging on my arm and guiding me quickly through an alley behind the newspaper building. A late-model silver Toyota Land Cruiser was parked in back by the loading dock. Samantha stopped in front of it and fished some keys out of her shoulder bag. "That's some vehicle," I said, surprised she was driving the newest L.A. car-of-choice for young macho movie actors and not-so-young clothing manufacturers. "It was Daniel's," she said, climbing aboard in the driver's seat. I got in next to her. "He leased it for the paper, but we mostly used it to go skiing in Tahoe."

She started the car straightaway and we backed around the building, slipping through the town via a series of alleys that ran parallel to the Redwood Highway, taking care to check at each cross street for squad cars or police barricades. Samantha was a skillful driver and in a few minutes we were out on 101 again. Halfway down to Willits, we stopped briefly at a convenience store, then continued on another thirty miles or so until I directed her up the road toward Gabriel's. I was intending to stake him out, perhaps get a photo of his basement, but less than halfway up, not far from where we had been kidnapped by the Guardians, I spotted a vintage black Morgan snaking down the mountain toward us.

"Bubblegum man?" said Samantha.

"It's him," I said, ducking out of view as the car bore down on us.

Samantha pulled into a fire road, turned around and followed after the Morgan, speeding rapidly downhill. In a couple of minutes, we had caught up with it, hiding discreetly behind other traffic as it proceeded south on 101.

"It's the guy you were talking about last night?" she said with some astonishment, after I had explained things to her in more detail. As we approached Willits, our vehicle was forced closer to Gabriel's, which had slowed as the highway narrowed to a two-lane road. "The best friend who slept with your wife?"

"The very same. Cute, huh?"

"From this angle?" Samantha lowered her head closer to the windshield and squinted. "Not bad . . . if you don't mind my saying so."

"Oh, not at all . . . just as long as he dies at fifty-three from terminal masturbation warts," I muttered to myself as the Morgan turned left just before the Willits main street. Gabriel headed down another three blocks and pulled up to the side of a small building. A sign out front read NORTH COAST VETERINARY CENTER.

I signaled Samantha to drive past and park out of view, around the next corner. She stopped by a wrecking yard and we walked back. By the time we returned, Gabriel had already gone inside somewhere. I stepped closer to the front of the veterinary center. Its windows were covered with black shades and it was eerily quiet within: no sounds of dogs being inspected or parakeets having their wings clipped. A windowless Ford van was parked in the driveway.

I walked over to Samantha, who was standing by the side of the building, about halfway down the driveway. "Great place for a pot farm," I said. "They probably grow it in the garage out back where they keep the old Dobermans."

"Not out back. Underground. It's the best place for a 'sea of green.'"

"'Sea of green'?"

"Six-foot tables of high-production grass . . . all dwarf plants." She pointed to a low cellar door at the end of the building. "Force-grown under sodium lamps. They get a crop in forty-seven days with this seed called AK-47."

"You know a lot about this," I said.

"I'm practically a local girl," she said with a smile. "But I don't smoke it anymore. Last time I had a hit of this stuff I thought my grandmother was coming after me with a meat cleaver."

I knew what she meant. Walking softly, I wandered down toward the cellar door and peeked carefully through the cracks. A blast of searing white light came from the thin sliver and I cupped my eyes to see, just barely able to make out what looked like the edge of a closely grown bonsai garden, the "sea of green," beneath a network of plastic pipes and other paraphernalia including what appeared to be ceramic heaters attached to the ceiling. There was an intense stench, too, coming through the door, almost sickening, like three months' worth of left-over fish trapped under some garbage in a Dempsey Dumpster. This was apparently not bubblegum but the high-speed AK-47 itself.

I heard someone moving about inside and imagined he was carrying a real AK, but it was no time to get tentative.

I walked back past where Samantha was standing over to the Morgan. Its convertible top was down and I easily leaned in and yanked out the starter wires. The Ford van was more difficult. The doors were locked and I had to slash the tires with my pocket knife. Then I walked over to a juniper bush, broke off a large branch and headed down to the cellar door, planting myself squarely in front.

"Drug Enforcement Agency!" I yelled, banging hard on the door with the branch. "Open up!"

15

THE WORST NIGHTMARE OF MY LIFE was always that Simon was Gabriel's son. I had no proof of it. I was never sure I actually believed it and our matching physical characteristics (Simon's and mine) made me think it was ridiculous, but the paranoid fantasy often came back to haunt me over the years and even now, with my foot planted metaphorically on Gabriel's neck, I could not entirely escape the thought. Was it the memory of that self-satisfied smile on his face one afternoon twenty-one springs ago when I picked up Suzanne at his New York apartment after a business meeting or was it simply normal male paranoia?

This morning I continued to scrutinize his features, his pale complexion blotched red with fear and embarrassment, looking for similarities to my son as he paced anxiously behind the Ford in terror that I would have him arrested. I never could see a specific resemblance and I couldn't see any then, but still something in me wanted to stick a hypodermic deep in his veins and suck out the DNA to know once and for all.

"I don't know why you're so sanctimonious," he was saying. "You used to smoke more of this shit than anybody but Rado and Ragni. Whatever happened to those stoned conversations we used to have about how the biggest dope peddlers in the country were General Foods and Philip Morris? About how your average pot farmer was just the modern equivalent of a nineteenth-century country gentleman rustling up a bit of moonshine for his friends?"

"I'm just here for some information, Gabriel."

"I don't have any to give you." He looked from me to Samantha, who was sitting on the steps of the veterinary center holding the Kodak FunSaver 35 ("The Film That's a Camera") I had bought at the convenience store halfway between Willits and Garberville. It was the sight of this supposedly recyclable item photographing his "sea of green" that had sent Norman B. Pinsky, doctor of veterinary science and born-again gentleman farmer, running for his life across the abandoned lot next to his center and down the next street, tripping and falling like the Little Tramp himself. The same camera had also frozen Gabriel as surely as the barrel of an assault rifle when he emerged from his cellar farm with his hands up, as full-blown a coward as any in his film scripts. "I'm just trying to live my life," Gabriel continued. "You think it's easy to be a Hollywood screenwriter at fifty? The way things are nowadays, all those twenty-five-year-old Wall Street retreads running things, making lobotomized pabulum for the masses. Do you think they care if you attended film school in Paris, if you saw *Nights of Cabiria*? Most of them don't even know who John Huston is, let alone Fellini. Culturally, it's more engaging to grow pot. At least you learn something about botany!"

"I have more urgent problems than your career at this

moment, Gabriel. Now are you going to tell me where Claire Hannin is or am I going to have to have you arrested?"

He gestured vaguely and took a step closer to Samantha.

"And don't even think about taking that camera. I may not be exactly Mike Tyson, but I've got enough hatred for you saved up to break every bone in your body." I slammed the branch on the hood of the Morgan for emphasis, leaving an unsightly dent.

"Easy now, Moses. You don't really have any proof, you know. There are not exactly any books for this."

"Who needs proof? The police can seize all your possessions the moment you're a suspect in a drug case and prove it later. It's called asset forfeiture. Ms. Backus is an expert, but I'm sure you know all about it."

"My, my. Now the self-righteous Mr. Wine himself supports the dismantling of our Constitutional rights—"

"You better fucking believe it!" I said, bashing in both his headlights. "Where is she, Gabriel?" I walked around the back and smashed in his brake lights. This was getting to be fun. "And come to think of it . . . while you're at it . . . I'd like to know why this is such a secret too. A cowardly motherfucker like you who is willing to screw his best friend's wife for a couple of years should be willing to sell out Claire Hannin at the drop of a hat. . . . So talk, Gabriel, or . . ." I surveyed the Morgan for more possible targets, gouging little nicks in the finish with my pocket knife as I went. Gabriel looked mortified.

"If you pour some sand in the fuel line," said Samantha, "you'll wreck the engine forever."

"Good idea," I said, and popped the hood. "Then we can just call the police and—"

"Okay, okay. I'll tell you."

I stood still and waited.

"I don't know where she is," Gabriel said. "Only her boyfriend does."

"Who's that?"

"Lawton Stanley."

"Lawton Stanley?"

"Yes. . . . I know it sounds crazy but it's the truth. . . . Chemistry comes where you least expect it, Moses. You should know that. . . . If you don't believe me, go see him. He's always down at the Chateau Montreux in Napa."

"The Chateau Montreux?" I'd been drinking their cabernet for years. "What's it got do with Stanley?"

"He bought it after his wife died with all that FOXAM funny money he got from Sean Handler. Stanley was sick of the lumber business anyway. If you want to find out about Claire, he's the only one who can tell you."

"If you're lying to me, Gabriel," I said, "I'll come back and do to you what I should have done seventeen years ago."

I left Gabriel with his car problems, got into the Land Cruiser and headed south with Samantha toward the Napa Valley. But we were barely out on the 101 when my beeper went off. I recognized the number as Nancy's.

"Do you want me to pull over?" asked Samantha.

"It's a friend. I don't want to deal with it now," I answered, keeping the gender neutral.

"Woman friend?" said Samantha. I obviously wasn't slipping anything past her.

"Seems pretty far away at the moment," I said.

The beeper went off again, within five minutes, but this time, I didn't recognize the number, although from the 707 area code, it was local. "I better deal with this one," I said.

We drove off into a truck stop and I dialed the number on a pay phone. Suzanne was on the other end, at the Honeydew general store. She sounded about as stressed out as I'd ever heard her since the days of our divorce, and it took her a moment to articulate.

"Moses, it's getting crazy out here! The moment they heard the Guardians were blamed for Springer's murder, everyone went ballistic, particularly Karin. I think they're planning something extreme."

"What do you mean?"

"I don't know exactly. They don't talk when I'm around. This morning they were looking at some maps down by the river. Bill's gone off someplace for supplies. . . . What're *you* doing?"

I glanced at Samantha, who was watching me from the cab of the Land Cruiser. "On my way to wine country."

"What?!"

"Your old boyfriend led us there. He's gone into the high-tech marijuana business."

"I can't believe it! You're still wasting time getting revenge on Gabriel. Your son's in trouble!" Her anxiety had turned into anger. "And who's the 'us' you're talking about?"

"Someone who worked for Springer. A reporter. . . . Look, I'm not interested in Gabriel. I'm—"

"Yes, you are! You're—"

"I'm trying to find out what the fuck's going on!" I shouted.

"No, you're not! Who is she?"

"What?!"

"The reporter. Who is she? Don't lie to me, Moses—I know you! Ever since we split up it's been one after the other. No wonder I did what I did. It was fucking self-defense!"

"Oh, come on. This isn't—"

"You're the most selfish person I've ever met!"

"Stay calm. All right?"

"Stay calm? You're the one who's going wine tasting with some bimbo when your son's life is in jeopardy!"

"She's not a bimbo, for crissake! She went to Brown!"

"Oh, great! Are you going to tell me her IQ too? I hope she's over twenty-one!"

"I don't have to tell you anything! You're the one spending your life with some retarded carpenter who gives body rubs to horny divorcees!"

"Fuck you!"

I was about to say fuck you too when something told me this had gone far enough. Maybe it was the telephone trembling in my hand. Who knows? But I shut up. Still, it was Suzanne who spoke first. "Moses, I'm going to cry," she said. I could hear it in her voice.

"Okay, okay," I said. "I'm sorry. I didn't mean it. Really."

"What're we going to do?"

"We're doing what we can. I'll . . . try to figure out something. Tell Simon . . . or Karin . . . not to do anything nuts until they hear from me. I'll try to get through to you on the Internet. Or call me if something happens."

I hung up and walked back to the Toyota, climbing in beside Samantha. "Who was that?" she said, pulling out. "You look awful."

"My ex."

"You sure you want me along on this? I could drop you by a car rental or . . . "

"No, that's okay," I said. "Normally I'm not like this—

at least, I don't like to think I am—but ... I don't much
feel like being alone at the moment."

"I can understand that," she said.

We continued down 101 along the Russian River to
Geyserville and turned left on the state road that mean-
dered through the Alexander Valley and on into Napa. It
was lined with vineyards on both sides, the historic names
that long ago gave lie to the myth that America was a land
of tasteless Babbitts drinking cheap beer and eating cheese-
burgers. Normally, Napa was my getaway of choice for a
self-indulgent weekend but on this trip we proceeded
directly past my favorite northern Italian deli and the precious hardware store selling more varieties of corkscrews
than you ever dreamed were invented, turning right
through the fields of old-vine zinfandel grapes along
Sulphur Springs Creek. There, at the foot of Mount St.
Helena, stood the magnificent Chateau Montreux, a winery
built in 1885, according to a plaque above the gate, by a
California state senator, in the style of a seventeenth-century
French chateau; a Chinese pagoda was later added, sitting
on an island in the middle of a private, man-made lake.

We drove through the gate and stopped in the guest
parking area. The main entrance to the building had been
cordoned off and the sole access was through the wine-
tasting room. Only a handful of tourists were walking in
and out. It was off-season and, at the thirty dollars plus a
bottle, Chateau Montreux did not normally attract the
Disneyland crowd anyway. Samantha and I entered a cavernous space dominated by a large crystal chandelier and
several oak fermentation barrels. An elderly couple were
sampling a Winemaker's Reserve by a counter display of
vintage wines and jogging outfits with the vineyard logo.

"Are you tasting?" said a balding man behind the

counter. He took out two clean glasses and placed them in front of Samantha and me, next to a small bucket for expectorating our leftovers. "We're pouring a chardonnay, a cab and a white zin."

"We'd love to but"—I leaned in closely and spoke in a low voice—"we're aficionados and we were wondering if we could speak personally with Mr. Stanley about obtaining some of his '91 pinot."

The balding man stared at me a moment, then smiled. "You must be Mr. Wine. Mr. Stanley's been expecting you." I flushed with embarrassment. "You have a wonderful name for visiting the Chateau Montreux, by the way," he added, while dialing a number on the house phone. "Tell Mr. Stanley, Mr. Wine and a friend—"

"Ms. Backus," I interjected.

"Bacchus and wine," he said, and then into the phone, "Ms. Backus . . . are here to see him."

Five minutes later Lawton Stanley walked into the tasting room. In contrast to the staid attire he'd worn at the funeral of Leon Erlanger, he was dressed in a loose-fitting work shirt with his sleeves rolled up and a pair of well-used jeans. With his long silver-flecked hair and wire-rimmed Armani glasses, he looked every bit the Wall Street gentleman gone politely boho. He greeted Samantha and me, shaking our hands firmly. "I'm sorry you can't be here under more auspicious circumstances," he said, opening a double door and leading us down a corridor into the main part of the building. "We're having a Winemaker's Lunch this afternoon. The chef from Stars is making his trademark squab. Perhaps you'll stay."

"Wish we could," I said. "But I'm under a little pressure, as Gabriel Levine may have told you. I imagine he called."

"Ah, yes, Gabriel. Amusing fellow. An old friend of yours, I understand."

"In a sense."

"He knows everybody around here, after working on that movie. Is it ever coming out?"

"I wouldn't know. . . . I guess he told you I'm interested in locating Claire Hannin."

"Yes, he did." Stanley slowed to a stop. We were in a room of giant metal vats, where, according to posted signs, the crushed grapes were inoculated with yeast before fermentation. "Claire's a private person," he said. "Her life experience made her that way."

"What do you mean?" I asked, though I had some inkling what he was talking about.

"You might say, Mr. Wine, this area of California's had a recent midlife crisis. Some of us who all along thought one way, now think another. Others have . . ."

"Reversed field as well?"

"You might say. Obviously, I'm not that interested in board-lengths anymore. I'm down here spending my time measuring the residual sugar in a liter of chenin blanc."

"Doesn't sound unpleasant. What happened to Claire? She had that unfortunate accident in the car, if that's what it was."

"Maybe she began to see life in more complexity too."

"Is that when you two met?"

"No, even before then. She was leading a demonstration in front of my ranch near Garberville and"—he smiled—"I invited her in for tea."

"Did she ever tell you anything about a school?"

"A school?" He shook his head. "You must have been talking to Daniel Springer."

"As a matter of fact . . ."

"Poor Mr. Springer. He had his theories, didn't he?" He glanced fleetingly at Samantha before continuing. "It's ugly how they're blaming his death on your son and his friends." Stanley started walking again. We followed him through a door past some elegant conference rooms and a private dining room where a long table was set with cut crystal and vases of iris and daffodil.

"Who do you think killed him?" I said.

"I'm not an expert in that. Murder's your business, not mine, Mr. Wine."

"If you had to theorize."

"I wouldn't want to but—" He stopped himself in mid-sentence and guided us to another door at the end of the corridor. "I want to show you something." He pushed through the door and ushered us into a formal garden under construction. "My little bit of Tuscany. I sent a land-scape architect to the Villa Patraia outside Florence to make a perfect copy of Buontalenti's design."

"You were talking about your theory. . . ."

"Well, yes . . . obviously I was trying to avoid making an accusation . . . especially when I have no proof whatso-ever, but . . . you may have heard of a group called California Forest Protection."

"I ran into them."

"Vigilantes of the 'wise use' movement."

"So I gather. Where do you think I could find them?"

"Not easy. They wouldn't be vigilantes if it was." He smiled. "They're not stupid. They've gone underground. But there's a man named Platt—with two *t*s—who used to be a member, lives outside of Willits on Sacramento Road. He did anyway." He looked at his watch. "And now, you'll have to excuse me. I must prepare for my lunch guests. . . ." The lake with the pagoda was right in front of us, but he steered us in the other direction, opening a gate. "You won't mind if I don't walk you to your car." He gestured across the driveway and waited for us to leave, but I didn't move.

"What about Claire Hannin?" I asked. "How can I contact her?"

"I'm sorry, Mr. Wine. Claire and I have an agreement. I can't give out her address."

"You can imagine how important this is to me, Mr. Stanley."

"Yes, I can." He stood there agonizing a moment. "I'll tell you what—you have an answering service or a beeper or something?" I nodded. "Why don't you give me that number and I'll ask her to get in contact with you."

"You've got to do better than that. My kid's life is on the line here."

"Mr. Wine, I gave my word to the woman I love. You're lucky to have that much."

Stanley spoke with a boardroom finality, as if that topic had been dismissed by the CEO and there was no revisiting it. I had no choice but to give him my beeper number and leave.

I asked Samantha if I could drive and got in behind the wheel. We headed north along the side route to avoid traffic at a speed thirty miles above the limit. It was well after noon and all I could think of was Simon and his friends back in the Lost Coast in despair over having been accused of a horrendously brutal murder—and this time, making it worse, without a jot of mitigating accidental circumstances. It was easy to understand their anger, even to sympathize with the desire for revenge. But I was petrified that whatever they were planning would only hasten their own destruction. And I was even more scared that the person instigating it would be my own son, acting on his own behalf or, dare I think it, on behalf of the very people who were supposed to be looking for him.

I was reaching a level of paranoia I couldn't contain. I was near panic and I had no idea what to do about it. Call a lonely pay phone in the middle of nowhere when Suzanne was obviously long gone? Leave e-mail through some Internet remailer in Finland? But what did I have to say? I didn't have a shred of information except for the onetime address of a member of a fringe group.

"Relax," said Samantha, catching my mood. "You're doing all you can."

"Maybe that's the point," I said, pressing harder on the accelerator.

We made it back the sixty-five miles to Willits in well under an hour, stopping only at a gas station to look up the address of a Platt with two *t*s on Sacramento Road in the most recent phone book—it was number 34, first initial S.—and then slowing only in the last mile as the traffic began to stack up. In another half mile, we came to a full stop. "Shit," I said, sticking my head out to see past the long line of cars formed in front of us. "Roadblock." I had visions of state troopers checking my driver's license again, the name Wine now popping out at them like Dillinger or Capone. I turned to look around. Behind us, the driver two cars back was staring at me and frowning while talking on a cell phone.

"Who knows this Land Cruiser," I asked Samantha, "other than you and Springer?"

"Everybody knows everybody around here," she replied.

"Is there a back way out?"

"Turn," she said, and I made a quick U, averting my

eyes from the other drivers and smiling in the desperate hope that a pretense of ignorance would somehow distract them. At the end of the line of cars, Samantha pointed to a fire road that went up at about a forty-five-degree slope. I hesitated before turning and slid the transmission lever into four-wheel drive, slowly guiding the car upward. It worked. For the first time I was bouncing over the ruts in a vehicle that was built for them. We climbed for a couple of minutes, then plunged into a gully and then climbed again, up an ever steeper incline that took us to the top of the ridge. The village of Willits suddenly appeared below us and then disappeared again, its few paved streets intermittently visible through an oncoming ocean fog, as if the town itself were engaged in a collective game of hide-and-seek.

"Where's Sacramento Road?" I asked Samantha, arriving at a fork in the fire road.

"It *was* over there," said Samantha, holding a county map in one hand and pointing with the other to where a thick cloud was settling in like a cat in the depths of a canyon. I followed her directions down toward it, becoming more apprehensive of what was waiting for us as we descended into the increasing whiteness. By the time we reached paved road our visibility was no more than a car-length and the first houses loomed up at us like holographic images. I had slowed to read their addresses when I saw the silhouette of a car bearing down on us, its yellow headlights flaring in the mist. Then I heard the dull, muffled thud of a shotgun in the fog. I slammed on the brakes and ducked, pulling Samantha down with me as the shotgun fired again, riddling the back with bullets as tires blew out and the Land Cruiser spun out of control.

16

I ALWAYS WANTED TO BELIEVE I could communicate openly with my sons. We wouldn't be like previous generations, where chasms of austere traditions created an unbridgeable gap. We would be friends and yet I would still able to be their father, dispensing advice and Band-Aids when the situation arose. So why had this happened? Why this extreme exaggeration of everything I stood for—or, even worse, this complete rejection of it? Why, suddenly, did it seem like a stranger had sprung from my loins? Was rebellion necessary for every generation, no matter what? Had we . . . had I . . . boxed them into a corner and given them no maneuvering room to differentiate themselves, standing approvingly in the background when they bought their first condom or Bogarted their first joint? Was this supposed open communication simply a convenient self-aggrandizing lie I told myself and them? Had deeper forces, older than Abraham and Isaac and as immutable as our DNA, been at play all along and finally come back to haunt me?

I didn't have much time to debate these issues—not that

I would have come to any conclusion—as I sat tied to a kitchen chair in a house somewhere on the road back into Humboldt State Park. Samantha and I had been taken there in a Jeep Grand Cherokee—the vehicle whose yellow lights I had seen—by the tall, handsome man and his mustached buddy, who apparently was S. Platt. Moving with professional speed, they had pulled us from the disabled Land Cruiser at gunpoint before we had the slightest chance of resisting. We were both tied up and placed in the back while Platt drove and the tall man kept his pistol dangling ostentatiously over the seat. We were met at the door of this house by the woman with the dirty-blond hair. First they secured me to the straight-backed chair, tying my wrists to its legs with laundry cord; then all three took Samantha off into another room. In a few minutes, the two men returned.

"What has your son said about us?" said Platt as soon as the tall man shut the door behind him.

"My son? Nothing."

"You're not going to tell us you haven't seen him?"

"I'm not going to tell you anything."

He looked over at the tall man, who seemed unimpressed with my response. "What did your son say about us?" Platt repeated.

"I didn't talk to him."

"You didn't talk to him? You expect us to believe that bullshit?"

"I didn't talk to him," I said.

The tall man nodded to Platt, who stepped aside, and walked toward me. He was apparently the leader. "Mr. Wine," he said, turning a chair around and sitting opposite me with his arms over the back. "I dislike the use of excessive force as much as you do, but as you can see, I can apply it effectively where required." I certainly could see.

The choke hold he used on my neck to get me into the back of the Cherokee would have worked on a sumo wrestler. "We know you have been with the Guardians," he continued, "and we know your ex-wife is still there."

"You seem to be very well informed."

"Up to a point. . . . So I would like to ask you again. What did they tell you?"

"They or my son? You're not being very specific."

"Let's begin with the general. Did they tell you who we were?"

"No," I said.

"Now, Mr. Wine. I'm not an idiot and neither are you. I assume you've been asking questions about California Forest Protection ever since you met us in the London Grove."

"Of course. You're a private security organization operating here in Northern California. Most of the lumber companies pretend you don't exist, but they're probably happy you do."

"Is that all?"

"I doubt it. You seem to be rather skilled at tracking my whereabouts. Who told you? Lawton Stanley?"

"Stanley?" The tall man laughed. Then he got up and started to walk slowly back and forth in front of me. It was a minute or two before he spoke again. "Perhaps it was someone much closer to you who informed us of your whereabouts."

"What's that supposed to mean?" I snapped. The hell of the situation was biting into my guts.

"There are six members of the Guardians at this moment. One of them is obviously keeping us abreast of your activities. Do you know who that is?"

"No and why would they do that?" I asked, running

their names down in my head—Max, the failed yuppie; Sheila, the Brit; Hector, the junior computer whiz (he had the capability); Bill (he had made that phone call); Karin (how could I trust her?); and Simon.

"By the time you find out, Mr. Wine, it will be too late. Besides, if you wanted to report them, what would you be reporting—what the authorities already know." There was a low peep. "I believe that's your beeper," said the tall man.

I shrugged.

"Aren't you going to answer it?"

"A little difficult at the moment." I tugged at my wrist.

The tall man reached down and unclipped the beeper from my belt. "707-555-0181 . . . mean anything to you?"

I shook my head. In fact, I did recognize it, from Suzanne's earlier call from the Honeydew general store, but there was no point in broadcasting it.

"Do you believe him?" said Platt. "I don't." He walked over and started to pat me down, pulling out the computer printout and glancing through it. "The son of a bitch is carrying around information about cassette box bombs," he said to the tall man. "'The device is commonly used in Lebanon,'" he read; then he turned to me. "Where'd you get this?"

"It came from Daniel Springer's computer. You know him?"

He slammed me across the face with the back of his hand, snapping my head backward.

The tall man reached for a wall phone, glanced at my beeper again and punched in the number. "Who's this?" he said into the phone, then turned to me. "Sounds like your ex." He thrust the handset against my ear.

"Hello," I said. I could feel blood trickling down my cheek.

"Moses! Who was that? Are you alone?" I didn't say anything. "Help me. Please! Come quickly! They're gone!" She sounded hoarse. Almost frantic. I looked up at the two men, who were staring at me, convinced they could hear everything she was saying almost as well as I could. "Simon and all of them . . ." she continued. "Disappeared and left me here ten minutes ago!"

The tall man removed the handset from my ear and hung it up. "I guess that leaves you with a dilemma," he said, taking the printout from Platt and perusing it. "You're certain no one told you anything else about us?"

"Nothing. I swear. . . . Would you mind letting me out of here?"

"You're sounding desperate, Mr. Wine," said the tall man, amused. He turned to his partner. "I'm going to talk to Ms. . . . what's her name?"

"Backus," said Platt.

"Right. Backus," repeated the tall man. He sounded skeptical. "Maybe *she* can be more informative."

"I'll watch this creep," said Platt.

"I better keep this." The tall man pocketed the printout and left.

I looked around the kitchen, which contained an aging stove and refrigerator and a fading blue Formica table. Outside, through the window, was the redwood forest. It seemed a long way away. I waited for a while, watching as Platt helped himself to a beer.

"You ever hear of Alan Turing?" I asked finally.

"Turing?"

"He was my idol when I was a kid. The guy who broke the Nazi code in World War II."

Platt swilled his beer. "What's that got to do with any-thing?"

"That's why I was able to break into Springer's computer. Get that printout."

"Any fucking nine-year-old could do that."

"You're right there," I said, smiling and shaking my head. "Actually, all I had to do was open Word for Windows and search on 'terrorism' and up came the whole file . . . with all the stuff on that bomb school and everything." Platt stopped drinking and looked at me. "I didn't even get a chance to read it all. It had one of those little icons on the top saying it was going to be faxed."

"Faxed?"

"Yeah, to the *New York Times* and some other papers. I don't remember exactly when. Sometime this week?"

"Fuck!" said Platt, and walked out of the room, shouting, "Larsen!"

I stood up and went to the window, still tied to the chair. I thought for a split second of Samantha, guilty about abandoning her, but then turned around and jumped backward, chair and all, into the glass. The window smashed into a thousand tiny safety pellets, which rained on me as I crashed on the concrete below. I had landed on their driveway. I heard Platt and Larsen yelling inside. "Kill the fucker!" Larsen said. I picked myself up and started to run/waddle toward the woods across the road, crouching low and keeping the Cherokee between me and the house. I could hear them coming out the front door. I lowered my head even farther and bolted for the trees. I made it there quickly, but I immediately pitched straight over a steep incline I hadn't seen and fell, rolling over myself as the chair crunched between my ribs and the ground. A couple of chair legs and an arm broke off and a piece of splintered wood went deep into my side. Doing my best to ignore it, I struggled to my feet again and kept running. I could move more easily now because most of the chair had shaken free. I pulled my hands out of the rope. Some shots went off. I didn't look back but darted around a boulder and sped farther into the forest, pushing myself as hard as I could remember, feeling my heart thump as it told me, No, no. This is too much. You can't do this anymore. But I had no choice.

After what felt like an hour but probably was closer to fifteen minutes, I came to a halt at the base of an old-growth tree and leaned my head against it. I stayed there for a moment, catching my breath beside its comforting bark and listening for my pursuers. They seemed to have gone or given up. The forest was ominously silent, cool and damp, but I felt safe. Then I heard the sound of a car, backfiring and sputtering up the mountain and I realized I had run away from the road on one side only to run toward it again on the other end of a switchback. I spun around, rushed through a group of trees and stopped, looking through several more to see a pickup chugging over the ridge with a load of manure in the back. I ran out in front of it and waved my hands. "Emergency!" I shouted. "Save me! I've got to get to Honeydew!"

Suzanne was sitting on the curb in front of the general store as the pickup pulled into Honeydew. Her shoulders were slumped and her head buried into her chest like an old woman, but she sprang to her feet, revived, before I was halfway out of the truck. "Moses, thank God you made it," she said, hurrying over to me. "I'd given up. . . . Who was that on the phone? It sounded like they were going to kill you."

"California Forest Protection," I said, wrapping my arm around her shoulder and squeezing her briefly. "I don't think they're on our side. . . . What's happened to Simon?"

"They've been gone for almost an hour. They were carrying chemicals."

"Good Christ! What kind?" She shook her head. My heart started pounding all over again. "Do you know what they're planning?"

"Burn something . . . blow something . . . they wouldn't tell me, I can promise you."

"Whose idea was it?" I asked, not sure I wanted to know.

"Karin, Simon, Hector, Bill . . ." She gestured in frustration.

"No instigator?"

"It looked unanimous at this point. All I know is they didn't want me involved."

"Where'd they go?"

Just as she pointed toward a small trail that ran north into the woods, four military helicopters, flying in formation, roared overhead in the same general direction.

"What do we do, Moses?" said Suzanne, panic in her voice.

"First call Jacob." I walked over to the pay phone and punched my credit card code followed by his number. But he wasn't in. I left a message with the answering machine: "Jacob, immediately send the following to N2690@earthlink.net—'Stop everything. You're being set up. Pop.'"

"Who's setting him up?" asked Suzanne.

"I hope *someone* is," I said, hanging up. "It's the only chance we have." Then I dialed 911 and told the operator there was an extreme emergency at the clapboard house by the stop sign on route 328 into Humboldt Park. They should look for a Ms. Samantha Backus.

"Who's that?" said Suzanne. "Your reporter friend?"

I nodded. "I left her in a bit of a mess. . . . Let's go. We'll try to catch them."

I took Suzanne by the arm and we walked quickly down the street toward the trail.

"What did you learn about those forest protection people?" she asked.

"Not much. They're very concerned about what *we* know."

"And what's that?"

"Not a whole helluva lot as far as I can tell. . . . From the sound of things they had something to do with a bomb school."

"Now what?" said Suzanne, exhaling. "Was Simon involved in that too?"

"I don't think it's possible," I said, trying to reassure us both on this at least. "It was several years ago."

Simon and the others were nowhere to be seen when we reached the trail. We continued on, moving as swiftly as we could through the dense forest, taking off our shoes in order to ford a stream that was fifteen feet wide with no logs to cross it. A half hour later we were traversing a brutal series of switchbacks along the south slope of a granite outcropping. It was late afternoon, but the sun was beating down hard on us.

"This used to be easier," said Suzanne. I grunted in agreement, wiping my forehead with the inside of my dirt-caked sleeve. "Remember Mt. Donner? Simon was on your back in that Gerry pack and still we made it up the east face in three hours."

"Twenty minutes behind Gabriel," I said.

"That's right. He was along on that trip, wasn't he?"

"He was on most of them," I said, the bitterness coming through despite my gasping for breath. I could still remember catching up to him on the edge of a stream, flyfishing, the kids marveling at the delicacy of his touch as he flicked his line after the elusive trout.

Suzanne paused for a moment and looked back at me. "Now he's a drug dealer. Isn't that enough revenge for you?"

"And what am I? Forty-nine years old and still a detective."

"What do you expect?"

"I don't know," I smiled at my own self-pity. "Governor of California? CEO of Microsoft?"

Suzanne smiled too. "I think you did all right. You have an interesting life. And you're not a bad guy after all. . . . I don't know how I could go through this without you."

"I don't know either. Without you. This is hell."

There was an embarrassed silence for a couple of minutes as we continued on up the ridge.

"I'm sorry for what I did back then," Suzanne said, almost inaudibly.

"You are?" She had never said that before. "So am I. I mean it was as much my fault. Maybe more. I didn't know what we had."

"Neither of us did. . . . Look," she said. We had reached the top of the outcropping. She was pointing across the ravine in front of us, where six figures in ski masks were making their way uphill between some tall bushes. They were a mile away or more. Beyond them, a couple of helicopters crisscrossed the sky, apparently oblivious of their presence. The figures disappeared in some foliage, then reappeared again on the other side of a boulder, heading for the top of the next ridge. I wondered which one was Simon, which Karin, which ones had chemicals strapped to their backs or attached to their utility belts. From this distance, it was impossible to tell, but they moved with a purpose, a strange majesty, as if they were on a mission of tremendous importance, a liberation movement overthrowing a dictatorship in a Third World country.

"Maybe we should let them go," I said. "Give them the freedom to do what they want."

"Is that what you really think?" asked Suzanne.

I hesitated a moment, but my response was definite. "No," I said. "Years ago, sure . . . but not now."

We started down the other side of the outcropping into the ravine. Simon and his friends were no longer visible at the top of the ridge and we redoubled our efforts, descending the switchbacks at a near run while staying beneath the branches of the nearby trees to avoid the attention of the helicopters and whatever other arms of the law were about. At the bottom, the afternoon sun had dropped out of sight, leaving us in a deep shade as we crossed the ravine and began our ascent on the other side. But even without the sun it was no easier. A helicopter roared so low over our heads that the trees shook all around us. We froze on the trail, watching it disappear. I took a breath, trying to ignore a growing sense of desperation, and continued on. Every step was deliberate and painful. The younger group must have been gaining ground every moment and would soon be unreachable. Part of me wanted to give up. But halfway up the next ridge, whether from blind will or a discharge of endorphins, I had a sudden burst of energy. My legs felt strong and supple, rejuvenated, and I ran up the rest of the way ahead of Suzanne.

At the top, I stopped and took another deep breath, staring out at the valley beneath me. There, nestled among the redwoods several hundred yards below, past a small rise and then another dip in the land, its aging nineteenth-century façade outlined against the last glimmerings of the setting sun, was the main mill of the Allied Lumber Company.

17

I REMEMBER THE FIRST TIME I hit Simon, because I threw up afterward. It wasn't a very large heave—I was on a diet at the time and my stomach contents were low—but what little I had was deposited in the sandbox of the Echo Park Alternative Center for the Child, a progressive nursery institution still run by us holdouts in a sixties co-op style, although it was already the late seventies.

It had been my day as parent to assist the teacher in looking after the children, an odd occupation for a neophyte detective who was spending much of the rest of the week tracking down reluctant witnesses in police brutality cases. But there I was, doing my best to participate and helping the kids to apportion their toys, which were shared equally. "They're everybody's!" was the creed of the institution. Needless to say, theory and practice did not always mesh. "It's *my* everybody's!" the kids would shout, asserting their jurisdiction over certain items associated with their own family lineage—or with some imagined proximity to it—while pulling the item forcibly from the hands of their peers and battering them over their heads with it in a distinctly noncooperative manner.

Simon was engaged in such an activity that day, wrenching a plastic tool kit given him by my father from the hands of a girl named Sundown and bopping her squarely on the nose with the hammer while yelling the ever popular "It's *my* everybody's!" at the top of his three-year-old lungs. For a moment I almost laughed, but when I saw Diana Weinfeld, the teacher, staring at me as if I were the worst kind of social reprobate, I grabbed Simon around the waist, carried him out of sight behind the jungle gym and gave him a hiding out of a Harriet Beecher Stowe novel. "You have to learn to share!" I shouted perhaps a dozen times while whacking him hard on the fanny. I mixed this with some idiotic statements, like "Everybody's is everybody's! Don't forget it!" (which certainly would not go down in the history of idealistic rhetoric), and then added some extra whomps on the side of his leg for good measure. When I finally put him down, the little boy was sobbing miserably. He staggered a couple of feet and collapsed on the seesaw. It was then that I was overcome with nausea and left my paltry souvenir in the dirt of the school sandbox, right next to an unwanted broken plastic spoon that was clearly and indisputably "everybody's."

I hadn't thought of this episode in years, but it was the first thing that came into my mind as I was standing opposite Simon, realizing that I might have to fight my full-grown son. I wasn't enchanted with the idea on many levels, the most obvious of which was that he was about three inches taller than I, with a remarkably muscular chest from years of paddling a surfboard against treacherous ocean currents. Beyond that, he had just been born strong,

as if he had inherited the genes of some Russian wrestler
lost on an obscure branch of my or Suzanne's family tree.
Even as an extremely shy fifth grader, he had been power-
ful enough to break the arm of the school bully in two
places, simply by picking him up by the T-shirt and tossing him into the gym wall.

None of this was reassuring, but it paled by comparison to the emotional pain of having to lift a finger to my
own blood. But I didn't seem to have a choice. It was now
practically dark, and Suzanne and I had come down the
ridge a half hour before, climbing up again and descending into a gully I had noticed from above, when we saw an
old storage shed off in the trees. We stopped and stared at
it a moment. It was quiet all around except for a single
bird and a dim, almost inaudible humming noise that
probably came from the mill down below. No one seemed
to be around, but I decided to approach the shed anyway,
with Suzanne a few feet to my rear. We were less than ten
feet from the door when the Guardians appeared from
behind the trees. Before I could even consider an escape, I
felt an arm around my neck and another around my waist.
Someone else had Suzanne in a hammerlock. We were
being dragged into the shed.

"I can't believe you did this, Pop," said Simon in a fury
moments after we were inside. We had been pushed
against a wall, standing opposite him, Karin and Bill. Max
watched from the corner. Hector and Sheila, a few feet
away, guarded the door. "You fucking well know you're
not wanted here—neither of you. You're not responsible
for me and I'm not responsible for you. That's over. Why
can't you get that through your heads?"

"What're we supposed to do? Let you burn down a
lumber mill?"

"You don't have the slightest idea *what* we're doing."
He glanced over at Karin, who nodded. She was standing
to his right in front of several canister belts. Leaning
against the wall behind her was a green flag with the
Guardians logo next to a pile of small wooden boxes with
copper strips on top.

"It doesn't look like you're about to establish a day care
center," said Suzanne.

"That *would* be your solution, wouldn't it?" said Simon.

"Simon, this is crazy," I said. "You're all being manipulated."

"Manipulated?! . . . You expect us to listen to—"

"I don't care want you want to listen to," I shouted.
"You're going to listen!" I looked around at all of them.
"What you're planning now and whatever you've done
before . . . you've been goaded into it. . . . Someone in this
room is a government agent."

"What knee-jerk bullshit," said Simon. "You think
we're so stupid we . . .?"

"I just came from California Forest Protection. They as
good as told me you've been infiltrated."

"Fuckin' company stooges," Simon muttered. He
turned away in disgust.

"That's the kind of lie they'd put out," said Hector.

"It wasn't a lie," I said. "That's what Springer was
investigating. It was on his computer."

There was an uncomfortable silence. Finally Karin said,
"If there's any government agent in the room, it's me."

"No, it's me," said Bill.

"I'm the government agent," said Max.

"No, it's me," said Sheila.

Soon they were all chiming in: "It's me. It's me. It's
me."

The only one who didn't say a word was Simon. Finally he turned around. "Yeah, it's me," he said, staring straight at me. "I'm the one."

A helicopter whirred in the distance.

I glanced over at Suzanne. She looked as if she was going to be sick. I felt the same way.

"We can't waste any more time," said Karin. She turned toward the door, then checked her watch, took a step forward and addressed the others. Clearly, she was taking control. "Full darkness," she said. "We have to get started."

"Do you know anything about a school?" I asked her.

She ignored me, signaling to Hector, who picked up a canister belt and strapped it on. Simon grabbed one of his own and headed out. Everyone was moving back and forth now, in and out of the shed, carrying equipment.

"There was some kind of bomb school around here," I said, following along with them. "I don't know what it was, but Claire Hannin knew about it."

"She sure did," said Karin. "They almost took her leg off." She stacked the wooden boxes alongside the canisters.

"The CFP were involved. Maybe teaching." I kept after her. "Who were the students?"

Karin stopped and looked at me. We were standing outside now, just beyond the door. "What difference does it make?"

"I don't know exactly. The police say Claire Hannin blew herself up in her own car. I'm sure it's connected. Daniel Springer was doing research on the school when he was killed."

Karin stared at me, the first hint of confusion betraying her façade of militant self-confidence. "What was he trying to find out?" she said.

"Give me some time," I said. "I'm trying to figure it out."

"He's already had time," said Bill.

"That's right," said Karin. "Plenty." She turned to Simon and smiled, touching him on the sleeve. He smiled back, the sound of helicopters audible once again in the distance.

"Just a few days," I said. But no one bothered to answer. A wind came up, as if blown at us from the rotor blades of a chopper, the leaves shaking with a high-pitched noise like a thousand rattlesnakes. Suzanne clutched her stomach. The rest of us stood there frozen until Bill said, "Look," pointing through the darkness to the next hill. Three black choppers with long military fuselages were headed in our direction like ominous flying objects out of *Batman*, their giant searchlights beaming down on the trees, darting back and forth the way they do over South Central L.A. when police are after a stolen car or a drive-by killer. Simultaneously I noticed several dark land vehicles—were they also military?—coming down the highway toward the mill, their bright headlights low to the ground like the Batmobile itself. I took a half step backward. The air had an acrid, metallic smell, like an unwashed beaker in a chemistry lab. The wind became suddenly chill.

"Who warned them?" said Karin, gesturing vaguely to the marshaling forces while surveying our group until her eyes alighted on me and stopped. I could see the deep lines of suspicion on her brow in the reflected light of the military vehicles. She glanced over at Bill, who hesitated, then shrugged as if to say it wasn't worth it. Karin nodded and turned downhill. "Time," she said. The others picked up their remaining equipment. One by one, they started

off—first Hector and Sheila, then Bill, then Karin. Then
Simon. He reached for the last box of what I assumed to be
explosives when Suzanne said, "What're you doing?" in a
peculiarly calm voice that reverberated back eighteen
years. In my head, I was standing in the play yard of the
Echo Park Alternative Center for the Child when Simon
froze guiltily for a moment and looked back and forth
between Suzanne and me. We stood there fifteen feet
apart, an isosceles triangle of mother, father and child.
Simon bent for the explosives again.

I knew I had to stop him. I ran one step and dove for
him, tackling him around the legs while pushing him as
far from the box as I could. He was as strong as I expected
and it was like trying to fell a bull or a stallion, but with
my adrenal glands pumping like a steam engine, I managed to pull him down. He fought back instantly, slamming into me with his elbows and snapping forward, trying to slip out, but I held on with the last ounce of
strength I had. We rolled across the ground back toward
the shed, his friends coming after us. "Go!" he shouted
confidently, "leave us! I can handle this!" as he grabbed
me around the back and yanked, flipping me over with a
spine-rattling jolt, planting his knees on my shoulders
and pinning me firmly to the hard earth. He waved Karin
and Bill away with his hand and stared down at me. Out
of the corner of my eye, I could see them all going, heading down the hill as I gasped for air. I felt as if I were
going to spit blood.

"You're too old for this, you dumb fuck!" said Simon.

"And you're an imbecile for doing it!" I replied.

"That's what you really think, isn't it? You pretend to
respect everything I do, but you don't at all because you
don't think I'm smart enough!"

"That's not true. I—"

"Yes, it is. You never have! You never thought I had the brains to figure things out for myself!" he said, grabbing onto my shoulders and shaking. "But the point is I do," he continued, pulling back on my vertebral column until it bent like a crossbow. "You just don't see it! I made this decision for myself!"

"Oh, *really*?" I said. Something about my sarcasm must have reached him because he froze for a second, waiting for me to continue. "Then tell me one thing," I asked, though I still dreaded his response. "What the fuck were you doing with Agent Bart's telephone number?"

"Who's Agent Bart?"

"The FBI agent in charge of your case. The one whose phone number was on your calendar. It was in your handwriting!"

"How the hell should I know? You're the brilliant detective! You figure it out!"

He twisted hard on my arm again. I was about to scream when I bucked upward and kicked him straight in his upper abdomen, sending him flying backward. "You little bastard," I said, jumping up and running for him, but he was already up again himself, circling me, his mother staring at us both with an expression of stunned alarm. I took a wild swing at him and missed. Then another.

"Not bad for a geriatric case," he said, a smile beginning to cross his face.

"I'm not dead yet," I said. I lunged for him again, grabbing onto an arm and pulling it behind him, trying to secure a hammerlock. "You're not going down there!" I yelled. "Never!" I added, when we heard a burst of small-arms fire from below. We both stopped for a second and looked down as searchlight beams criss-crossed the hill-

side. Fifty yards below a half-dozen state troopers were
running to where a woman's body was sprawled across a
rock.

Simon screamed in agony and bolted for her.

"No! Don't!" I shouted, running after him with all I had
and intercepting him just below the shed. He tried to pass
me both ways but I shifted back and forth like a line-
backer, anticipating his every move. He was furious, desperate to get to her, but I had to stop him from getting
down there if it was the last thing I did. I kept pushing
him farther and farther toward the trees, trapping him,
when, totally frustrated, tears streaming down his face, he
ran around me through the woods, found another trail,
and raced down the hill toward the rock. Pushing his way
through the surprised troopers, he bent over Karin, clutching her to him, talking to her and cajoling her to stay alive.
She looked at him for a moment, touched his cheek and
said something before her head flopped backward.

"Simon! Go away!" I yelled, but the advice was futile
and far too late, almost absurd. I watched impotently as
the troopers surrounded them, lifting Karin from his arms
and placing his wrists in handcuffs.

18

THE INFURIATING THING about conventional wisdom is that it is often correct. I spent my life rebelling against it—it felt like a box to me, restricting my freedom—but in the end I would usually have to succumb. The conventional wisdom about a crisis is that you can't just sit down and cry—you have to disassociate yourself from the horrible reality of your pain in order to cope with the immediate situation and then allow yourself to go to pieces later on, when you have a chance. And that is how I behaved that night, riding with Suzanne in the back seat of a CHP squad car the twenty or so miles north from Glasgow to Eureka. We were in the rear of a caravan of five vehicles, two of them CHP, two Humboldt County Sheriffs and one from the National Guard, which apparently had been drafted for the occasion. Simon was two vehicles in front of us in one of the sheriff's cars but I still could catch an occasional glimpse of his silhouette if I leaned forward. Once, at a stoplight, I even saw what might have been the glint of his handcuffs, reflected in the rearview mirror.

I didn't have any cuffs of my own at that point, but I had no idea whether I would be formally booked and was making notes in my head about what I could and couldn't say and whom to contact if more than one phone call were allowed. If I could make only one, I knew it would be to my old friend Jack Koufax, the defense lawyer with the famous family name who had long ago given up denying he was related to that most renowned of all Jewish sports heroes, the onetime pitcher for the Los Angeles Dodgers. Although Jack spent much of his time in recent years defending bunco artists and crack dealers, he had distinguished himself in the sixties and seventies in several important political trials and I figured he would be the perfect man for the job. More important, he knew Simon from the old days—our kids grew up together—and I knew he would be sympathetic. Then I thought about what I should do about the media, whether I should call Andrea Yamaguchi at the *L.A. Times* and try to put a spin on the situation so Simon and his friends were not portrayed as a group of young lunatics with Molotov cocktails. But what could I say? I didn't even know what they were planning. When Karin was shot twice in the front and once in the back, the box she carried was also hit. But nothing blew up as far as I could tell. I didn't have much time to find out. Suzanne and I were accosted by a pair of young highway patrol officers less than a minute after Simon was captured by the troopers, and we followed the officers voluntarily to their car. At that point, out of the corner of my eye, I noticed Hector being escorted into a similar vehicle with Max. Apparently Bill and Sheila had still not been apprehended as we approached Eureka, although it was clear, listening to the police band, that some kind of manhunt was in progress for a male and a female Caucasian, both in their twenties and considered armed and dangerous.

By this time the Humboldt County Court House was in front of us, a dull California stucco affair of early sixties vintage that also contained the county sheriff's department and the jail. As we descended into the garage, I looked at Suzanne. We had barely spoken but had held hands tightly the whole way. I knew she would be cool in a crisis, just as she had been in the 1973 earthquake, when our bedroom wall fell in, and a year later, when we came home to find an angel dust addict in our living room waving a semiautomatic in one hand while dismantling the stereo with the other. She would be cooler than I, in fact. I always cried, when it was over, but she never did.

Indeed, she was steady as they came a half hour later, when we stood in the claustrophobic foyer of the sheriff's department jail division opposite a homicide detective named Pirelli. He informed us we would not be able to see Simon that night, although it was only eight-forty in the evening. He was still being booked and after he was finished with that and given his prison clothes, it would certainly be long past the nine o'clock lock-up. And in any case, visiting hours were between eight and three daily, with exceptions made only on verified petition of a licensed California attorney—not an out-of-state one like Suzanne. Simon would be permitted his one call, however, and I gave Jack Koufax's number to the detective. I asked him to tell my son I had already left word with Mr. Koufax's service that he'd be calling. Pirelli nodded and stuffed the number in his pocket. Also tell him that we love him, said Suzanne. It didn't look as if the detective was about to do that. But he did assure us we personally were not being charged with anything. Even though,

unlike Ms. Greenhut, I was unable to show valid identification (I didn't bother to explain my wallet was in the pos-
session of California Forest Protection), my identity had
been vouched for by Special Agent Bart of the Federal
Bureau of Investigation and we were both free to go.
Apparently, Bart was not following through on the RICO
indictment he had been threatening.

I certainly didn't ask why and we walked through the
security doors, down the stairs and out the side exit of the
court building without saying a word. As we hit the street,
I began to fall apart. Suzanne pointed out a Best Western
on the next corner and we started for it, when I noticed the
reflection of the jail window in the office building across
the street. A uniformed guard was staring out through a
thick pane of wire glass, his burly arms crossed compla-
cently in front of him. I looked away, overcome by the
grim reality of it all and cried out suddenly, almost like an
infant, clutching Suzanne's arm as we hurried down the
sidewalk to the motel. When we walked through the door
into the lobby, I was sobbing and had to avert my eyes
from the clerk while Suzanne filled out the check-in form
and gave him her credit card. I was able to choke it back
only until we got to our room, where I wept privately for a
while. But even that didn't last. My only consolation was
that if it turned out Simon was an FBI plant, at some point
they would have to let him go. But that was *some* consolation.

"Can you sleep?" I said to her later. The lights were out
and we had been tossing around in adjoining queen-sized
beds for an hour or so.

"No," she said, her voice strained, barely audible. I had
become increasingly aware of her pain as I lay there listening to her, my thoughts racing from my childhood to the

events of the previous hours and back again, lingering
briefly on the early period of our marriage and then plum-
meting forward toward the divorce, the attempted recon-
ciliations, the endless shuttlings back and forth of the children on their weekend schedules, Jacob telling me that
Simon would never remember the good times, that he was
too young, Simon and I shooting baskets at the schoolyard
in Laurel Canyon the first time he beat me, Jacob coming
out, Simon hating it and then reconciling, the three of us
skiing, Simon drawing cartoons of cute little animals with
the big lost eyes of Tweetybird when my father died.

I turned over and looked at Suzanne. "Is this the worst
day of your life?" I asked her.

"Yes," she said. A minute later she added, "Try to sleep."

"I don't think I can," I said, sighing more loudly.
Suzanne laughed gently and shifted over on her side.

"Why don't you come over here?" she said, patting the
mattress. I climbed out of my bed and slipped in next to
her. She wrapped her opened arms around me. I slid mine
behind her back and held her to me, my lips brushing
briefly against hers and then meeting them more solidly.
Our bodies folded together, our legs fitting one between
the other in the old way. It felt safe and familiar. In a short
while, I was inside her. We were making love for the first
time in over fifteen years, moving back and forth with an
intensity and abandon I couldn't remember experiencing
when we were younger. I had always wondered what it
would have been like to be with Suzanne again. But in a
situation so unique, so extreme, there was no way to
know. All I knew was at this moment it felt like the solution to everything.

"Is this a mercy fuck?" I asked her when we stopped
for a moment.

"For both of us," she said.

I fell asleep shortly afterward. The next thing I remember was my father in his hospital lab. It must have been a dream because I was a little boy of about seven, tugging at his white lab coat while he experimented with the caged animals. "Help me, Daddy. Help me," I was saying but he wouldn't respond. I shook and pulled his coat until he finally turned around. He opened his mouth and tried to speak, but no words came out. He reached out to me instead, his hands and arms wounded with deep gashes, one lonely tear of blood running down his right cheek. The sight of him that way awakened me and I sat up with a start. It was dawn and there was no way I would go back to sleep. Suzanne awoke a little later and we went to have our morning coffee in an all-night diner.

We were the first on line for visitors' hours and were able to see Simon at about eight fifteen that morning. We were sitting at a table in a small attorney's room when a sheriff's officer let him in. Simon wore a loose-fitting gray prison uniform and handcuffs. He sat down opposite us and another officer came and stood behind him.

"She's dead, isn't she?" were the first words he said, as if confirming what he already knew.

Suzanne and I both nodded anyway and gave him the details. Karin had been taken unconscious to the intensive care unit of Humboldt State Hospital and never recovered. Simon blanched when we told him. Suzanne reached across the table to comfort him but the officer signaled it wasn't permitted.

"Did you reach Jack Koufax?" I asked.

He shook his head. "Maybe Mom can do it."

"You need a real criminal lawyer," Suzanne said. "It's early. He'll call."

Simon nodded, adjusting his wrists against the bindings of the handcuffs. I could see he was fighting back tears. It was unbearable to see him that way.

"Be strong," I said, and then I regretted it. Why should he be strong?

"Don't worry, Pop," he replied anyway. "I'll be okay."

Then we sat there for a moment. There were many things I wanted to ask him but with the guards present, monitoring our every word, I didn't know how to formulate the questions. And since Suzanne was not a member of the California bar, there was no immediate way to have our conversations protected by attorney-client privilege.

"How'd they find us so easily?" said Simon finally. "I don't get it."

"I don't either," I said. The guard tilted his head with interest. I glanced sideways at him, then looked pointedly at Simon. "It was just the middle of nowhere," I continued. "How could we all show up at the same time?"

"Because of that Chinese restaurant," Simon said suddenly. I stared at him curiously. What was he talking about?

"Everyone's crazy for that moo goo gai pan," said Suzanne, naming a dish that was a family favorite when the kids were little.

"I didn't think it was so hot," said Simon.

"Where'd you like it better?" I asked him hopefully.

"In Garberville there's a place, across from the hardware store. But I think it's closed now."

"The Cantonese place?" I asked, not having the slightest idea what he meant and not having seen a Chinese restaurant in all of Garberville.

"Uh-huh," he said. "Karin liked it." Then he started to look sad again. We stayed there for another fifteen minutes making small talk. Suzanne promised to get him some surfing magazines and some watercolor paints, if they would let him have them. And I told him the basketball scores I had read in that morning's paper. It all seemed absurd. Then the guard indicated our time was up.

Nicholas Bart was waiting in the jail foyer when we emerged.

"Because your son is being indicted under interstate anti-terrorism statutes," he informed us, "he's being moved down tomorrow to the federal facility at Terminal Island. I'm sorry to have to tell you this, but I guess he'll be closer to home, won't he?" Bart looked in my direction. "For you, anyway, Mr. Wine."

"I'd go anywhere to defend him," I said.

"I'm sure," said Bart.

The truth was I knew Terminal Island well, in the Los Angeles Harbor by San Pedro. I had visited it many times, interviewing inmates, occasionally even in the maximum security area, where they kept the capital cases and the big-time drug dealers. It wasn't the far side of hell, like Pelican Island, but it was close enough to it to make life barely worth living for any middle-class white boy, no matter what kind of shape he was in.

"What about bail?" I asked.

"That's up to the judge," said Bart. "You know that. Arraignment's some time early next week. Of course in terrorism cases . . ." He shrugged.

"He isn't Sheik Omar Abdel Rahman."

"I know that, Mr. Wine. But there are laws in this country. They apply to our own citizens as well as to foreigners."

I stared at Bart for a moment. Then I glanced at Suzanne

before returning my gaze to the FBI agent. "You sure you never met my son?" I asked him. "He had your phone number."

Bart frowned. "Really?"

"This was stuck to the calendar in his apartment." I took the Post-it from my pocket and showed it to him.

"How interesting," said Bart. "That *is* my number. . . . But I have no idea why he would have it. Perhaps he wanted to confess."

"That would be strange. He told me he had no idea who you were."

"Do you believe him?" Bart smiled before I could formulate a reply. "Well, you know your son better than I do. . . . And it would be a little late, in any case." He started to escort us out. "Everything's different now. But he does have the opportunity to cooperate, if he wants to. The U.S. Attorney might recommend leniency for such a young defendant. Who knows?" We reached the door. Bart held it open for us and looked at me a moment, then gestured to the Post-it still in my hand. "Why don't you let me have that to run through the lab?"

"I don't think it's necessary," I said, slipping it back in my pocket. I took Suzanne by the arm and we hurried out.

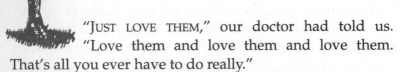

19

"JUST LOVE THEM," our doctor had told us. "Love them and love them and love them. That's all you ever have to do really."

We parents of the Echo Park Alternative Center for the Child all took our children to the same pediatrician, a tall lean vegetarian in Silver Lake with a Jewish Afro and a benign smile who reassured us we were all part of nature and that our kids would grow up strong and true if we gave them lots of affection, plenty of breast milk and not too much meat. The pediatrician became something of a local legend and his office—with its posters by pacifist Sister Mary Corita warning that "War Is Not Healthy for Children and Other Living Things" hung next to Huichol Indian yarn paintings—became something of a community center as well. When our kids were sick, we rushed them over and he told us not to panic, just to give them a hug and a kiss. When we were concerned about disciplining them because they had a problem at school or with their peers or, later, because they wandered off without telling us or broke their curfews, he told us not to worry. It was just developmental. And he didn't believe in curfews anyway. Or punishment. Or discipline in general for that matter. He believed, as we did mostly, in treating children with respect as our equals. He looked with skepticism on the child-rearing advice of Dr. Benjamin Spock, our parents' guru, who was much too scientific and rigorous, you might even say Prussian, in his approach, and who, worst of all, had abjured the sainted breast milk in favor of bottles and canned formulas. This was tantamount to a capitalist conspiracy, the pediatrician once told me. Thank God or Krishna, Spock eventually recanted and took the side of our generation in its struggles for peace and justice.

When the families split up, as most of them inevitably did, the majority of the parents continued to see the doctor individually to provide some continuity in their children's fractured lives, seeking his counsel whenever their kids were in crisis, up to and even after college. He was a kind of security blanket in an exasperatingly changing world. The instinct to consult him about Simon even flitted briefly through my head as Suzanne and I emerged from the Humboldt County Court House that morning. But I didn't consider it for long, and then with a certain grim irony, because it hadn't been more than six months since one of the doctor's own daughters had been arrested on sensational charges of running a high-priced call-girl operation for Hollywood moguls and stars; the doctor himself was subsequently indicted for laundering his daughter's ill-gotten gains. Such were the fruits of permissive child-rearing. Or were they? But this wasn't the time to debate the fine points of developmental psych. It was the time to act. And quickly.

So, back in the motel room, Suzanne and I decided to separate. She would return to Los Angeles and help set up Simon's legal defense while I would remain in redwood

country to find out what I could before the arraignment
and deal with whatever Bart meant by "cooperate." The
thought of my son as a government stool pigeon spending
the rest of his life in a witness protection program was
only slightly more appealing than his spending the rest of
his life in jail. And if he wasn't really a stool pigeon and
had been a provocateur all along, then what? Where did
they put those people? Did they get to go live out their
lives as "national heroes" on the government dole on
some tropical island? Would I ever want to go visit him?
This prospect was only slightly less appealing to me then
my son marrying a Nazi. I hated Bart for even making me
think about these things, delusional as they may have
been. And I hated myself for thinking about them.

But by then I had almost become used to being in a per-
petual state of self-torture. After our discussion, I picked
up the phone and called a cab for Suzanne. Then I dialed
Jacob in New York and filled him in about what was going
on. He had already heard part of it on the news and was
highly agitated when I called him. He had been blaming
himself for what happened all night. He told me he had
picked up my earlier warning message from his answering
machine fifteen minutes after I left it and sent it on immediately via e-mail using a remailer as instructed. But a few
hours later he had been notified that there was no such
Internet address. That's when he started to blame himself.
Had he got the address wrong? Had he misused the
remailer? What had happened? I told him not to worry—it
would have been about a day late anyway—and urged him
to come out to Los Angeles and join his mother. We would
need all the moral support we could get. He said he would.

Then I walked downstairs with Suzanne and waited
with her for the cab. The weather had turned gloomy,

threatening rain. We stood there a couple of minutes, staring at the dark clouds rolling in off the ocean and sharing a sense of mission, when I broke the silence.

"About last night," I said.

"I told you—a two-way mercy fuck. It won't happen again." She gave me a smile that was almost playful under the circumstances.

"Right," I said, barely able to smile back but trying anyway. She noted my confusion and continued to smile at me as if to say "Lighten up. We both know it's for the best in the end."

I nodded without speaking. It *was* for the best. "By the way," I continued, taking one step further into the abyss, "you promised to tell me something if I found Simon. I really didn't do it exactly, I know—find him—but I'd still like your answer."

"To why we broke up?"

I nodded.

"But you already know." I didn't say anything so she went on, sounding slightly impatient. "We were never like real married people, a husband and a wife. We were always more like brother and sister."

"We were?" I sounded more startled than I was.

"Come on, Moses. We had everything in our marriage but true passion for each other."

"That's not so bad."

"I guess, in a way but . . . surely you know what I'm talking about. It wasn't the sex. God knows we had that. But we were never intimate with each other the way lovers are. We both deserved better." There was no point in arguing, even if I had wanted to. She had said what was as close to the truth as you can get in these matters, and I knew it as well as she did. But that didn't stop me from putting on a wan expression. "And stop feeling sorry for yourself," she continued. "I wouldn't believe you anyway. . . . Besides, having a good sister can be a lot better than a lover in a lot of ways. In fact, it can be one of the best things in the world."

Her cab pulled up and I reached into my empty pockets. "Lend me a few hundred bucks," I said.

"Sister to brother?"

"Don't worry. You'll get it back."

"We're both working for the same cause here," she said, counting out some bills. "What about your license? What're you going to do if you need a car or something?"

"I think I have someone who can help me."

She hesitated, looking at me knowingly and smiling again before she got into the cab. "Say hello to her for me," she said. I nodded and we waved to each other as she drove off.

I walked back inside and called Samantha Backus. I had been worried the whole time that something terrible might have happened to her, but kept forcing this possibility into the back of my mind, because I had so much to deal with and because there was little I could do at the moment anyway. I prayed my 911 call had worked. In any case, I told myself that those characters from California Forest Protection were probably less reckless than they seemed. I hoped they were anyway. But I was still in my third or fourth cold sweat of the last twenty-four hours— or my fifth or six—as I listened to the phone ring in the offices of the *Humboldt Herald*, the tension increasing with each successive ring. I didn't calm down, and then only the slightest bit, when someone finally picked up on the other end and buzzed me through to Samantha's extension without the slightest hesitation.

"Backus here," she responded quickly.

"It's me," I said, relieved. "Moses."

"Oh, great," she said, sounding relieved as well. "I've been looking for you all over. I tried your beeper and—"

"I don't have it anymore. That and a few other things."

"That's no surprise. How are you? Are you all right? How's Simon?"

"I'm okay. Simon's okay too, I guess, for someone who's in jail and whose girlfriend just died. It's hard to tell what's happening. . . . How about you?"

"Fine now. Those two guys came back an hour or so after you left and almost killed me trying to find out where you'd gone. They didn't believe I didn't know anything. Thank God the police came at the last minute and scared them off. Someone must've called 911."

"Thank God. Listen . . . can you help me?" She agreed immediately. I asked her for some information I needed, some back newspapers. She promised to see if she could find them.

Little more than an hour later she came roaring around the corner in the Land Cruiser. Remarkably, it appeared all repaired. I got in next to her and touched her shoulder. "Thanks," I said. "Really."

"No problem," she replied. "I like you. I'd help you even if you didn't make the 911 call." She turned to me with a teasing smile that in a normal situation would have completely revived my spirits. Even in this one, it lifted them a bit, at least temporarily. "Besides, I told you a half-dozen times now," she continued in her gently mocking voice. "I'm a reporter. I'm exploiting you, remember? Don't ever forget that."

"A reporter, right," I said, studying her a moment

before turning behind me to make sure she hadn't been followed. No one seemed to be there. "You sure got someone to fix that quickly," I continued, nodding to a new rear window that replaced the one that had been shattered with bullets only the day before.

"Like I said—small-town life," she replied, still smiling. "We know everybody. You'd be surprised what I could get fixed."

"I guess I would," I said, wondering exactly what she meant.

"You would. I promise. . . . Now where to?"

"Know any Chinese restaurants around Garberville?"

"Nearest one I know's the Yellow Panda five miles north of town. But I think it's closed."

"That's the one," I said. "Go there."

She gave me a puzzled look but shrugged and pulled out anyway, gesturing toward the dashboard. "I found those back papers you wanted. I didn't have to go to the morgue. Daniel kept copies in his desk."

"I'm not surprised," I said, reaching for the two newspapers folded on top of the dash. I unfolded the first one, the *Humboldt Herald* for June 14, 1990. A banner headline was blasted across the top of the front page: REDWOOD SUMMER HORROR! Beneath that, and just above a photograph of a smoldering Volvo of mid-seventies vintage, was the subhead MAN DIES, ORGANIZER INJURED IN CAR EXPLOSION. Trying to keep the paper steady in the jouncing Land Cruiser, I glanced through the accompanying article, a brief factual account of the incident. Claire Hannin, thirty-nine, chief organizer of Redwood Summer and Northern California chairperson of Earth People, had been seriously injured by an explosion of unknown origin while starting her car in the parking lot of the Quick-o-rama Laundromat in Willits.

Accompanying her at the time was nineteen-year-old Ned
Sayles, a marine biology major on his summer break from
UC Santa Cruz, who died instantly. An investigation was in
progress. This was followed by personal assurances from the
Mendocino County sheriff that he would leave no stone
unturned in ascertaining the cause of this tragic event. The
article closed with a short history of the Earth People.

I went on to the second paper, dated December 9, 1990.
The lead articles were a banal discussion of whether public
funds should be used for the coming Garberville Christmas
Pageant and a report of the medalists at a blind-tasting of
Mendocino County vineyards. Down in the lower right-
hand corner were the first few paragraphs of a story by
Daniel Springer. The headline read, BLOODSTAIN SPREADS
OVER REDWOOD SUMMER. The article began with a review of
the case, then jumped to the third page, where it detailed
the accusations and counteraccusations among the police,
the FBI and the quickly disintegrating Earth People about
who caused the bombing, still unsolved after six months.
Claire Hannin herself was under continued suspicion for
accidentally setting off the bomb in her own car but,
according to Earth People spokesman William Brindle, the
true culprits were a nefarious group of "anti-environmen-
tal vigilantes" known as California Forest Protection.

"I wonder if that's the same Bill," I said.

"Bill?"

"One of the Guardians. He's still out there as far as I
know." I gestured vaguely into the giant trees that were racing past us. Then I looked back at the article again. It went
from the case to describing a memorial birthday service
held in Garberville for Ned Sayles. His family had come out
from back east, several branches including his grandparents, his father and his sister, a high school student.

Apparently his mother had died young. At that point, late in 1990, Ned would have turned twenty, Simon's present age. There were a few more paragraphs but I was starting to feel carsick, so I put the paper down and opened the window. It had just started to rain and I closed it again quickly.

A few minutes later Samantha pulled up in front of the Yellow Panda, which was closed until the beginning of tourist season in May.

"What're we doing here?" she said.

"I don't know. Looking for a hardware store."

"There isn't one."

She appeared to be right. The only buildings on the street across from the Yellow Panda were an abandoned warehouse and a lonely souvenir stand, also closed until tourist season, its carved Smokey the Bears and Rudolph the Red-Nosed Reindeers looking like lost Christmas decorations in the rain. I exhaled in frustration. Maybe I had misunderstood Simon when he talked of a Chinese restaurant and a hardware store. Maybe he was just playing a game, trying to distract the sheriff's guard from our conversation or himself from the frightening reality of what was happening to him. Or, darkest of all, he was just sending me on a wild-goose chase to get rid of me.

But then I noticed a low, one-story building about fifty yards to our right. It had the words "Reforestation Supplies" printed in fading green letters on gray corrugated siding. If it wasn't a hardware store, it was the closest thing to it in the vicinity.

Samantha drove down to the building and we got out and ran over to its wire-glass front door, knocking quickly while huddling under an overhang against the rain. No one answered. I peered through the glass. It was dark inside, with no furniture visible except a couple of chairs and a

desk with papers stacked high on top of a computer monitor. We knocked again and stood there another minute or so
when a tall, stooped man some years older than I appeared,
staring at us from deep inside. In a red Basque beret,
ancient huaraches and a black turtleneck so threadbare it
must have fed half the moths in the county, he looked like a
refugee from San Francisco's North Beach circa 1958. "What
do you want?" he said, shuffling toward us. His voice was
less suspicious than matter-of-fact, but commanding nevertheless.

"I don't know," I said. "My son sent me."

He continued up to the door and looked me straight in
the eye. "Who's that?"

"Simon Wine."

The man nodded and opened the door, stepping aside
and beckoning us in. We stepped into a cold, damp room
with a bare concrete floor. "Who're you?" I asked.

"Amos Manling."

"The founder of the Earth People?" asked Samantha,
impressed. So was I. I was surprised I hadn't recognized
him immediately. He had been a public figure for decades,
a legend of his generation, like Stewart Brand or Timothy
Leary. But who would have expected to find him here in
the middle of nowhere?

"Sit down. Sit down," he said, gesturing to the chairs.
They were black canvas sling backs out of the fifties.
"Would you like some tea? I've got Lemon Zinger,
Almond Sunshine, and an oolong from Tibet if you're into
caffeine. You must be going out of your mind." He waited
for us to sit before continuing. "Your boy's in enough trouble to disrupt the entire solar system!"

20

"THE ENVIRONMENTAL MOVEMENT died after Red-wood Summer," said Manling. "At least in its present form." He was pacing back and forth in front of us professorially while we sipped the tea he insisted we take with lemon and Sucanat, a preparation of granulated sugar cane juice made without additives. "And it should have. We had already won."

"Won?" I interjected skeptically.

"Of course. You're from Los Angeles, aren't you? Even there the air's cleaner than it was twenty years ago. And the electric car's right around the corner. The water's cleaner too. Practically everywhere. That's a fact. If the environmentalists would just celebrate their victories instead of whining, they'd go even further and faster on top of that. Don't you agree, Ms. Backus? We make our fellow creatures wise through positive reinforcement, not hectoring them all the time as if they didn't live on this planet too." He smiled at Samantha, staring unabashedly at her hips and legs, which were wrapped tightly in a pair of jeans. "Would you like some more tea? Or perhaps I can

interest you in some Armagnac in this cold weather?
They're extremely good in combination—Larry Fer-
linghetti's favorite."

"I'm fine," she said.

"Corso and Kerouac favored straight bourbon,
although they made a show of taking ayahuasca and such
things. But it was all bullshit."

"How do you know Simon?" I asked, quickly before he
rolled on to a history of the Beat Generation and the Angry
Young Men.

"Surfing," he said. "I used to go watch the surfers.
They're the future, you know, in harmony with the elements, yet above them. . . . Of course there's always a risk,
out there on the big waves . . . sharks, currents."

"You're right about that. My son's in pretty deep water
at the moment."

"Yes, he is," said Manling. "Deeper than you think." He
made a sudden stop in his peregrinations and looked at me.
I gazed back at him and frowned. How much worse could
it get? Being accused of two murders was deep enough as
far as I could tell. "I'm afraid his life is in danger."

"What're you talking about?" I said. The words came
out in a near stutter.

"He learned too much, I imagine," said Manling.

"About what?"

"About what Karin Sayles knew. Poor girl."

"Karin *Sayles*?" Finally I heard her last name, which
made an instant connection. "You mean Ned Sayles's sister?" I said.

"Yes, of course," he replied impatiently. "Who else
would I mean?"

"And what did she know?"

"Ah, that I can't tell you, Mr. Wine. I wasn't intimate

with her like your son. She was a very willful young lady.
Determined to play out her own agenda."

"What was that?"

"Vengeance against an impure world. The agenda of all
ideologues—Lenin, St. Sebastian, John of the Cross."

"That's all?" I said.

"All I know."

I glanced over at Samantha, who was sitting immobile
with the tea in her hand. "You've got to help me more
than that, Mr. Manling."

"I'd like to but . . ." He shrugged apologetically.

"You know what I'm going through, I should imagine.
As well as anybody." He looked at me curiously. "You're a
father too. You and Claire Hannin had a child, didn't you?"

"How'd you know that?"

"Claire has a daughter. You two were together. She
idolized you. Who else would it be?"

"Why don't you ask Lawton Stanley?" he replied, his
voice suddenly rising.

"I tried."

"Then try again. . . . Look, Mr. Wine, I'm telling you
what little I know because I think you have an interesting
son. I met him one time at Ocean Beach when Claire and I
were still speaking to each other. He talked about you actually, as if you were some kind of ideal he could never live
up to. I don't know if he was angry about that or just rebel-
lious, but he seemed vulnerable to me, almost innocent. I
was hoping he wouldn't be manipulated by one side or the
other, but it sounds like he was. I told him if he were ever in
trouble I would try to help him and that's probably why
you're here. The only thing I can tell you now is that if I
were you, I would look into the background of Ned Sayles."

"What's that?"

"I heard he had a drug problem. More than that I can't say. I might have learned more but I never wanted to. You can destroy beautiful things if you look at them too closely." Manling half-smiled and turned toward the front of the building. "Quite a rain out, isn't there? You better get started if you don't want to get stuck in the mud." He headed for the door. It was obvious we were being dismissed and we got up and followed. "Very pleased to meet you," he said. "And even more pleased to meet you, Ms. Backus, although you didn't say much. That usually means you know more than the rest of us." We all shook hands and I was about to leave but Manling held on to my arm and leaned in closer. "Radio said your boy's being arraigned in Los Angeles. That's a long way. I hope he's not going by road."

"I don't know."

"Let me know if I can help. I never answer my phone, but you can leave a message or e-mail me on the Well under the name of Alcibiades."

"Thank you."

He released my arm and stepped aside. Samantha and I rushed through the rain to the Land Cruiser and climbed in. I thought I should go see Stanley again, so I asked Samantha to head down to Napa. "I've got to talk to Bart," I told her as we pulled out. She offered me her cell phone and I dialed straight through to the sheriff's office. This was no time to quibble about the security of cellular lines. I left word for him and he called me back in less than five minutes.

"Hello, Moses," he said.

"Hello, Nick. Are we on a first-name basis now?"

"Why not?"

"I just want you to know that I have some reason to believe my son might be in danger."

"In danger? He's in solitary confinement in the sheriff's jail."

"He's traveling tomorrow, isn't he? If anything happens to him, I'm holding you responsible."

"I am responsible. I'm in charge of the case."

"You know what I mean."

"No, I don't. . . . But if you have any evidence . . ."

"I'm terrified someone's going to kill my son, Bart! Don't you understand?"

"Yes, I understand," he replied in the calm voice of someone talking to a madman.

"Just make sure nothing happens to him," I said.

"I'll do my best."

"You damn well should. It's your job!"

"That's what I said. Didn't I? . . . Besides, your son's our most important witness. We would never let anything happen to him."

I said good-bye and hung up. "Can we go any faster?" I said to Samantha. We were heading back once again on the 101 to the Chateau Montreux. "Not unless you want to end up like that," she said, gesturing to a VW that had skidded off the highway in the rain, its driver clutching what looked to be a dislocated shoulder as a cop spoke into the intercom of a nearby squad car. "That won't help matters."

"No, it won't," I said, and picked up the cell phone again, punching in another number. It rang several times without answering until a nervous voice answered on the other end.

"Hello."

"Hello, Gabriel. It's Moses."

There was a long silence punctuated only by the persistent squeak of the windshield wipers. "What do you want?" he said finally.

"I need your help. I want to know about Ned Sayles."

"Who's that?"

"Come on, Gabriel. You've been around here for years. You knew Claire Hannin. You must've known Ned Sayles. He had a drug problem too, if that refreshes your recollection."

"Still trying to ruin my life, Moses? That's not very generous. You should've given it up a long time ago. I probably did you a favor in the long run anyway, if you think about it."

"Some favor."

"You don't think so. But there was more happening between you and that woman I saw you with the other day than I ever saw between you and Suzanne in seven years of marriage."

I glanced at Samantha, who was concentrating on the road. "Look, this isn't about me. It's about Simon. Do *him* a favor and tell me what you know about Ned Sayles. I'll never bother you again as long as I live. I swear."

There was another silence as the wipers squeaked away.

"I'd do anything for Simon," he said finally. "He doesn't deserve to suffer for what went down between us. But . . . "

"But what?"

"You're on a cell phone."

"Shit, Gabriel."

I clicked off. We pulled over into the nearest rest stop and I dialed him again from a pay phone behind a row of semis. The rain was coming down in sheets and I covered my head with the back pages of the *Humboldt Herald* when he picked up a second time. "Tell me about Ned Sayles," I said.

"He got away with murder."

"Come on. Ned Sayles blew up."

"I know, I know. But before that. He was this rich kid from Manhattan. Father's one of those lawyers who represents corporations against the Environmental Protection Agency, weaseling out of regulations, that kind of thing. Works for Sean Handler, among others."

"*Karin's* father does that?"

"Karin?" I could hear Gabriel's surprise echoing mine through the telephone speaker. "I see you've made all the family connections."

"I'm beginning to," I said. "So I take it the . . . son was in full rebellion against his lawyer father."

"To put it mildly. Ned Sayles was the kind of kid who would lie down in front of a bulldozer to stop them from clear-cutting a forest. Or tie himself to a saw bed in the Allied Lumber Mill the first day FOXAM took over."

"And he was into drugs."

"Well, we've all got our weaknesses." I thought I heard Gabriel chuckle on the other end. "Of course, Ned *was* a little excessive, as he was in everything. Or so the rumor goes."

"What was that?"

"That he was kind of a Johnny Appleseed—you know, gave out hundreds of free bricks of sinsemilla every week from a van parked behind the information center in Redwood National Park. Or distributed it to the tourists in Bodega Bay in old bait boxes. They say he wore a Norwegian fishing cap and jodhpurs."

"He never got into trouble?"

"Not that I knew about."

"All that time he was working for the Earth People, right alongside Claire Hannin. . . ."

"That's right. Did you find her, by the way?"

"Not yet." I stood there stock-still, feeling the rain soak through the newspaper. The water was beginning to roll down the back of my neck. "What else didn't you tell me?"

"Nothing," said Gabriel. "I didn't know the guy personally. . . . But I think I told you what you need to know."

"I guess so," I said. I heard him clear his throat nervously on the other end. "Moses, I, uh. . . . I hope you're not going to broadcast where you heard any of this. I only told you because of Simon. I'm, uh . . ."

"I know. You're in the business. . . . Good luck, Gabriel." I started to hang up, then I said, "Sorry about the Morgan."

"It's okay. I can buy another one."

I hung up and climbed back into the Land Cruiser beside Samantha. "Flood warning," she said, indicating her radio, which was tuned to the weather band. I looked over at the next hill where little rivulets were starting to cut notches in the mud between the oak trees. A stream of murky water already ran along the side of the freeway, a particularly exuberant tributary cutting across the concrete beneath an underpass. A couple of cars fishtailed slightly as they moved through it, spraying water. For a moment I considered turning around, but I wouldn't have known how to face myself if I had.

"Let's go," I said. Samantha headed out onto the highway. But as we drove through the storm, I started to feel increasingly anxious about Simon. Would they be moving him earlier in this weather? Would they decide to fly him down instead or choose the even safer but pricier Amtrak? Would I be cut off from him? It was the kind of agitated feeling you have about your children when they're three, the agitated feeling that never goes away, like in the Jewish joke about the old man who proudly introduces his son by saying "Mine's fifty-four!" Only now I had justification for my possessive paranoia.

I picked up the phone and tried Bart again, but this time he wasn't in. I got a guard on the line and started yelling "I'm Simon Wine's father! I've got to know. Is he there? Is he there?" until the guard relented and told me that Simon was there but that I couldn't speak to him and I hung up. I saw Samantha looking at me. "He's all right?" she asked. I nodded but I didn't calm down. I stared through the windshield turning over everything in my mind—Karin and Ned Sayles, the bomb school, Bill and the remailer, Claire and Lawton, Sean Handler and the FOXAM Corporation, Daniel Springer's notes, the Jack London Grove, the CFP, Leon Erlanger, Gabriel, Suzanne and my children. I chewed on these names and images over and over again like grains of rice in some ritualized macrobiotic diet. But I couldn't make anything of them. They were all one inchoate mess to my addled mind. And as we drove for the second time through the gates of the Chateau Montreux, I had a brief fantasy that I was entering a retirement home and that I would once and for all be relieved of my responsibilities.

21

"THIS ISN'T THE GREATEST TIME. I'm about to lose a half million worth of petit syrah to root rot."

"Mr. Stanley, I—"

"And isn't the point, after all, that your son spiked a tree, or helped to spike it, and that a man died because of that?" I was standing with Samantha in Lawton Stanley's office as he spoke, staring through a leaded-glass window at his rain-soaked vineyards. "That renders the rest of this meaningless, doesn't it, speaking as one father to another?"

"One father to another, Mr. Stanley—my son's not guilty. He's a pawn."

"A pawn?" said Stanley, not hiding his skepticism.

"His only crime's wanting to make the world a better place."

"You believe that?"

"I damn well believe it," I said, my voice rising to cover whatever doubt I had. I wondered if I had been successful. "I want to see Claire Hannin immediately. Amos Manling said you'd know where she is. And I don't want to give her my beeper number. I don't even have a beeper any-more. I want to talk to her in the flesh and I want you to take me to her now!"

"I don't have a reason to do that," said Stanley, "even if I could."

"Yes, you do," said Samantha. "The Eureka Savings investigation."

"I don't know what you're talking about," said Stanley.

I didn't either. I looked over at Samantha. "Think back, Mr. Stanley," she said. "Government agents came to your office. They made it very difficult for you. It was about taxes, I believe. You don't want that to happen again."

Stanley stared at her, his expression turned suddenly wary.

"Don't worry," she continued, "this is for our uses only."

"I thought you were a journalist, Ms. Backus."

"I am." Samantha smiled.

Stanley seemed about to say something, then changed his mind. He sighed and glanced out at his vineyard. "Wait here," he said, and walked out.

"How'd you know about *that*?" I asked Samantha.

"Deep background," she said vaguely. "Just be glad I did." She turned to Stanley's bookshelf and took out an old volume, frowning as she read the spine. "He likes Steinbeck, I see. I've always found him a little boring. How about you?"

"I guess you don't want to talk about it," I said.

"What?"

"How you knew about that."

"That's right," she said.

Stanley returned a few minutes later, handing us each umbrellas and telling us to follow him. We headed through the chateau and out a side door toward the man-made lake with the pagoda, the one he had steered us away from on our first visit. It had three islands and, moored to a wharf, an old Chinese junk that was being buffeted by the winds. We crossed over a bridge of wooden struts leading to the center island, containing the pagoda. The floor of the bridge had become slippery in the rain and for a moment it seemed we were characters in an Oriental line drawing, clutching our umbrellas in one hand and holding the ebony railings in the other while we made our way through the hostile elements. Stanley led us up to the heavy bronze doors of the pagoda, opening them with a large set of keys. We followed him inside, climbing a set of rickety stairs. Halfway up, Stanley stopped and unlocked a smaller door, ushering us into a room that looked like the prow of a ship with semicircular windows giving out on a view of the entire Napa Valley. Through the torrential rains, I could see thunderbolts cracking across the top of the local foothills, rattling the window glass and shaking the pagoda itself. It was disorienting and only after a moment did I notice we were not alone.

A woman in a plain linen shift with a knit blanket in her lap was seated in a rocking chair next to a daybed. She was staring straight in front of her unblinkingly at the wall with her mouth half open and her tongue frozen against the back of her lip. A daddy longlegs was crawling up the back of her arm toward her shoulder.

"This is Claire," said Lawton Stanley, brushing the insect away and adjusting her blanket. "I had to make sure she was dressed before I allowed you to see her." I tried to have a closer look at the woman but it felt too much like prying. Claire Hannin was the first true catatonic I had seen outside of a textbook or documentary footage of a mental hospital. I turned to Stanley, who was supporting himself on the headboard of the daybed. He had changed before my eyes from the confident industry captain gone boho to a broken man who had lost his lover in a way perhaps more brutal than death. "I'm sorry," I said, but he waved me off; he was clearly the type of man who equated sympathy from others with defeat. "How long has she been . . . ?" I gestured toward Claire as a flash of lightning illuminated her face like a strobe. A particularly intense thunderclap reverberated through the valley.

"Ever since the bombings, she'd go into these strange retreats. I thought she'd get over it. But last year on her daughter's birthday, we went for a ride in that air balloon out of Yountville . . . the one that goes over all the vineyards. . . . When it came down, Claire wouldn't get off. We had to lift her. . . . Not even Amos Manling knows."

"What happened to her daughter?" asked Samantha.

"In school. Back east." Stanley leaned over Claire, touching her shoulder and whispering reassuringly in her ear, before turning back to us with a desolate expression. "There have been many victims of these North Coast wars. I always thought I was one of the bad ones, but Claire was the worst. She's so guilty about her own violence, she won't let herself move."

"What'd she do?" I asked.

"It's not what she did. It's what she started. . . . She never guessed the extent of it. Neither did I, in my own way. From my side. I think that's what might have brought us together." We stood there a moment, listening to the storm, when he asked rhetorically, "You've seen enough, haven't you?" He walked toward the door. "Come on and I'll give you a taste of the Napa Valley's first one-hundred-dollar chardonnay. You probably need it. I've been living with this horror for a while, but you've only known the extent of your son's involvement for a few days."

Five minutes later, we were in his study sampling his chardonnay. "This is a Valley of Lies," he said, indicating the bottle, which had his signature on the label. "Who knows if it's worth a hundred dollars? Or even ten. . . . But someone was going to put that price on a chard sooner or later. It might as well be me."

I rolled the wine around in my mouth and swallowed. I had no idea what it was worth either but it went down as smoothly as mountain water and he was right, I sure needed it. "What about Claire?" I asked. "What made her give up nonviolence?"

"She never really did. But when FOXAM took over, there was no one to talk to anymore. Before then, they could come to my house and have a demonstration, boil me in effigy in the hot tub. But what do you do with a holding company? Make a bonfire of the junk bonds? She was incredibly frustrated. I could see it in her. Ten years down the drain. She was ready for something new."

"Bomb school?"

"Oh, yes, the CFP. There were accusations they started something like that. I never believed it."

"Just about the time the Guardians of the Planet were established."

"Claire didn't have anything to do with that. I would have known. She had her own ideas on what was to be done. And she wasn't a double agent either, if that's what you're thinking." Stanley smiled almost superciliously as he looked at me. "Mr. Wine, I hope you're not one of those tiresome conspiracy theorists."

"Someone from the Guardians studied bomb making with those guys. Who? Ned Sayles?"

"I doubt that too. I knew Ned Sayles's father. Ned despised everything he stood for. That doesn't make him a very good candidate for a double agent, does it?"

"What do you think?" I turned to Samantha, who shrugged. "There's got to have been someone," I said.

"You *are* one of those conspiracy theorists," said Stanley, this time unable to suppress a laugh. "Life isn't an Oliver Stone movie. It's usually pretty much the way it appears, unfortunately. The thug on the street who looks like he might mug you is usually the one who does. . . . As a detective I'm sure you know that. You should also know . . . sadly . . . that your son's actions are more than likely precisely what they seem. He got involved in a radical group and played his role as he was asked."

"I refuse to believe that."

"Believe what you want. Two men and a young woman are dead. Claire Hannin has paid her price, so have I. Now it's your son's turn. My advice to you is get him a good lawyer."

"I already have."

"And what does he say?"

"Nothing yet. I have to give him some ammunition." I started to pace.

Stanley smiled at me, then turned to Samantha, who was standing in front of the bookshelf, finishing her chardonnay. "Are you as much of a conspiracy buff as your friend?"

"I'm not sure," she said.

"Mr. Wine, like so many of his era, seems to have once again chosen the FBI as the root of his dilemma. A little knee-jerk, don't you think?"

Samantha shrugged.

Stanley continued to look at me skeptically. "Frankly, I

think you're just looking for a cop-out for your son."

"I wish I were. Unfortunately, I think they assume Simon knows everything I just told you and probably a lot more."

"And of course he doesn't," said Stanley.

"No, he doesn't."

"Otherwise, he might be guilty of something himself."

"He's not."

Stanley looked at me coolly. "You know, Mr. Wine, some people think we all get the children we deserve. . . . I don't want to be rude, but in your rush to paranoid judgment, have you ever considered that your son could just as easily be a government agent himself? If Ned Sayles joined the ecology movement to rebel against *his* father, what would be the most natural rebellion for your boy? . . . More?" He lifted the hundred-dollar bottle of chardonnay to my glass. I declined.

22

WHEN SIMON WAS FOUR MONTHS OLD, we were invited to a barbecue at the home of our old friends Art and Nina LaRusso in East Los Angeles. It was the midseventies by then and while most everybody in our crowd had been trying to make peace for some time and to some degree with their radical student pasts, the LaRussos had gone the other way, further left. To everyone's astonishment, they had exchanged their conventional bourgeois occupations and grad-school degrees for working-class jobs—he on the assembly line at Buick, she as an information operator at the phone company—moved from an artsy beach neighborhood in Santa Monica to the heart of the Chicano barrio and joined a group anachronistically named the California Communist League.

When Suzanne and I arrived at their house that afternoon with the infant Simon taking his first outing in his new stroller and the four-year-old Jacob in tow, we discovered we had been invited to a recruitment party for this league. Art and Nina greeted us warmly, but very few of the old crowd were there, most of them already having been pronounced hopelessly reactionary for the purpose. Instead, groups of friendly black and Latino families picnicked on ribs and tamales while the revered leader of the league, an older black man named Nelson, spoke of the necessity of sacrifice for the coming revolution. A table of political literature in those little red plastic covers had been set up behind him featuring, as I recall, *The History of the Labor Party of Albania* (Albania being the last socialist country extant yet to take that final catastrophic rightward turn into revisionism). Its General Secretary, Comrade Enver Hoxha, Nelson informed us in his speech, was the world's leading exponent of pure communism and should be an inspiration to the working people of California.

This was all a bit much for me, but Art and Nina insisted we meet Nelson, bringing us over as a family to their leader, who treated us all avuncularly as potential model workers at an as-yet-unbuilt utopian labor camp, clapping us on the back and telling us how great it was we were friends of that marvelous progressive couple the LaRussos. Then he looked down at Simon in his stroller, saying, "The future is yours, young fellow! . . . It is a boy, isn't it? . . . Dare to struggle! Dare to win!" Simon, who was asleep, did not react. "Did you hear me?" said Nelson, raising his voice. "Comrade Stalin loves you! Comrade . . . Hoxha loves you!" Simon blinked awake and started chortling and looking around. "See. A born revolutionary," said Nelson proudly, smiling and dangling a copy of Hoxha's little red book in front of the four-month-old, who promptly began crying, puked all over it and reached for his mother, clutching for some brightly colored gypsy earrings she was wearing. Suzanne picked Simon out of the stroller, wiping his mouth and trying to comfort him. "You better be careful of this boy," said Nelson. "He has reac-

tionary tendencies." I thought he was joking until I saw
the scowl on his face. Art and Nina looked embarrassed.
As we left a few minutes later, I said to Suzanne, "Maybe
it wasn't such a great idea to bring him."

I often wondered what it had meant for my kids to be
exposed to such bizarre events when they were tiny, what
it meant to them as they grew up. Sometimes it seemed
meaningless. Children were so much smarter than we
were anyway. They could detect their parents' bullshit a
mile off. But other times it felt as if every minor hypocrisy
had been magnified across the spectrum of their lives.
Who knew what really happened at those points, what
chain reactions were set off? I ruminated on them, but I
never came to a conclusion. This particular memory had
surfaced from my unconscious when Samantha asked me,
"What do you think about what Stanley said?" We were
back in the Land Cruiser, heading north. She was at the
wheel again while I stared bleakly into the storm.

"About Simon being a double agent?" I replied. "The
nightmare inside a nightmare."

"Do you believe it?"

"Why would I?" I said, glancing at her. I couldn't read
her expression and I wondered if she could read mine—if
she knew the idea was never far from my awareness, that
it continued to resurface like an indestructible monster in
an arcade game, no matter how many times and how hard
I tried to annihilate it. Every time it looked as if I could
ignore it, something or someone reminded me. Even the
sainted Amos Manling was suspicious Simon was being
manipulated. And ever since his surfer buddies told me
about the break-in at PG & E, about how surprised they
were he had gotten away with it so easily, so was I.

I was filled with questions I couldn't answer. Had an

agreement been made back then, allowing Simon to escape prosecution in return for his cooperation in the apprehension of the Guardians of the Planet? Was he deliberately made the fall guy when the chain saw flew back into Leon Erlanger? Were they able to convince him his idealism was misguided? Or rather, as Stanley had indicated, was I the cause? Were the values I espoused crumbling not only in the society around me, but in my own family as well? I didn't want to believe it, but what was Simon doing? Where had he been that night in the Lost Coast when he separated from the Guardians?

I couldn't resist reaching into my pocket and pulling out the now tattered, little yellow Post-it, scrutinizing it out of the corner of my eye. Was that really his handwriting? Had someone copied it? Had someone tricked him into writing Bart's number and then affixed it to his calendar?

"If you don't think it's so," said Samantha, observing me as I stuffed the Post-it back in my pocket, "why do you look so worried about it?"

"How would you feel if your kid was accused of being an FBI stoolie?"

"Depends on the situation, I suppose. . . . To some people they're more popular than journalists."

"To some people," I said, glancing at Samantha a second time. She was still hard to read. "I better find out what's happening." I motioned to a convenience store, which had suddenly appeared in the driving rain, and Samantha pulled over.

We went inside and she bought some Evian while I used the pay phone to call my voice mail. There were several messages from Nancy in escalating order of coolness, followed by one from Suzanne about thirty minutes later. She was at Jack Koufax's office and wanted me to fill her in

on what was happening. I dialed the number there and
Suzanne and Jack both got on the line. I reported on the little I'd learned and then Jack spoke with his lawyer's voice.

"Whatever you do," he said, "make sure Simon doesn't
say anything without me."

"I know. I know. I'm on my way to see him now. I'll
remind him."

"Also make sure they read him his Miranda rights
and—"

"What kind of business do you think I'm in?" I asked,
annoyed.

"Meanwhile, I'm petitioning for a change of venue.
Southern District's not the best place for us. It's stacked
with Reagan judges."

"Moses . . ." It was Suzanne. "Remember I told you my
partner was on the Internet all the time?"

"Yeah, with the divorce."

"Right, André Dalton. He's been fishing around for
us . . . He ran a search on Nicholas Bart."

"At the FBI server?"

"No. Not there." She hesitated. "You're on a pay phone,
aren't you?"

"Yes, yes."

"I can hear the storm. The news says it's crazy up there."

"It is. . . . So where'd he search?"

"Couple of places. He got into the national college
alumni records. Bart got his degree at the University of
Colorado. Majored in chemistry, minored in sociology.
Three point two grade point. He uses his mother's maiden
name, by the way."

"Fascinating. What else?"

"André also got into his brokerage account at Dean
Witter." Samantha walked up. She offered me some Evian

but I shook my head. "Bart must be some kind of financial genius. It's quadrupled since 'ninety-one."

"What'd he invest in?"

"Stocks, bonds, the usual stuff."

Samantha's cell phone beeped and she took it out of her purse and answered.

Suzanne continued, "A couple of Pacific-rim mutual funds. Point is, almost everything went up."

"Maybe we should get some tips."

"It's for you," said Samantha, holding up her cell phone.

"I'm going to have to call you back," I said, and hung up, switching to the cellular. "Hello."

"Hello, Moses. I hear you've been looking for me."

"Speak of the devil." It was Bart.

"What can I do for you?"

"Nothing now. I'm on my way up there. Just make sure I can see my son."

"I don't know if it's possible at this time."

"What do you mean you don't know if it's possible? You're the agent in charge of the investigation."

"Just what I said. I don't know if it's possible. Your boy's been under a lot of stress. He's come down with something."

"What?"

"We think it's only a bad flu. We hope it is anyway. I'll have to speak with the doctors. He's being moved to a medical facility."

"What medical facility?" I looked at Samantha standing three feet away from me, trying to piece together our conversation.

"I can't hear you, Moses. You're breaking up. Could you say that again?"

"What medical facility?" I shouted into the cell phone.

"St. Agnes."

"St. Agnes?" I glanced at Samantha, who nodded. She knew where it was.

"Yes. He should be there within the hour."

"So will I," I said. I was about to sign off when I thought of another question. "By the way, did you catch any more of the Guardians?"

"A young woman named Sheila James was brought in this morning."

"She was the only one left?"

"I believe so."

"What about William Brindle?"

"William Brindle?"

"Late twenties. Tall. Blond. Birdlike face. They call him Bill."

"I'm afraid we haven't apprehended a Bill Brindle."

"I'm not surprised," I said.

"What's that supposed to mean?"

"Whatever you think. I'll be seeing you, Mr. Bart."

"Indeed," he said as I pushed "end" and handed the phone to Samantha. I called Suzanne back and told her what had happened. Then Samantha and I headed out of the store. Outside, the conditions were worse, a clogged drain having turned the parking lot into a small lake. "Sometimes Northern California's the gloomiest place in the world," she said as we rolled up our pants and waded across to the car. I felt the water trickling down the inside of my shoes and soaking my socks. "No kidding, " I said. "Siberia for the sixties." We climbed into the Land Cruiser and sped off, spraying a muddy wake behind us like water-skiers going through a sewage outflow.

A half hour later we were passing through Willits. Thunderclouds were nestled in the valley, making it seem almost nightfall although it was only three in the afternoon. We continued on into the country of the tall trees. They were darker still in the storm, almost funereal, as if we were driving through a tunnel into the underworld. Maybe it was the surroundings, maybe it was the unbearable tension of the last few days, but suddenly, from far inside me, I let loose the deepest, most painful wail of my life. My body shuddered and my stomach buckled in on itself and I banged my head on the dashboard as I increased the wail. It became a shriek of desperation. Soon I was almost ululating like an Arab over the coffin of a loved one.

Samantha was so taken aback she nearly lost control of the car. "You must love your boy a lot," she said, smiling in embarrassment as she swerved back into the lane.

"Yes," I said, immediately putting a stop to my bizarre behavior. I felt embarrassed too and tried to think of a joke to diffuse the situation, but all I could come up with was something lame about children being more consistent in my life than women, so I censured it and sat up straight instead, staring at the waterlogged highway. "Miserable, huh?" I said.

"We'll manage."

A blinking yellow light was signaling a detour around a flooded area. I turned and looked at Samantha, who was concentrating once more on the road. "What're you going to do when this is over?" I asked.

"Write about it."

"And after that?"

"Find something else to write about, I guess." I continued to stare at her in the dim light. "What's the matter?" she said. "Why're you looking at me that way? Don't you believe me?"

"That's not it," I said, not prepared to deal with that

question right now. "I just wanted to thank you. I couldn't do this by myself."

"I don't know. You're a detective. You're used to working alone."

"Not on this," I said and faced forward again. Up ahead, I could see the sign for St. Agnes Medical Center caught in the beam of our fog lights. Samantha turned and in a few minutes we were pulling up at the front of the medical center, a small two-story brick building tucked into a redwood grove with a green cross and a small statue of the saint, presently dripping wet, by the emergency entrance. An ambulance sat idly in the driveway next to a busted pickup truck and an old Volvo. It was the kind of rural facility I hadn't been in since Jacob broke his arm at tennis camp in the fourth grade.

We entered via the emergency room and walked past a woman with a crying baby to an elderly receptionist behind the counter. "How do you do, ma'am?" I asked her. "Has the party from the sheriff's department arrived yet?"

She stared at me concerned. "Has there been an accident? We've been expecting a lot, but I guess everybody's being sensible and staying off the roads."

"No, it's about a prisoner. They're supposed to be bringing him here for medical attention."

"I haven't heard about that," she said, frowning. "I'd call the triage nurse, but she's off putting sandbags behind her house. She had a mud slide in her living room three years ago that ruined all her furniture including her grandmother's best ottoman. Maybe I should notify the attending physician? He's up in Eureka at his daughter's scout meeting."

"That's okay," I said, taking a couple of steps away and

turning toward Samantha. The rain was beating against the clinic window like a squadron of drummers in a marching band.

"Suspicious?" she asked me.

"From the start."

"Then why'd you want to come here?"

"I always thought the best way to find out which direction a hurricane's blowing is to put yourself in the eye."

"Punch yourself in the eye is more like it," she said.

I walked over to the window and tried to look out, but the glass was misted over. There were some yellow reflections glowing in the water droplets and I wiped the window with my sleeve and moved closer to see what they were—the headlights of a car stationed about a hundred feet down the road. The lights went off immediately.

"You're right," I said to Samantha, who was now standing beside me. "I did punch myself in the eye."

"Let's go," she said.

"Go?"

"You want to be in a hurricane? Let's be in a hurricane." She was already heading for the door and I had no choice but to follow her out into the storm. She started running for the Land Cruiser and I went along with her, stride for stride, moving toward the driver's side when she cut me off.

"I'll do it," she said.

"But—"

"I've got the keys. Don't be such a fucking sexist. It's my car."

She unlocked the doors and we got in, she on the driver's side and me on the passenger's. "Besides," she said, turning on the motor. "You don't have your driver's license. I wouldn't want you to get in trouble."

"Didn't the CFP take yours?"

"I have a special hiding place for my purse under the floorboards," she said flatly as we pulled out. Within seconds the other car was right on our tail. I turned around and looked straight into its headlights.

"It's the Cherokee," I said. "They're out to kill us."

"I imagine," said Samantha. She floored the engine and the Land Cruiser shot forward, fishtailing briefly before sending a plume of water splattering all over the windshield of the Cherokee. Then she caught hold of the cement, barreling forward and leaving the other vehicle skidding on the country road.

"Good work," I said. But then, unaccountably, she slowed, waiting for it to catch up. "What're you doing?" I asked, as the Cherokee bore down on us. Suddenly I could see the silhouettes of my friends from the CFP—Platt and Larsen—outlined through their muddy windshield. A third figure I guessed was their woman friend was barely visible in the back.

Platt leaned out the passenger side, raised his shotgun and trained it directly at our rear window.

"Jesus! Turn!" I shouted.

Samantha smiled. "Relax," she said. "Trust me!"

I heard the shotgun go off just as she crunched down into four-wheel drive and turned left straight across a field into the trees. The Cherokee skidded out, then continued after us. We were headed toward the steep ridge of a canyon and she pointed the Land Cruiser upward along what might have been the remains of a fire road, but the water was coming down too fast to tell. Samantha kept going anyway and so did the Cherokee, right up along the side of the canyon, swerving back and forth on the nearly invisible switchbacks until we hit the top and skittered across the rim of the canyon with the Cherokee right behind us. Ahead of us, a river of mud flowed through a notch toward the valley floor below, sheer walls of granite blocking the way on either side. I had no idea how we were going to get out of this when Samantha suddenly slammed on her breaks, downshifted and spun around in a 180-degree turn, the Land Cruiser slipping out of the way like a shadow boxer as the Cherokee slid forward out of control, hitting its breaks with a piercing squeak. Seconds later, the Cherokee was face-forward in a mud bank and we were barreling down the hill again in the direction we had come.

I stared at Samantha in appreciative awe. "Where'd you learn to do that?" I asked, although I already had a good idea of the answer.

"I told you—country girl," she said.

"Which country?" I replied. "Quantico, Virginia, or D Street in Washington?"

But she didn't answer that one. She had slowed down and we were both looking back in the direction of the Grand Cherokee. It had already backed out of the mud bank and was speeding off into the storm on a road that led directly into the redwood forest.

"Now where're they going?" I said.

"After your son. They want to make sure he's dead before we get there." She threw the Land Cruiser into reverse and did a broken U, heading after them. "No matter which side he's on."

"Which side *is* he on?" I looked at her, holding on to the dash as we jounced over the ruts. "*You* ought to know."

Samantha glanced at me. We were already in the trees now, the Cruiser's headlights beaming through sheets of rain into their giant trunks. "Frankly," she said, "I'm not sure."

23

SAMANTHA BACKUS'S REAL NAME WAS Samantha Faber and she was a special agent of the FBI assigned to internal investigations. Although I had suspected it for a while, even before she had exhibited such detailed knowledge of Lawton Stanley's tax problems, I found out officially a few minutes later as I sat with an open map of California on my lap. The Cherokee had seemingly vanished into the night, and Samantha, still at the wheel, showed me her government identification card.

"You fooled me for a while," I said, staring at her photograph beneath the holograph.

"You're not the first."

"Yes, but I'm supposed to be a professional."

"If you're worried about your image, I'll—"

"No, no. That's okay . . . What about the rest of your story? Brown . . . Paris . . . ?"

"All true," she said, returning the card to her purse.

"Then what made you . . . ?"

"Join the feds? . . . When I couldn't get that job on the

Trib, I took a position as an investigator for the U.S. Customs Service. One thing led to another and . . ."

"You like what you do?"

"Shouldn't I?" She looked at me a little annoyed, catching the edge in my voice. "I like fighting crime, yes."

"Inside and outside the Bureau?"

"Everywhere. . . . Look, we're wasting our time here," she said, gesturing to the map. "I thought you were trying to figure out which way they'd be taking your son."

"There's only one way." I folded the map. "If they don't bring him down 101, they'd have too much explaining to do."

"I hope you're right," she said.

We turned north at the highway intersection. I watched her as she drove, trying to understand her better. This was a whole new generation. When I was her age, the thought of working for a federal investigative agency was tantamount to joining the KKK. But she seemed perfectly at ease with it, as if she had a job with Ben & Jerry's or Apple Computer.

"So this internal investigation," I said, "I take it, it has to do with Nicholas Bart."

She nodded.

"How long has it been going on?"

"For a while, but we don't have anything substantive. He's a hard bird to catch."

"Does he have a connection with the CFP?"

"Not documented."

"What about the bomb school?"

"He might've started it, but no one's been able to prove it."

"You mean the FBI didn't organize that?" I said archly.

She glanced at me. "We're not in that business."

"I'll bet."

"We're not."

"You used to be."

"Not anymore."

"How do you know?"

She went silent for a moment before she said, "I think you're living under the assumptions of another era."

"Maybe Bart is too."

"He's thirty-four."

"Then why are you investigating him?"

"People go wrong, even in the Bureau."

"Thank you, Director Hoover."

"That was uncalled for," she said.

"Sorry," I said. "Maybe I *am* living in the past." I smiled. "But I'm going to be fifty in a few weeks."

"You don't look it."

"Thank God."

She laughed, diffusing the tension, and we drove along for a few more miles without talking. The weather, which had let up for a while, had turned worse again and I could see the water level rising as we crossed a bridge over the south fork of the Eel River. There had been no sign of the Cherokee for some time, but somehow I felt it was still close. "Actually the investigation cleared Bart over a year ago," Samantha said, breaking the silence. "He's a smooth operator. I don't have to tell you. . . . But then I started over again, by myself, quietly. . . ."

"Lone wolf? That's risky, isn't it?"

She chose her words carefully. "You could say you're not the most popular person in the Bureau when you reopen the investigation of another agent."

"I guess you're not," I said, hearing the tension in her voice. "What's Bart's motive for all this?" I asked her.

"Does he hate environmentalists so much he can't stop himself?"

"I don't think he gives a damn."

"Then what made you suspicious of him again?"

"You."

"Why me?" I said. I stared at her, but I couldn't see very well. She had dimmed the dashboard lights for better visibility.

"Before we met, he insisted you were some kind of retro sixties asshole willing to hang anybody to get your kid off."

"And after?"

"Well . . . you are kind of retro, if you don't mind my saying so."

"Thanks," I said.

"But you're not an asshole. . . . Unfortunately, you made sense."

I wasn't entirely satisfied with her explanation, but there was no time for casual discussion. A yellow warning light was flashing at us and Samantha slowed as a CHP officer in a slicker, standing in front of a police barricade, was caught in the Land Cruiser's headlights. He walked toward us with his hand up. Samantha rolled down the window.

"Road's closed," he said. "You've got to turn around."

"This is an emergency," said Samantha.

"So's everything, lady," the cop replied. "There've been three bad accidents already. We don't need any more."

I tensed. Was Simon one of them? This storm was certainly convenient. They couldn't have planned things better. "This woman's FBI." I gestured to Samantha. "You've got to let us through!"

He stared in surprise at Samantha, who reached in her

purse again for ID and showed it to him. "Sorry, Agent
Faber. You can go ahead, but I have to warn you, you
won't get past the bend." He pointed out into the darkness. "Highway washed out fifty yards ahead. Eel River's
overflowed from here to Glasgow. And a tree's blocked the
road about a mile up."

"You didn't see a sheriff's vehicle go through?" I asked.
"With a prisoner?"

He shook his head.

"How about a Jeep Cherokee?"

"They haven't let anything through here in over an
hour but mud."

The officer walked off to deal with another car.

"Could they have gone through another way?" I asked.

"Those guys know the area better than I do," Samantha
replied. "They were born here." She reached for her cell
phone and dialed the sheriff's office in Eureka. Not surprisingly, the party with Simon had already left.
Identifying herself as FBI, she asked the person on the
other end to please try to get a hold of them on the police
band. It was an emergency. We sat there and waited until
the sheriff's officer got back on the line. No luck. The
prison van wasn't answering. Who knew where the
Cherokee was?

"They'll never let him out of there alive, will they?" I
said to Samantha, continuing before she answered. "How
far is it from here to Glasgow?"

"Couple of miles."

"Let's go."

"Wait," she said, stepping into the backseat and leaning
over to a steel locker in the storage area. "We'll need
these." She opened the locker with her keys, revealing a
.357 Magnum and a shotgun.

Before I could say anything, she handed me the Magnum and an extra clip and took the shotgun for herself. The gun felt heavy in my hand. And strange. It had been a while. But somehow the situation overwhelmed any qualms I had about firearms.

We climbed out of the Toyota and headed into the storm, the startled CHP officer watching us as we went straight around the barricade. We continued on the fifty yards to the bend in the road and stopped. The officer was right. It was impassable. The Eel River had overflowed.

"Worse than when my house flooded," said Samantha, staring at the oceans of black water that were pouring down the middle of Highway 101 like lava from an unseen volcano. We backed up and moved off the road onto higher ground, proceeding along the rim of a hill as we made our way north. It was hard to keep our footing with broken branches everywhere and the ground itself softened into an insubstantial mush. The night was almost impenetrable with a murky moonless sky of low dark clouds and no discernible lights on the horizon.

The course of the raging river shifted and the road reappeared, climbing up the next hill. We joined up with it and continued on, struggling against the wind. At the top, there was a sudden lull, as if we had finally stepped into the eye, and I could see more clearly, about a hundred yards or so down to where the river and the road united for a second time. Just beyond that spot, a huge fallen tree had blocked the highway just as the officer had told us. But trapped in front of it, and all by itself on the road, was a sheriff's van. Its headlights were on and, despite the storm, its driver's door and rear cargo doors were wide open as if it had been suddenly abandoned.

I touched Samantha's arm and we walked down closer

to it, coming to the side of the road. The van had halted within a foot or two of the tree and its motor was off. I could see the iron mesh behind the side windows. It was clearly a prison vehicle. We drew closer. Everything was quiet, the lull in the storm continuing. No one seemed to be in the vicinity as we crossed the road alongside the tree, continuing straight up to the cab of the van, when we both stopped simultaneously. In the driver's seat was a sheriff's officer I recognized from the Eureka jail, his inert body slumped over the front wheel. A steady stream of blood poured down his left cheek from the top of his head, which had been blasted away at what appeared to be point-blank range.

I held my stomach, trying not to be sick, and looked at Samantha who was staring at the ground. Silently, I walked around to the back of the van to the open rear doors. It couldn't have taken more than two or three seconds, but it was the longest, most terrifying walk of my life until I saw . . . nothing. The van was empty. No presence of the most frightening image I had ever conceived: the corpse of my son.

"Simon!" I screamed out, knowing that it might have been better to keep my mouth shut, but the immediate feeling of relief was so strong I couldn't stop myself. "Simon!" I repeated, scanning the forest around us. There was no response. Samantha and I started moving away from the van again, heading down the road. But we hadn't gone fifty feet when we stopped. Facedown on the ground in front of us was another body. I leaned over and looked. It was Bill Brindle. He had been shot in the back.

I sucked in my stomach again with dread when I heard an agitated voice. "Moses . . . thank God, you're here. . . . It's been crazy." It was Bart, standing by the bank of the swollen river, huge runaway redwood logs rushing past from the mill pond up in Glasgow. He wore a wide-brimmed rain hat and a heavy rubber storm coat.

"Where's Simon?" I demanded.

"I don't know. . . . I hope he's okay . . ." He took a few steps toward us, pointing to Brindle. "This terrorist from the Guardians hijacked the van and . . . "

"He's no terrorist! He's with you. . . . Or *was!*"

"Oh, Moses, please. Don't be ridiculous," said Bart. "The only one working with us is your son. . . . I thought you knew that by now. You're the one who showed me my number on that Post-it."

"You expect me to believe that bullshit, Bart? How come you just sent us on a wild-goose chase to that hospital?"

"I wasn't trying to send you anywhere. What're you talking about?"

"Your friends from California Forest Protection were waiting outside for us."

"They're not my friends. They're a bunch of disaffected crazies who formed some vigilante group." He shook his head in dismay. "And they weren't waiting for you. They were waiting for us. We were trying to get there ourselves." He gestured to the damaged prison van. "They wanted to stop Simon before he could talk. . . . I knew the police wire was being tapped. But I thought it was just the Guardians."

I stared at Bart. For a split second I almost believed him. "You know damn well the CFP didn't have to tap the police. You could tell them anything they wanted to know yourself!"

"Who told you that? Agent *Faber*?" Bart nodded to Samantha, who stood ten feet away with her shotgun at

her side. "The FBI malcontent? She investigated me for
five years until they made her stop. If anyone's working
with the CFP, it's her."

"That's why they kidnapped both of us? If I hadn't
called 911 . . ."

"Funny. I didn't see any kidnapping charges on the
police docket." He looked straight at Samantha, the rain
pouring down on us.

"I got away myself," she said.

"Moses, are you going to believe this nonsense? Help
me find your son. He was shot by that terrorist and—"

"Shot?!"

"He's out there somewhere." He pointed off into the
trees.

I felt as if my head were about to explode. "If you so
much as touched my son, I'll rip every bone from your
fucking body!"

I started to advance on Bart, who stepped backward
and pulled a .38 from under his coat. "Don't move!"

The three members of California Forest Protection
walked out from behind the trees. Platt and the woman
had shotguns trained on us. Larsen had a Magnum of his
own.

I froze in place, my right hand at my side with the barrel of my own Magnum aiming at the ground.

"Sorry it had to be like this," Bart said. "I was trying to
show you it was unnecessary. . . . Now drop that gun."

"Where's Simon?" I asked, seething with rage.

"I said, drop the gun," Bart repeated. "You don't seem
like much of a marksman anyway. And these gentlemen
were trained at the Marine antiterrorist school in
Quantico. Larsen was the leader of a SEAL team in
Kuwait."

"Was that before or after he taught the Guardians how to use explosives?" I looked at Larsen, who had his Magnum trained straight at my head.

"You better drop it," Samantha said to me. She raised her left hand in surrender and bent over, depositing her shotgun on the ground. I slowly lowered my shoulder and did the same, my pistol falling on the wet dirt with a dull thud.

"Slide them toward me," said Bart. We kicked our weapons a few inches forward. "Now back up." We took a few steps backward.

The storm had relented for a moment. It was almost quiet. Bart and his partners stood there staring at us. I suspected they were trying to figure out how and where to dispense with us. I also suspected it wasn't going to take them long. I started to go over my options, which didn't seem great, when a rock slide came down from the hill in front of us.

Everyone looked over. "That him?" said Platt.

"I thought he was shot," I said.

"Shut up," said Bart. He gestured to Platt and Larsen. "Everthing's under control here. Go have a look." He nodded into the woods. They lit out after Simon, leaving Samantha and me there with Bart and the blonde.

"Simon, they're after you!" I screamed, although I knew my voice would be drowned out against the howling wind. The rain was coming down harder again. Seconds later I heard some gunshots in the distance. Before I could do anything, the woman stuck the barrel of her shotgun against my chin. "You think you'll get away with this, you motherfucker?"

I said to Bart, "How're you going to explain killing all of us?"

"It's a stormy night," he said.

"No one's going to believe you," said Samantha.

"Who's going to tell them? You?" He circled behind her and wrapped his arm around her neck in a choke hold. "The government watchdog?" He pulled her to the ground, stepped away and kicked her so hard with his boot her jaw rattled as she flew backward. She clutched her stomach, gasping for breath. Her eyes fluttered shut.

Bart stared at her a moment, then turned to me. "Or you," he said, "the concerned parent?" He trained his pistol on my face only inches away from the shotgun barrel. I looked from it into the bore of the .38. Bart curled his finger over the trigger. "God save us from concerned parents." He was about to fire when Samantha suddenly rolled over and reached for his legs. The blond woman spun around. I dove for her, grabbing the shotgun as Bart fired twice. The first one went wild but the second one struck Samantha in the shoulder. She yelled, clutching it, and stumbled toward the woods.

I flipped over on the ground and fired the shotgun at the blonde. Her face blew apart in a hail of blood. Bart wheeled around, pointing his pistol at me. The shotgun only had a single bore. I threw it at him before he fired and ran with all I had for the trees. Several shots went flying past me as I slipped in the mud. But I made it to the forest and kept going, running for what felt like several hundred yards, yelling "Simon! Simon!" until I collapsed from exhaustion on the trunk of a redwood.

I stood there a moment, breathing hard and peering out in the darkness. I couldn't see anybody. I heard no sound except for the driving rain on the branches. Simultaneously, what must have been a thick fog was settling in all around me. The tree in front of me disappeared from view, followed by the fern bush only a few feet away. I was in a nighttime white-out.

Some more shots rang out from behind. I spun around. Then I heard footsteps coming in my direction. Two sets. They passed me and continued on, then stopped.

"Fuckin' soup out here," someone said. It sounded like Platt. "What happened to the FBI bitch?"

"We got her that time," said Larsen.

They headed back toward me. There was no way I could fight them. I needed to arm myself but how? I began to walk as quietly as I could back in what I thought was the direction I had come. But within fifty feet I was lost in the thick fog. I turned around in a circle, trying to orient myself. Desperate, I called out, "Simon! Simon!" and kept walking, not knowing where I was. Somewhere off to my right I could hear Platt say, "It's the father!" A couple of more shots went off. They started running toward me. I went the other way, tripping over some foliage and bumping into a tree when I felt a hand on my shoulder and froze.

It was Samantha. Her face was badly bruised and scratched and her jacket soaked through with blood on the left side. She stood there a second, struggling to stay erect. Then she collapsed into me and thrust my original Magnum in my hand. I dragged her over to a boulder and laid her down. More blood was flowing from her arm. Platt or Larsen had shot her a second time. But they hadn't been able to stop her, and she had retrieved the weapon.

I took off my jacket and was putting it under her head when a flashlight beam pierced the dark fog, striking me in the chest. I fired blindly in the direction of the beam, the Magnum recoiling furiously in my hand. The flashlight went out.

"Good try, Wine." It was Bart. "Now try this!" He pumped a series of shots in my direction as I dove for cover behind the boulder. "Hey, boys, he's over here!" he shouted, flicking the flashlight again as a signal. I could hear Platt and Larsen making their way toward us. Then another set of footsteps from the opposite direction. Simon! Where was he?

Everything went silent. I crouched down behind the boulder. All I could hear was Samantha breathing. Then the whispered word: "Pop!" I couldn't tell where it was coming from.

"The kid!" said Platt from somewhere not far off.

"Keep quiet!" I said in an urgent stage whisper.

Silence. A rustling of branches. Then bodies moved in my direction. They took the bait. I held my breath as Platt and Larsen drew closer. I stared into the night, straining my eyes to make out their silhouettes in the fog. The moment I saw the hint of an outline I jumped up and started firing, emptying my clip. They were already at point-blank range. They cried out, both clutching their chests in agony and pitching forward to the ground. Platt's shotgun exploded in the dirt. Then there was silence again. I looked over at Samantha. I couldn't tell in the darkness whether her eyes were open or shut.

"Well done, Moses," said Bart. He sounded about thirty feet away. "Good marksmanship." I backed against the boulder again and jammed the second clip in the handle. Immediately I started firing in the direction of his voice. There was another scream of agony, this one higher pitched. I held my fire. Listened. The rain had stopped. I stood there a moment, waiting. There was another rustling noise, then nothing. "Maybe a little too good," Bart said finally. He flicked on the flashlight, training the beam

around. Nothing was visible until it stopped suddenly on
the shredded, blood-splattered remains of a prisoner's
shirt. The fabric was clinging to the branches of a bush.
Protruding from beneath the lowest branch was Simon's
leg. I recognized his hiking boot.

The flashlight beam started to approach in my direction. "Helluva thing, isn't it," said Bart, "to shoot your
own son."

I dropped to my knees like a penitent. I couldn't go on.

Bart stopped about fifteen feet from me and looked
down. "I'm sympathetic. Really," he said. I looked up at
him and nodded. I knew he was going to kill me, but I
didn't much care. I spread my arms to offer him a target.
He stared at me a moment, then raised his gun when
Simon jumped up, bare chested, from behind the bush.
With a giant stride he leaped on Bart's back, clawing and
pulling at him. But Bart was stronger than I expected. He
shook Simon and threw him off, pushing him toward the
boulder and instantly aiming his .38. He had Simon
trapped against the rock about to kill him. Before he could
fire, I reached for the Magnum and blasted away blindly
with it. It struck Bart in the back. He gasped and pitched
forward into Simon, who caught him and deposited his
limp body on the mud in front of him.

I got up and walked over to Simon. His bare chest was
covered with blood. "Fuck this, Pop, huh?" he said, wiping it off.

"No kidding," I said, staring at him, incredibly grateful
he was alive. I grabbed him and held him tight. I glanced
over at Samantha, and saw that she was alive too. I was
relieved beyond words. Then I looked back at Simon.
"Where'd you learn to play possum like that?" I asked.

"You," he said.

 "Is it illegal to give a man the benefit of your expertise, Mr. Wine?"

I was sitting opposite Sean Handler in his office at the headquarters of the FOXAM Corporation on Figueroa Street in downtown Los Angeles. It was early morning—Handler had to be at UCLA for a nine o'clock class he taught in contemporary investment strategies—but I had already finished filling him in on the details of the case, both known and surmised, as far as I understood them. We had sat down together in the sofa area of his office at about seven thirty and talked over a breakfast of fresh orange juice, toasted bagels from I-N-Joy and some strong Viennese roast coffee.

I had begun by alluding to our mutual acquaintance Mr. Lawton Stanley through whose good graces (and Internal Revenue difficulties) I had been granted this interview. I knew he and Handler didn't much care for each other, but I guessed correctly there would be enough upper-class politesse on both sides to get me through the door. So I made the usual obeisances about what great guys they both were and then Handler and I continued on this social note, segueing to his high school days. This was because I inquired about a photo he had on his desk of his graduating class, all formally decked out in caps and gowns. Handler was particularly proud of that class, because several members had gone on to become famous, including a leading theatrical agent and an Oscar-winning actress—not to mention his own distinguished career as a mergers-and-acquisitions wizard, a veritable symbol of the 1980s.

"Must've been something in the lunchroom milk," he said with a modest smile. "But that's my real pride, my true bastion against life's inevitable adversities." He pointed to several family photos next to the graduation shot. Three attractive children were posed with Handler and his wife—a tall, equine woman of the Jewish-WASP type with short blond hair—over a number of years and in various locales, from Bel Air to what looked like the beach of some Mediterranean island like Sardinia or Sicily. "Cynthia and I have been together for twenty-six incredible years, watching the children grow up," he continued, pointing to each one individually. "Danny's already married himself, doing his residency at Mass General, Jennifer's prelaw at Dartmouth and Marcus, the youngest, is talking about following in his father's footsteps at the Wharton School of Business, heaven help him. But I don't mean to bore you."

Handler poured me another cup of coffee. I studied him a moment, trying to focus on the matter on hand. His stylishly tailored beige pants and pastel cashmere cardigan gave him the appearance of well-tended success associated with recently retired tennis pros or stock traders whose business interests required their full attention for only an hour or two a day. But there was something almost too trim about him, a hollowness around his eyes that gave him a slightly cadaverous aspect at odds with his age. He also took, I noticed, several different vitamins, including E and B complex, as well as some pills I couldn't identify, along with his breakfast, grimacing as he swallowed them down.

"I'm here about my son," I said finally.

"I've been told," said Handler. "Quite a frightening story. I've read the newspaper reports. How this FBI agent . . . Bart, is it? . . . tried to kill him by rigging a phony escape and all that. . . . But I'm sure you're relieved the U.S. Attorney is reconsidering your boy's indictment."

"Only some of it. He's still in serious trouble."

"With Jack Koufax in his corner, he should do just fine. Wasn't Koufax the one who got the racketeering charges dropped on Lou Mazzini? If he can do that, he can do anything."

"It's not exactly the same thing."

"Still, everything's in your favor. What an embarrassment to the FBI. Their own agents mucking around in High Sierra waters. Those things were supposed to be over in the days of COINTELPRO."

"Hmmm . . . well . . . could be," I said. "Maybe they were at that." It was then that I launched into my contention that it was money, not political ideology, that originally motivated Nicholas Bart to foment violence in the North Coast wars by creating a bomb school. This creation set off a chain reaction that led to the dementia of the activist Claire Hannin and, some years later, the death of the logger Leon Erlanger as well as the assassination of a reporter named Daniel Springer. A paramilitary group called California Forest Protection murdered Springer and blamed it on eco terrorists because Springer was about to reveal the CFP's and Bart's initial connection to the school. But none of this, I emphasized, had been instigated by the FBI itself. Not this time. Someone, to put it simply, had paid Agent Bart to do it.

"An impoverished civil servant," said Handler, weighing the possibilities. "Corruptible, I suppose. But who would want to do it?"

"Someone impatient with government restrictions on the use of the land, endangered species regulation, that kind of thing."

Handler smiled broadly. "Scarcely seems worth paying for, Mr. Wine. Those regulations are a thing of the past with our new Congress. Or soon to be."

"This was five years ago."

"I see your point, but still . . . a big risk."

"You think there's some deeper motivation?"

"Who knows? In any case, I don't know how I can help you. I've heard a description of poor, young Mr. Bart, of course . . . from the news reports . . . no one could escape it. But I don't recall having met him."

"This might jog your memory." I showed Handler a photograph I found in the files of the *Humboldt Herald*. It was taken on that Fourth of July when Handler came to Glasgow in his new Pendleton shirt to ingratiate himself with the locals after having taken over the Allied Lumber Company in a leveraged buyout. It showed a concerned Nicholas Bart helping a lumberjack fish the CEO out of the Eel River. Handler looked like a drenched river rat in the picture. It was something he and I had in common.

"That's Bart?" he said noncommittally. I nodded. "If you say so," Handler continued. "It wasn't my happiest day in the out-of-doors, as you can see. Came down with a flu I couldn't shake for weeks . . . if ever."

"There's also this," I said, passing Handler a copy of Bart's Dean Witter statement. He perused it quickly and returned it to me.

"Mr. Bart should be giving *me* advice," he said.

"That would be strange since three of those companies are yours."

"Were," said Handler. "For a short time."

"During periods in which people made millions."

"When they were on the right side."

"When they had the right information."

"What's that supposed to mean?" asked Handler, but I didn't answer. At that point he raised his question about whether it was against the law to offer someone free advice.

"Especially not to your own son," I said.

Handler stared at me with the dull expression of the prematurely dead. "What're you looking for here, Mr. Wine? Vengeance? That's a little banal. And redundant."

"Clarity, Mr. Handler. Just clarity."

He hesitated, trying to figure out, I imagined, how much I knew, whether I had seen the canceled tuition checks, the University of Colorado registration form with the father's name blank, even the Denver birth certificate for a male child, nine pounds, six ounces, of unknown patrimony. But what did it matter? "I was young," he said. "I wasn't going to let Phyllis Bart drag me down. . . . But I took care of him."

"I know."

"Sometimes it was hard. He wanted a lot, like all children. Sometimes he did things . . . to earn my love that perhaps he shouldn't have. But it's all over now. For him. For me." Handler took a breath and sat up straight in his seat. "The sixties were your era, Mr. Wine. The eighties were mine. You may be attempting a comeback, but unfortunately I cannot." He gestured to the pills that were sitting on the coffee table. "I'm in chemo for prostate cancer, which has already metastasized to the lung. I have at best six months to live. It's God's retribution for the sale of junk bonds." Handler looked at his watch. "And now I'm going to have to leave. I'm going to be late for class." He stood and walked to the door, holding it open for me. "Good luck, Mr. Wine. I'm sure justice will be served." He patted me on the back. "But whatever happens, it should be reassuring to you that you're not the only parent who didn't know his child."

"WERE YOU RIGHT?" asked Suzanne.

"About Handler?" I nodded. We were standing in my kitchen a half hour later. Simon and Jacob were in the dining room, eating breakfast cereal. The four of us had spent the previous night in my house, under the same roof for the first time in over fifteen years. I suppose it was inevitable—they didn't have a place to stay in L.A. and we were all scheduled to go over to Koufax's office this morning for a meeting—but it sure seemed strange, "the family of origin," as the shrinks call it, come together again. Nobody even mentioned it. We had tried to talk briefly about the case instead, but Simon was too depressed for that, so we passed the evening listening to music. Then Suzanne went to sleep in my guest room and the boys opened the convertible sofa. We were all in bed by ten.

"I guess the nightmare's finally ending," I said to Suzanne.

"I don't think I could have taken much more of it," she said.

"Me neither." I looked at her. "Did you ever think he was really guilty?"

She didn't answer right away. "Even if he was," she said finally, "we would have supported him anyway."

"Yes, we would," I agreed. I checked my watch. "We better talk to him now. Before Jack."

Suzanne nodded and we walked into the dining room, joining Simon and Jacob. No one said anything for a moment. "In case you're interested," said Jacob, breaking the ice with a sly smile, "Simon and I discussed it and we think it's a bad idea for you guys to get married again."

"What a relief," said Suzanne.

"Thanks," I said. "Now we better deal with the case." I turned to Simon. "I don't think it's going to be so bad. Bill Brindle was working for Bart. I assume he was also the one who told the Guardians the London Grove was on parkland."

Simon nodded.

"And I'm pretty sure he removed the warning signs that led to Leon Erlanger's death."

"I can't believe he'd do that," said Simon.

"Well, somebody did," I said.

The doorbell rang. Who could that be? I wondered, getting up to answer it. It was Nancy. She took a step in the door and saw everyone.

"I see I'm intruding," she said.

"That's okay."

"No, no. It's not. . . . Hello," she called out. The others waved back. Then she said, "I wanted to give you this." She handed me a check. It was a refund for our Vietnam trip from Wilderness Travel. "Also, I'm going to New York . . . modeling job."

"For how long?"

"I'm not sure. Maybe for good. NYU has a great psych department. I can finish my M.A. there." I looked back in the dining room, where everyone was watching us. "You've got things to attend to," said Nancy. She looked at me sadly and kissed me on the cheek. "Good-bye," she said, and left, closing the door behind her. I guessed it was forever.

I walked back into the dining room and sat down again opposite Simon.

"You don't think it was Bill who removed the warnings," I said.

He shook his head. It was then Simon explained to me how Brindle's belated guilty conscience had saved his life. Bill had been cooperating with Bart and the CFP in a plan to hijack the sheriff's van on the way south and kill Simon by staging an accident. But they were stopped earlier than intended by the felled tree (ironically the same natural event that allowed Samantha and me to find them). They were going to go through with it anyway, but Bill started to feel bad, watching his supposed friend about to be pushed into the Eel River with the van. He couldn't go through with it. So he opened the back door for Simon, who fled, and then Brindle was shot by his cohorts.

"So who do you think it was who removed the warning signs at the London Grove?" I looked at Simon a long moment. "Karin?"

He didn't say anything.

"Is that what you were trying to find out when you disappeared at the Lost Coast?"

"I didn't find out anything," he said. His head was down and he was staring at the tabletop. I could see he was near tears. "Maybe I didn't want to."

"You loved her."

"Yeah, but I didn't do everything I did because of her. Some of it was me. I had my own ideas. . . . And those troopers didn't have to shoot her. They could have caught her. They could have stopped her from . . ." His voice trailed off.

"Maybe," I said. "Who knows?"

He started to cry. Jacob, Suzanne, and I moved to get up simultaneously to comfort him, which made Simon smile. "I'm all right," he said, waving us off. And then he stood himself. "Let's go see that lawyer dude."

It was easy with Koufax. By the time we arrived, Jack had already gotten the U.S. Attorney, an old law-school buddy, to dismiss all charges with the promise that Simon would steer clear of any potentially violent organizations for the rest of the century. I flew up to the Bay Area with him the next morning and dropped him off at his apartment. Simon made me a cup of instant while I sat on a stool in his kitchen.

"How'd that number get there anyway?" I asked when he handed me the cup. I was staring at the calendar taped to his refrigerator.

"What number?"

"You know—Bart's phone number. On the Post-it."

"I don't know. Somebody," he said vaguely.

"Bill, I'm sure."

He shrugged and walked into the living room. I could see he wanted me to go.

"I want to work, Pop." He was looking at his easel.

"*Double Man?*"

He shook his head. "I have to do something else." I watched as he walked over to his desk and took out a creased Polaroid, propping it up on the easel. It showed

Karin, standing in a redwood forest. She wore a down vest and her lips were curled up in girlish laughter. She looked about twelve years old. Simon bent down and opened his paint box.

"Are you okay?" I asked.

He shrugged again. I stood there for a moment, waiting for something more, but he was already stirring his paints, staring at a blank canvas.

I said good-bye and started to leave when he came over and hugged me. We stood there for a while, holding each other warmly. Then I went down to my rental car and drove off, continuing on across the Bay Bridge to San Francisco to my second destination. In a few minutes I arrived at the Cal Pacific Medical Center in Pacific Heights.

Samantha Faber was in a semiprivate room on the third floor.

"I hope you like irises," I told her, arranging a bouquet of flowers I had purchased at a florist on Van Ness.

"I do. Thanks. . . . You didn't have to come," she said.

"I wanted to thank you personally."

"For what? I was just doing my job."

I shrugged and sat down on the edge of the bed opposite her. I was feeling oddly nervous.

"But I'm glad you did," she said, smiling. I smiled back.

"How was the operation?" I asked.

"Okay. They're supposed to release me on Friday."

"Planning on taking some time off?"

She looked at me and smiled again. She had a great smile. "Attractive, huh?" She pointed to a prominent yellow and gold shiner that decorated half the left side of her face.

"Very attractive," I said.

We sat there silently awhile until she told me there was something she needed to tell me. She had lied to me. Or fibbed at least. She had always been investigating Bart. The story that the special agent's bad opinion of me had reawakened her suspicions was just that—a story. "I was working with Daniel to get the goods on all of them—Bart, Brindle, the CFP."

"So you and Springer were always undercovers together?" I said, suddenly slightly hoarse.

She nodded. "From the beginning."

I shifted uncomfortably in my seat. I shouldn't have been so disturbed by this, especially since I had already suspected as much. But I knew why I was. I cleared my throat and asked: "Were you and Daniel Springer ever . . . ?"

"Lovers?" She shook her head in amusement. "No way."

"Good," I said. "That feels better."

"That's very old fashioned of you," she said. "For an ex-hippie."

"I'm an old-fashioned guy. . . . And I was never really a hippie. I only dressed that way."

Samantha laughed.